DRAGON GEMS
WINTER 2023

Published by Water Dragon Publishing
waterdragonpublishing.com

Cover design copyright © 2023 by Niki Lenhart
nikilen-designs.com

ISBN 978-1-959804-42-0 (Trade Paperback)

10 9 8 7 6 5 4 3 2 1

FIRST EDITION

FOREWORD

L ET ME TELL YOU A SHORT STORY about our Dragon Gems program …

We originally created our Dragon Gems short fiction program because many of our authors had short works that they wanted to see published. Some of their stories were related to the series they were writing; others were brand-new, mind-expanding and thoughtful ideas that made you think a lot in the space of very few words. Between our authors and some word of mouth, we received a small number of Dragon Gems submissions throughout the year, but it was enough that we had a steady pipeline of new short fiction to publish every month.

In Spring of 2022, we decided to promote the program and call for submissions more publicly. We assumed, at best, that we might double the number of submissions we usually received. That would be a good thing, as it would broaden our circle of authors published under the Dragon Gems program and increase its visibility.

On February 1, 2022, we opened submissions again and, on March 22, 2022, we were forced to suspend submissions because we — our editors and slush readers — simply could not keep up with the influx of stories that we received. During those six weeks, we received more Dragon Gems submissions than we had received during the previous *two years*. Even using our most critical criteria, we discovered that there were more stories that we wanted to accept for publication than we could publish individually in three years — and that was simply too long a time for us to make authors wait to see their story published. We do not do that for novel-length work; we certainly were not going to do it for short fiction.

So, after a lot of serious consideration and difficult discussions, we decided to transform our Dragon Gems program to also include quarterly collections of short fiction. What you hold in your hands now is the first in what we hope to be many of those quarterly anthologies.

It has been an unexpected and exciting journey getting here, and we hope you enjoy the many adventures and ideas that these authors now bring to you in these pages.

Steven Radecki
Managing Editor and Co-Founder
Water Dragon Publishing

CONTENTS

Emma Kathryn is a horror fanatic from Glasgow, Scotland. When she's not scaring herself to death, she's either podcasting as one half of the *Yearbook Committee Podcast* or streaming on Twitch as variety streamer *girlofgotham*.

•   •   •

"Little Gifts" is a story that's fairly different to most other things I write. I usually dwell in horror and dark tales, so it was fun to return to fantasy (a genre I loved when I was younger) and combine that with a "Goonies"/"Stand By Me" vibe. I like to think that teen me wouldn't have eaten food that appeared from a magical pool, but I really do love cake.

LITTLE GIFTS

EMMA KATHRYN

W HEN SAMMY HAD TOLD MARIE and Lara about the magic pool, they assumed he'd found a sinkhole. But this sure wasn't a sinkhole.

Three eleven-year-olds stood at the outskirts of the forest by the lake. The girls' mouths were agape as Sammy had pointed out his discovery, a blue and purple friendship bracelet dangling around his wrist dancing with excitement.

A shimmering disc of blue light, about the size of a manhole cover, sat in the earth between two old trees. It gave off a soft, melodic hum, as if it wanted to be noticed.

Usually during the summer, teens flocked to the lake for a swim. It was a miracle no one else had found this. Granted, the teenagers weren't really interested in venturing past the treeline. That was mostly reserved for the little kids, who still liked to climb.

"What the heck is that?" asked Lara, keeping a safe distance at all times. Marie was much closer but stayed with her back pressed against one of the trees.

"See those stones around it?" Sammy said. "They've always been here but the glowing and humming is new."

Marie peered closer. "Gosh, you're right! There's a circle of stones!" Sure enough, a ring of pebbles framed the pool. Some were smooth, some were mossy and some looked as if they'd been chiselled off of the side of a mountain. Absolutely none of them looked like they belonged here. A few toadstools sprouted around the outside of the circle. They looked like something out of a storybook and certainly not like any real mushrooms either of the girls had ever seen in real life.

"Don't touch it!" Lara said from where she was rooted to the spot. She toyed with the matching friendship bracelet she wore. Only she and Sammy wore them. Marie had refused. No-one would be wearing one when they went up to the big school at the end of the summer. "Please, Sammy, don't. Get back, Marie!"

Sammy laughed and gave Lara his signature grin. They'd known each other since their mums met at a toddler dance group. He'd always done that stupid grin when he knew he was on to something exciting. Like the time he found his big brother Daniel's Dungeons and Dragons gear and they spent winter break fighting beasts and running through forests with elves.

"Lara," Sammy said. "It's totally fine. Watch." He picked up a stone – certainly not one of the ones from the circle – and tossed it into the blue hole.

"No!" Lara burst as if he had just tossed a stick of dynamite down a mineshaft.

Nothing happened.

Marie giggled and joined in. Sammy and Marie threw about a dozen rocks into the pool that day. They only stopped when it started to rain. Marie ran home, yelling that her mum would go mad if she came home soaked through again.

Sammy and Lara walked home together. Lara didn't want to talk about the pool. But it was all Sammy wanted to talk about. They both tugged at their friendship bracelets as they walked. Sammy out of anticipation of it still being there tomorrow and Lara out of fear of it still being their tomorrow.

•　　　•　　　•

Sammy and Marie insisted that they return to the pool the very next day. They simply had to know if it was still there. Lara was livid. This was a waste of the school holidays. They could be going swimming or playing in the park or nagging Sammy's big brother, Daniel, to take them to the cinema. *Pirates of the Caribbean 3* was still showing at the local pictures.

When they reached the pool, all three of them gasped. Beside it, a neat pile of stones sat waiting for the children. Sammy and Marie immediately set about dismantling it, studying the stones and insisting that they had thrown this one or that one into the pool yesterday. Lara stood back and toyed with her long plait of brown hair nervously.

"I told you not to touch anything!" she whined. "Let's just go, let's not do anything else. We saw the pool; it looked weird and it did weird things. Let's leave it."

Sammy had had enough and dragged Lara over, pulling her down to sit on a protruding tree root.

"Lara, don't you know what this means?!" he beamed. He looked like when they found the map to the treasure room in the high elf castle back when they'd played Dungeons and Dragons. That game had been a lot of fun. It was hard not to smile when she remembered it but she was too scared right now. "We've found real magic!"

"Woooooooow," Marie said, wide-eyed and agreeing. Marie was prone to following whatever the coolest person in the room suggested. This was how she always got picked for dodgeball. For being a suck-up. Right now, Sammy was the coolest person in the forest so, on that day, whatever he said was gospel to her.

Lara rolled her eyes. "Maybe it's just the big kids messing with us?" she suggested.

3

"What about the pool then?" Sammy asked. "Why is it all blue and shiny and singing?"

"It's not singing. It's just making a noise."

"Nuh-uh," insisted Sammy. "I can hear music. Can't you hear it?"

Marie began to nod. "I can totally hear music." It was more than likely that Marie could not hear music at all. But rather the same humming noise that Lara was hearing. Lara stuck her tongue out at Marie and Marie promptly stuck hers back.

"I think we have to give it something better than stones," Sammy suggested.

"Like what?" Lara asked.

Sammy grabbed his backpack and rummaged around. As usual his idea of "supplies" was whatever his mum wouldn't notice him taking from the cupboard. He brought out a can of Irn-Bru soft drink and a packet of pickled onion Monster Munch. Lara knew that Sammy wasn't allowed Irn-Bru at home and his mum would go mad if she knew he had it (she was convinced it made him hyper) so this was probably just an excuse to get rid of it.

"What do you guys have?" he asked, turning to Marie and Lara.

Marie shrugged. She never brought supplies out of fear of bringing the wrong thing. Instead, she just took whatever the cooler kids would offer her. Lara sighed and pulled her backpack off and started looking.

"Chewing gum and a lunchbox pack of digestive biscuits," she offered. "But I'm not throwing anything. You have to do it."

"Perfect," Sammy said, throwing a quick hug around her. Lara rolled her eyes but she did enjoy the hug.

The three children stood around reverently as Sammy tossed the snacks into the pool. For a brief moment, Lara imagined that she could hear music.

Just like yesterday, nothing happened and they all went home.

•   •   •

When they next arrived at the two trees, a platter covered with a cloth was waiting for them. Sammy pulled it away to reveal an elaborately decorated silver tray of exquisite lemon cakes. They devoured them in minutes. They were delicious. Lara was only briefly worried that they could have been eating poison. That fear went away after she'd eaten her third one. Sammy slipped the silver tray into his backpack and took it home with him.

This time, Marie and Sammy threw down as much food as they could buy at the corner shop with all the pocket money that they had between them (£7.25). Lara had contributed to the buying of the sweets but, as usual, threw nothing.

•   •   •

The next day, before leaving the house, Sammy phoned round the girls. He insisted that each one had to bring something really special to the pool. Something that could be considered a sacrifice.

This was when Marie decided she wanted to bail. She said that one of the other girls in their class had invited her to the cinema and since they were all starting secondary school at the end of the summer, she had to 'extend her friendship group' in case they didn't all wind up in the same classes. This was code for someone cooler had finally come along.

Lara didn't know what had come over her. Three days ago, she had been yelling at Sammy not to touch anything. Today, she was picking out her favourite Katy Perry CD (Teenage Dream, of course) and preparing to throw it down a hole. Well, she had transferred the CD to her iPod Nano but sometimes her mum let her play the CD in the car so it was still pretty important to her. She also looked at her bookcase and took down her copy of The Hunger Games. Then doubled back and picked up Matilda as well. That would be plenty.

Lara and Sammy stood over the pool, staring at it tentatively. There was definitely music coming from it now. The blue didn't seem so bright today. In fact, it looked a little glassy today. As if there was something on the other side that was trying to show itself. In fact, Lara could have sworn that the stone circle was much bigger today. Big enough for a full-grown adult to easily fall down.

No gifts had been left in return today. Maybe whatever was in there didn't like Crunch bars or Fanta or salt and vinegar Chipsticks? Maybe yesterday's offering hadn't been good enough.

"I'm scared," Lara said.

"I know," Sammy nodded and took her hand. Their friendship bracelets briefly touched. They stayed like that just for a minute. Any longer would have been weird. When they let go of one another, they each wiped their hands off on their t-shirts.

Lara brought her CD and two books out of her backpack. Sammy brought out his copy of the video game Fable III and then carefully produced a painted miniature figure.

"Oh Sammy," Lara gasped. She could understand him throwing the game (his dad would believe him if he said one of the big kids had taken it and not given it back) but not the figure. "You spent ages painting that."

It was a tiny medieval ranger. Bowstring pulled back, ready to fire a tiny plastic arrow at any imagined beasts that may attack. The paint was messy in places but it was the first one Sammy had ever painted himself. Daniel had given it to him when he'd discovered the DnD equipment heist. Rather than going mad, his brother had actually welcomed Lara and Sammy to one of his games, taught them how to play and then showed Sammy how to paint miniatures. It had been the birth of a new hobby.

"This character met the elf king and was invited into the great treasure room," he said with admiration. "That's how amazing he was."

6

The wind whistled through the trees around them. The music caught the breeze and danced up to meet their ears. Something was definitely there.

"You ready?" he asked and they held their favourite things aloft. Lara nodded even though she was absolutely not ready. She clenched her eyes shut and let go.

The items fell into the pool with a soft noise that she couldn't describe. It wasn't like something falling into water or even like something landing on hard ground. More like something falling onto a bed of marshmallow.

Music swelled and the blue light suddenly got bright again. Lara stepped back and shielded her face. Even though her eyes had been closed, the light had seared against her eyelids. Staggering out of the way, she tripped over a tree root and the earth rushed up to meet her.

When she finally tried to look at what was going on, she saw Sammy standing bright-eyed over the pool. Reaching up from below was the most beautiful hand she'd ever seen. Supple fingers covered in fancy rings stretched out, beckoning for Sammy's touch.

"No!" she managed to yell before Sammy reached out but it was already too late. He'd seen the wonder beyond. Adventure called to him like a siren. The mystical hand took Sammy's little fingers and pulled him in. There was no fear on his face and he didn't scream. In fact, years later, Lara could have sworn that he went willingly.

Music and light cut abruptly, leaving Lara alone with the sound of the lake and the woods. Above her, a bird cried out. After what felt like far too long, Lara scrambled to her hands and knees and crawled over to the pool. It was gone. All that was left was a broken circle of stones.

Sammy was gone.

• • •

Police officers made her go over the story a million times. Every single one was convinced she was either lying

7

or that she'd made it up because her eleven-year-old brain hadn't been able to comprehend whatever had actually happened to Sammy. Search teams dredged the lake and obviously found nothing.

Marie had denied everything. She didn't want to seem like the loser who believed in magic. When the girls eventually started secondary school, they were luckily in different classes and never spoke again. Marie quickly became one of the cool kids and didn't want to remember the summer when they'd found a magic portal.

As for Lara, she quickly became the school's weird kid. Stories spread of what she'd done to Sammy. Some said she'd killed him, some said she sacrificed him to monsters that lived in the woods, and some said that she'd let some imagined local pervert take him away after he'd plied them with lemon cakes. The only person who was ever nice to her was Daniel. For a while, his mum had said his "stupid games" had put stories in the kids' heads. Lara knew that wasn't true. And anyway, Sammy's mum wouldn't even look her way. She clearly hated her and was convinced Lara knew something she wasn't telling everyone.

For six years of high school and four years of university, Lara kept her head down. It was only after finishing university when she finally found the courage to go back to their magical place again. On her own this time, without adults – parents, police officers, child psychologists.

Ten years later and she knew exactly where she was going. The remnants of the stone circle were still there. Right between two trees that weren't quite as massive as she remembered them being. Now, they seemed like wooden markers. Not the giant pillars stretching up into the sky that she had remembered.

She sat down cross-legged amongst the roots. She was too big to perch on them now. Opening the bag draped over her shoulder, she brought out some snacks – gum, Monster Munch, a can of Irn Bru (remarkably less sugar than it had all those years ago) – and some small items. A book of poetry that the first person she'd ever dated had given her, a class photograph from her last year of primary school, and a tiny gaming miniature. She had never painted hers but it still depicted a plastic cleric. Holding a book in one hand and a staff in the other.

All of these items were placed within the stone circle. The stones were even more scattered than they had been that day he had left. She had wanted to touch these stones for years. Around the time of the incident, crime scene tape held her back and then after that it was her parents holding her back and then it was a therapist. But now she was an adult and free of them all. Now these stones were all hers. She straightened them and adjusted them.

Then she adjusted them more.

And a little more.

And then a lot more.

As she moved the last rock – one of the mountain peak looking ones – a few degrees counter-clockwise, something shifted. Hand snapped back and she held her breath. Something began to hum. Tears filled Lara's eyes and she whooped with delight.

Blue light filled the dirt circle and the humming became music. All of the items she had placed there fell into the pool and vanished. Part of her wanted to reach through but she did nothing. She waited.

Over the next few hours, the pool got wider and brighter and the humming got louder and clearer. She could hear it now. It was strings – harps and violins and guitars. It all drifted out to meet her and washed over her like a healing salve. It told her everything was okay.

They were never there when the gifts arrived. She didn't know how long she was supposed to wait or if anything would even happen with her sitting here watching. But nonetheless, she waited. As the sun set and the moon rose, she stayed where she was. Time was worth sacrificing just as much as

CDs and sweeties. She had brought something to read and she had a sandwich. She could stay all night if she had to.

Sometime around midnight, the blue disc of light turned clear. Lara set aside her book and moved closer. She had never been this bold when she was eleven. Through the clear pool, she thought she could see people. Bright and shining gold flickered on the edge of her vision. What was she even looking at here?

Just like that day ten years ago, a hand reached up through the magic. It wasn't the ringed and delicate hand she had seen back then. No, it was definitely the hand of a young man and hanging from his wrist was a braided blue and purple friendship bracelet.

Lara laughed and cried at the same time. The hand beckoned her towards adventure and companionship. It had been waiting ten years for her.

She took it with ease and without a second thought for what she was leaving behind. This was the greatest gift the pool could ever have given her.

Richard Zwicker is an English teacher living in Vermont, USA, with his wife and beagle. Some of his over 75 short stories have appeared in "Heroic Fantasy Quarterly," "Mythic," "Cosmic Horror Monthly," and other semi-pro markets. Two collections of his work, *Walden Planet* and *The Reopened Cask*, are also available. In addition to reading and writing, his hobbies include playing the piano, jogging, and fighting the good fight against middle age. Though he lived in Brazil for eight years, he is still a lousy soccer player.

•   •   •

I wrote "New Cessations" in response to a prompt about "a magic spell that goes terribly wrong." I teach a high school English elective on "Science Fiction and Fantasy," so I thought I'd have some fun with fantasy tropes. As with many of my short stories, I tried to find a golden mean between comedy and seriousness, though I think comedy won out in this one.

NEW CESSATIONS

RICHARD ZWICKER

M AZRUS, THE ONLY WIZARD in Bungladore, woke with a start, knocking his protesting cat to the floor. This was the fifth consecutive night he'd dreamed of his death at the indiscriminate hands of Pokius, his archrival. Why was this happening? The two had not seen each other in months, and Pokius lived a week's march away. Was Pokius toying with him by transmitting unsubtle warnings, or was he sensing actual danger? It would be nice if dreams were more specific.

"Are you going to sleep now or practice your stoolball technique?" asked his cat Addy, her tail whipping back and forth.

"Sorry. If I could control my dreams, I would."

Addy spat. "Your dreams are my nightmares."

His heart still racing, Mazrus got up and poured himself a cup of wine. Perhaps he could use the time to study a book he seldom opened, The Dark Compendium. It was an ancient tome of black spells, the kind favored by Pokius, and it might offer insight into the rival mage. Though both wizards favored cloaks and waist-long beards, Pokius was in most ways his antithesis. His rival hadn't the patience to learn the methods of white magic, instead seeking a shortcut with black. Rather than trying to improve the world, Pokius's motivations were selfish and self-promoting. That made him dangerous, as the demons of black magic had their own agenda. Mazrus opened a trap door in his floor and pulled out a box. After undoing the sealing spell, he pulled out the dusty book.

The next moment the door of his cottage blew open with a crash, and Pokius leaped into the room. "Prepare for your doom, Mazrus!" he shouted. It was just like Pokius to tell you to prepare for something and not give you any time to do it. Clad in a black cloak, the hood reaching his eyes, the intruder brandished his gnarled python-headed staff. A burst of energy knocked Mazrus off his feet. By instinct he created a protective shield around his body. The impact of the two forces produced a blinding flash.

"Have you no decency, attacking a wizard when everyone should be sleeping?" Mazrus gasped.

"Decency?" echoed Pokius. "What has decency to do with a mage of the black arts?"

Point taken, thought Mazrus, though he could barely hear his adversary over the onslaught of energy. If he was to overcome Pokius, he had to retrieve his staff, which he kept near his hat rack on the other side of the cottage. He inched in that direction. His shield diminished, and he felt the increased heat of the bombardment. As his hands closed on his staff, all went black.

•   •   •

Mazrus awoke sprawled on the floor, Addy licking his face. Pokius was gone. How long had he been unconscious? He peered out his window. The moon shone high overhead, but that didn't tell him anything as he hadn't noticed its position when he went to bed.

"Thanks, Addy," he said, wiping his wet bearded face.

"You're not welcome," said Addy. "I get more hair in my mouth licking your face than I do when I give myself a bath."

"How long was I unconscious?"

Addy yawned, her mouth opening wide enough to swallow a hen. "Do I look like a water clock? A long time."

Mazrus flexed his aching muscles. They screamed he was too old for this. "The more pertinent question is why didn't Pokius kill me?"

"I have a theory on that, but it'll cost you a saucer of milk."

Pokius grumbled and poured the milk, which Addy lapped up greedily.

"I think it was on his to-do list, but he postponed it when I autographed his face with my claws and left a tattoo of my teeth on his leg," she said.

"As always, I am in your debt."

"That may be, but I was unable to prevent him from stealing that book you were reading."

Mazrus stiffened, remembering what he had been doing prior to the attack. "The Dark Compendium? How could he have known I was going to take it out? He must have put the suggestion into my head. This is bad, Addy."

"Don't blame me. I'm just a cat."

In the wrong hands that book was a danger to the world. He had to get it back, but how? Bungalore was sandwiched between a mountain and a thick forest, and there was only one road out of it. Eventually, this led to a choice of three roads. He hadn't heard a horse approach prior to the attack, and like most wizards, Pokius preferred to walk. By foot Pokius could not have yet reached that intersection, but Mazrus had no way of catching up to him. Once his rival left the connecting road, he could be anywhere. A woodcutter lived on the outskirts of the village. Mazrus could cast a spell that would alert him to intercept Pokius. But the woodcutter slept like a log, and it would take more than a message spell to waken him. He could try to levitate him out of bed and drop him on the floor, but being so far away from him, that could risk bodily injury. At any rate, it was doubtful the woodcutter's superior size would be enough to stop a wizard with a dangerous book.

Mazrus had another book that might help. He retrieved a dusty tome called The Forbidden Book of Spells, hidden in the frame of the bed. He'd never used it because its unifying themes were "DON'T DO THIS!" and "IT'S ALWAYS HARDER TO UNDO SOMETHING THAN TO DO IT!" In the index he looked up "fugitive apprehension." Not having the fugitive in his sight limited the options to two. He could destroy part of the connecting road, leaving an abyss. That was not without drawbacks. If the abyss was too deep for Pokius to climb down and back up, he could simply go around it. If it was too wide to go around, he could climb down.

The other option was more extreme: he could stop time. For this, the warning "DON'T DO THIS" was underlined followed by exclamation points. The book explained: "One might think nothing could change while time is stopped, but what doesn't stop is the one casting the spell. The changes the mage undergoes during the time-stop could have infinite repercussions once time is resumed."

He didn't like the sound of that, though there was a 50/50 chance that the changes would be improvements. There was no chance of Pokius doing something good with The Dark Compendium.

Mazrus looked at the spell. He need only chant approximately a hundred words in a dead language he didn't fully understand, then shout the final word. Another fifty words and a different final one would undo it. He slowly read the summoning passage, half hoping his pronunciation was good enough for it to work, half hoping it wasn't. He stumbled three-quarters of the way and had to start over. When he got to the final word, he shouted, "Constipatus!"

It seemed nothing had happened, but how could he tell? Everyone else would be frozen in time, while he could move as usual. Addy! She was asleep on the bed. He tried to rouse her. He couldn't. It worked!

He copied down the undoing spell, grabbed his coat, and set off into the night. Stopping time when it was too dark to see was an added annoyance, but it couldn't be helped. As he trod down the connecting road, everything looked as usual. The cottages sat dark and still. The stars shone. There wasn't the slightest breeze, but that wasn't unheard of. He began to doubt his spell but assured himself that not even Addy would have ignored his attempts to rouse her.

The second proof that the spell had worked came about a mile from his cottage. On the edge of the road he saw a fox watching him, except it wasn't. It peered at the other side of the road, about to cross, when his spell froze it. "You'll get to your destination soon enough," he hoped.

Two miles later he came upon Pokius. The spell had stuck him into an uncharacteristically thoughtful expression, his mouth agape, his bushy eyebrows and lengthy brown beard accentuating it. The malevolent hate Pokius generally exuded was absent.

The dark book lay nestled under Pokius' right arm. With some effort, Mazrus dislodged it. "This book was not meant for you, Pokius," said Mazrus. "I'm pretty sure it wasn't meant for me, either, but at least I have the sense to recognize that."

As Pokius had already overpowered him once that night, Mazrus put some distance between the two of them before reciting the counter-spell. It wouldn't take his rival long to figure out who had taken the book from him, but that was all right. Once he got home, Mazrus would give it a more secure hiding place.

Of course, without Pokius in front of him, he wouldn't be able to tell if the undoing spell worked, but as soon as he got to the spot where he'd left the fox, he'd know. In the dark he had to make sure he didn't walk right by it.

He didn't, almost tripping over it. To his horror, the fox remained in the same position. The undoing spell had failed! In his haste, he must have copied it wrong. He increased his pace, assuring himself that he would rectify things once he got home. The silence of the woods unnerved him. Under normal circumstances, there was always the feeling that something bad might happen. Far worse was the possibility that nothing would happen ever again.

When he got home and found Addy frozen in place on his bed, he rifled through the Forbidden Book to the time-stop spell. The undoing spell was exactly as he had copied. He repeated the chant. Addy didn't move. "Not much of an undoing spell, is it?" His casual remark belied the seriousness of the situation. How many lives would be altered because of his recklessness? If he were forever out of sync with the rest of the world, he'd have plenty of undistracted time to think about it.

He spent the next two days — or what would have been two days if time wasn't stopped — feverishly searching for a counter-spell. There was no way to reverse time, which was just as well, as he might not be able to stop that. He hadn't the power to go back to the previous day and safeguard the book. Only one spell held any hope: one that gave temporary sentience to a wall or a plant. Could he use it to reanimate someone who was frozen, a wizard with more experience than he? But what if in so doing, he permanently altered the personality of the mage? The spell was meant for objects without sentience. And besides, there were no other more experienced wizards within a day's walk.

Then he got an idea. What if he granted sentience to the book of spells itself? Somewhere within the book lay the answer. If he couldn't find it, the book could. He turned the page to the animating spell, chanted the words, and said, "Cognizantus!" Mazrus felt gut-punched, as if the animation had been extracted from his body. He fell to a chair while the book rose three feet as if riding a wave. It flung itself open, then slammed on the table, where it abruptly closed.

"Whew, I felt naked," it said, articulating the words like a scholar.

"From being open? What's the point of a book if it's not read?" Mazrus asked.

"Would you like your every secret exposed to prying eyes?"

"No, but I'm not a book."

"But you are your secrets. I am a repository for forbidden spells. If a spell is within my pages, it should not be used."

"Well, that's the point," said Mazrus. "I need your help in undoing a spell."

"Which one?" asked the book, its voice dripping with condescension.

"I stopped time."

"Oh no! What don't you understand about 'Do not do this!' Did you think I was kidding?"

Mazrus explained how Pokius stole The Dark Compendium. "I felt I had no choice. I chanted the undoing spell, but it didn't work. Why don't you just tell me how I can solve the problem?"

"Because you can't! It involves more power than you apparently have."

"There was nothing about that in the spell!"

The book flipped open to the first page and highlighted a sentence. "Read it."

"'It's always harder to undo something than to do it.' But you didn't say it was impossible."

"Because it's not." The page wavered upright. "Are there any other wizards in the neighborhood?" asked the book.

"Just Pokius. I wouldn't trust him to say abracadabra."

"Well, you'd better find someone or you'll be spending the rest of your existence talking to me."

Mazrus saw that, once again, he had little choice. Despite his exhaustion, he once again set out into the woods. When he reached the statue-like Pokius, he cast the animating spell. Mazrus's legs buckled and he winced in pain, the combination of too many walks and spells. A look of recognition then hate filled his archrival's eyes.

"How did you get here so fast?" Pokius asked.

"You're welcome," said Mazrus.

"I don't know what you're talking about, but if you think you're getting The Dark Compendium back, you're..." Pokius realized he was pointing at Mazrus with the hand the book had been in. "Where is it?"

"Where you can't get it. It pains me to say this, but I need your help."

"Of course you do, but forget it."

"To retrieve the book, I did a time-stop spell."

Pokius laughed. "Not even you would be stupid enough to do that."

"You asked how I was able to get here so fast. Anyone's fast when everything else is still. The only reason you're moving is because I animated you."

Pokius raised his hand to test the air for a breeze. He detected none. "You're serious. Undo the spell at once."

Mazrus explained that the only way that could be done was if the two wizards pooled their power together. "Together, we could solve this ... right now."

"Very well. It seems to be my cross to bear to straighten out your messes."

Pokius had never straightened out any mess that Mazrus had made, but he let that go. "Here's the spell," he said, holding up a piece of paper. Together they chanted it, then waited.

"Not exactly definitive," said Pokius.

"There was a fox frozen in the middle of the road a couple of miles closer to the village. If it's gone, the spell worked."

"That's two miles out of my way."

"You want to take a chance that time is still stopped? Let's see this through, then we can get back to the important business of trying to outdo each other."

"The implication that I measure my performance by you is insulting," said Pokius.

"Whatever you say."

They found the fox still in the middle of the road.

"What do we do now?" Pokius asked, his tone querulous.

"I have some resources in my cottage," said Mazrus.

When they entered Mazrus's cottage, he introduced Pokius to The Book of Forbidden Spells.

"You animated a book before you animated me?" Pokius bristled.

"You chose to steal The Dark Compendium instead of me?" Forbidden countered.

"Please," said Mazrus. "We must work together." He explained to Forbidden that the combined force of the two wizards had been insufficient to undo the time-stop spell.

"You'll have to find a more powerful wizard," said Forbidden.

"If I take one more step tonight, I'll find my death," said Mazrus.

Pokius straightened up. "There is an alternative. We could summon a demon and harness its power."

"Bad idea!" said Forbidden. "You start letting in demons, there won't be a world to save."

"You have a prejudiced view of demons," said Pokius. "They can be reasoned with."

"Sure they can," said Forbidden. "But they won't do anything out of the goodness of their non-existent hearts. All they want is to increase their power and dominion, neither of which is something anyone else should want."

Pokius shrugged. "This is what I expect from The Forbidden Book of Spells. All you can say is 'can't,' which doesn't solve the problem. Certainly within your pages lies a spell for summoning a demon."

Forbidden snapped shut. "You'll not get it from me."

"You mean to tell me you don't know a spell to call a demon? I thought they were your pals?" said Mazrus.

"I haven't memorized it," said Pokius.

"There's got to be a better way," said Mazrus.

"I'd be happy to hear it," said Pokius. "It could take us a month to locate another wizard, while we could raise a demon in minutes." He glared at Forbidden. "And if you don't wish to be part of the solution ..." He turned to Mazrus. "What did you do with The Dark Compendium?

"That book is written in the old languages," said Mazrus. "It would take me days to translate a single spell, and even then, I'd get it wrong. Do you know those languages?" He feared the answer.

"Not as well as I would like. I was thinking we can animate The Dark Compendium."

"Absolutely not!" said Forbidden. "Two animated books is a crowd."

"I don't know if I have another animating spell in me," said Mazrus.

"I can do it," said Pokius. "Get the book."

"Why don't you just put another suggestion spell on me to get it out?"

"You know that won't work if you're aware of it."

Something had to be done. The Forbidden Book of Spells didn't have an immediate solution. It was possible The Dark Compendium would. Mazrus thought summoning a demon was a terrible idea, but between him and Forbidden, they might be able to stop Pokius before he went too far.

"All right." Mazrus went to a closet and pulled out The Dark Compendium.

"That's where you hide it?" asked Pokius.

"I didn't have time to figure out a proper hiding place," said Mazrus.

"This idea is as intellectually unsound as asking the dark lord if he can put your soul to better use," said Forbidden.

The two wizards ignored Forbidden while Mazrus placed The Dark Compendium on the table next to it. Pokius recited the animating chant and said the magic word. Instead of rising like a wave, the Dark Compendium shook violently, seemed to lose its shape, then converged back into a book.

"Did it work or did you just gave it a headache?" asked Mazrus after a few moments.

"Silence," said Pokius.

An oily, cultured voice emanated from the book. "I am in your debt for granting me sentience. How can I serve you?"

"We need your help in undoing a spell that has stopped time," said Pokius.

"And you shall get it. Existence is pointless without progression."

"More power than we possess is needed," said Pokius.

"Anything that's done can be undone. With assistance."

"From a demon, no doubt," said Mazrus.

"I would recommend a couple, just to be sure. Here is the page to summon the first one." The Dark Compendium flipped to the middle of its contents.

"Isn't there another undoing spell we could use?" asked Mazrus.

"I'm afraid not."

Mazrus was surprised to see Pokius's hands shaking. "Are you willing to go through with this?" Pokius asked.

Mazrus had taken a step he shouldn't have with the time-stop spell. This could be even worse. Caution was a luxury he had forfeited, however.

"Proceed."

Pokius recited the chant. It was a powerful spell because even before he got halfway through it, the floor shook, as if a massive entity was pushing against it. Mazrus felt dizzy as guttural voices filled his ears. Pokius finished the spell by chanting "Liberatus!" The floor cracked, revealing a smoldering abyss. Mazrus grabbed onto his front door to keep from falling in. Pokius grasped onto a bending floorboard as his body hung over the hole.

"Divertus Constipatus Reversurus!" Mazrus screamed. A wail filled the cottage as he felt the abyss sucking them down. Pokius screamed and shot out his hand to grasp his rival's. His eyes filled with fear, he echoed Mazrus's spell. A grinding sound like misaligned gears cut into the noise, indistinct at first, then louder and more dominant. Feeling his head would burst, Mazrus wrenched Pokius onto what was left of the floor and shouted "Returneth!" The room lurched forward like a death throe. A cacophony of cracks and groans filled the air as the boards of the cottage wrenched back into place. The Dark Compendium burst into flame, Pokius screamed, "No!" and Mazrus was thrown to the floor. A few moments later, Addy was licking his face.

"You diverted the demon's power against the time-stop spell and sent it back," said Pokius, also on the floor. "How did you know it would work?"

"I didn't."

"You shouldn't have burned The Dark Compendium. We may have lost some spells forever."

"That was my doing," said Forbidden. "Burning a book is against my principles, but it had to be done."

Mazrus collapsed into a chair. Somewhere in the world there might be another copy. There would always be evil and ignorance with spells to tempt them. "In my opinion, you've earned your sentience," said Mazrus.

"That may be, but I'm going to surrender it. Books were made to encourage sentience, not be sentient."

"Are you sure?" asked Mazrus. "It's handy having you around."

"I'll remain. Just make sure you use me properly."

"How can I use you properly?" asked Mazrus. "After every spell you have, it says, Do not use!"

"Exactly. I am a reminder to anticipate what might go wrong and make sure it doesn't. That's what you need to stop. Not time. Magic isn't always the answer."

With the excess of spells cast that day, Mazrus didn't need to be told that twice. The book then closed itself and, muffled, voiced the undo spell for sentience, and lay still.

Mazrus looked at Pokius, who scratched his beard.

"What needs to stop is our rivalry," said Mazrus.

"And your pontification." Pokius sat upright on the floor, leaning back in a vulnerable and thoughtful position. "It's my nature to be a lone wolf, but it's not impossible to teach an old wolf new tricks. Perhaps next time I borrow one of your books, I will ask."

Mazrus would believe that when it happened, though as the delayed sun poked a ray over the horizon, he felt anything was possible.

Micah Castle is a weird fiction and horror writer. His stories have appeared in various magazines, websites, and anthologies. His novelette, *Reconstructing a Relationship*, was published by D&T Publishing in 2022. His forthcoming debut novel, *The World He Once Knew*, will be published by Fedowar Press in 2023. He can typically be found somewhere in his Pennsylvanian home reading a book.

●　　　●　　　●

"Heirlooms in the Cinders" is a quasi-sequel to "The Gallows", published back in 2021 in "New Exterus: Volume 1", and both are highly inspired by death metal band Slice the Cake's album "Odyssey to the West".

HEIRLOOMS IN THE CINDERS

MICAH CASTLE

"AND YOU WANT ME to retrieve what?" May asked, hand resting on the hilt of her sheathed sword sitting across her lap.

The man adjusted his collar, glanced around the tavern, eyes stopping on a passing waitress whose bosom nearly spilled from her gown.

"Hey!" She slammed her first onto the table, ale sloshing from her tankard. "Get your eyes off her tits."

He shook his head, adjusted his glasses. "Yes, yes; sorry." He took a gulp from his tankard, wiped the froth from his lips. "My client lost a family heirloom when Malum fell. Very precious, very expensive. They'd like for you to retrieve it."

Malum was a two days travel by horse, and the stories she heard made her imagine a desolate place that no one should be riding into. But her purse was empty and work was difficult to come by, especially for a woman. People only wanted men sellswords; broad shoulders, bulging muscles, fat stomachs and battle scars.

She had scars but none they could see, and her petite frame and fair skin made it appear as though she were meek, but those who had been on the receiving end of her swordplay discovered otherwise.

"Must be paying a lot of coin for such a task," she said.

The man rummaged in his trousers, then set a hefty leather pouch onto the table. "This is only half; the other will be given upon return of the heirloom."

May snatched the purse, and weighed it in her hand while the other grabbed her drink. She took a swig, set it down. "And what's this heirloom? A crown? A ring? It'd be ash by now."

"A necklace, in fact," he said, removing a twine-bound scroll, untying it and laying it flat before her. "In a home bordering the Fall. Here's a painting of it."

She leaned forward. Ornate silver, branching off like vines around five opaque, milky jewels, two small ones flanking a larger one in the middle. "And this is worth the price?" She looked up at the man, his gaze drifting towards the waitress again. May groaned. "If you don't stop staring at her tits, I'll cut your eyes out."

He stammered, facing her. Forehead flush. "Yes, sorry. The price is adequate for the job."

"And if it's not there? Or I don't find it? There were many homes in Malum, many probably now lost in rubble."

The man nodded. "They're certain it'll be there; at least the stones, which are all they truly desire. And if you return empty-handed, then we'll part ways without complaint."

"And the coin?"

"You can keep the half you already hold. A token from my client."

Someone who can lose such an amount must have heaps more, May thought. Who the hell is his client?

May sat back. If she had been any other sellsword, she would take the coin and run, but she honored her work, honored the skills her father passed down unto her before his passing; proud of being one of the few women sellswords, showing that men weren't the only ones capable of using weaponry.

"It's a pact, then," she said, finishing off her ale. "Where shall we meet once I return?"

He glanced at the waitress again, back to May. "Here, we'll meet here. Just tell the barkeep you've arrived, and he will reach me."

•　　•　　•

She left the tavern at dawn, riding her horse hard towards the rising sun. Burning orange filled the sky, tinging the clouds pumpkin pink. Frost melted from grass crunching under hooves, and soon their breaths were no longer coming out as mist. Autumn was ending, and winter, the season she despised the most, would soon be upon them.

By evening, she came to a withering oak, bowing over a babbling creek. The sky awash in violet, clouds orange. She tied the mare to the tree, then scavenged dry leaves, fallen twigs and branches, dumping them into a pile. Using what little flint and steel she had proved enough to spark life into the kindling. May hunkered by it, palms out.

Should've purchased gloves before I left, she thought. A heavier cloak, too.

Night fell, casting pitch over the stretching plains. If it weren't for the dim circle of fire light, she wouldn't have been able to see her own hands out in front of her. More kindling was gathered, branches broken from the tree. But despite the roaring fire, the unabated chill crept into her bones.

May unpacked the horse and spread out her feather-bed, a luxury she stole from a traveler after a night spent together eons ago, by the flames. She draped a threadbare quilt over her horse. She couldn't feed him, or herself, but at least she could provide some warmth.

The sellsword laid down, curling her knees to her chest, and wrapped her cloak entirely around herself. Only her head was visible.

Gradually, she fell asleep.

It was mid-afternoon when she entered a small village. May debated the entire ride if she should spend her newly-earned coin. She wanted to save it until she had the full amount, use it then, but her grumbling stomach and the horse's whining grated on her until her temples throbbed.

Just a little food and water, for the both of us, then, we'll be on our way.

Shoeless, laughing children ran through the mud, muck splashing up their bare legs. Women leaned in their crooked doorways, their muted gowns dirty with what seemed like flour. Hollow eyed men waded through the trickling crowd, others staring, standing, aimlessly in alleys, as though lost in the haze of some tonic.

She came to a tavern at the end of the road.

"Red Dragon Inn," she read the sign aloud. Raising a brow, and glancing about, she could find nothing resembling a dragon.

Name matters naught, she thought, tying the horse to a post out front, and entering.

A dim fire flickered within a cobblestone hearth, casting a faint glow over the empty tavern. The tables and bar had a sheen of grease, and the aroma of roasted boar lingered from the back. May's mouth watered.

She knocked on the countertop. "Hello?"

"What's it?" a man groaned, limping out from a backroom. His bald head and drooping, second chin carried the same coating as the tables. "What'd you want?"

"A few slices of pork, water, and some carrots for my horse."

"Got coin?" He scratched his stained armpit.

Without revealing the purse, she removed two gold pieces, and set them flat onto the bar. "This ought to do it."

The man snorted, as though he were a pig himself, and snatched the coin and shoved them into his trousers. "Wait 'er."

In little time, the tender came back carrying a hide of sizzling pork, four thick carrots atop, and a tankard of water. He slammed them down, and before she could thank him, he trudged back through the door.

She ate quickly, leaving nothing left of the meat and water. Even the plate was licked clean of fat and salt. May used the hem of her cloak to wipe her mouth. Outside, the horse was whining and when she left the inn, she discovered why.

Two men stood around him, one holding his tether and running the back of his hand down his snout.

One of the men, leaning against the post, noticed her. "Oh, nice horse you have 'er."

"Very nice; very pretty," the one petting him said.

"Get away from him," May demanded, her grip on the bundle of carrots tightening. She passed the one man and shoved the other away. He stumbled, but righted himself before falling into the muck.

"Ladies oughtn't be traveling all alone," the man said from behind her. "It's dangerous out 'er in the plains."

May turned and he pressed against her, his flesh and stained clothes reeking of piss and ale; breath rancid with turnips and onions. She felt a bulge against her. He licked his dry lips, grinning, revealing yellowed, crooked teeth.

"And you're going to protect me?" She laughed. "Or will it be him?" She pointed to the other man, who still stood dumbly in the street, his gaze fixated to the horse's rear.

"Hey, Oates!" the man shouted. "Get 'er eyes off that damn horse and do something."

Oates shook his head, nodded. "Aye," was all he said, coming up to May's side.

"So both of you will protect me, is that so?"

"Uh huh," he said.

"No sword or dagger, bow or arrow, not a weapon on you. But, I'm guessing you two are the type who're good with their hands?"

"Oh, yes; yes ..." Oates said, a lisp hinting his words. Rose his blackened hands, long, knobby fingers spread. "Very good with our hands, very good."

"Then carry these." May shoved the carrots into his palms, and with her other hand drew her sword, quickly bringing it up to the other man's throat. The blade sheared away some of his stubble.

He raised his chin, clenched his teeth.

"Still want to protect me?" She glared into his wide eyes. "How good are your hands against a blade?"

"We don't want 'ne trouble," he got out. "Just was having a pull, that right Oates?"

Oates held the carrots as though he didn't know what to do with him. He feverishly nodded.

"A pull?" She lowered her sword. "Is that all?"

The man sighed. "'Aye, just a gaggle. Nothing serious."

She rammed the hilt into his stomach, bowing him over, and smashed it up into his nose. Cartilage broke like twigs, and blood streamed over her hands. He toppled over, holding his face, cursing.

May turned to Oates, sheathing her weapon, and wiped the blood away on his shirt. With clean hands, she retrieved her carrots. "Now leave me to feed my horse."

Not a word was said as Oates gathered his friend and they disappeared into an alley. Not even those who were audience to the incident said anything as they passed by. Everyone continued on their way as if it had never occurred, and May did, too, as she fed her horse.

The road led from the village into rolling plains of high grass and giant slabs of jutting stone. Day gave way to night, and she rode under the star speckled tapestry. The men from the village hadn't rattled her, but she didn't want to chance coming upon more, especially smarter ones. Usually they traveled in packs of five, six, and carried weapons. She was good with a sword, but knew her limits. Six men, likely in a tonic haze, would overtake her with ease.

Night turned to twilight, twilight into sunrise. Clouds hid stars, and the sun washed away the moon. May climbed a rise, pulling the horse's reins behind her. He had become too exhausted to carry her uphill. When they crested the hill, she smiled as fear trickled down her spine.

Beyond the fields, perhaps a day's ride, lay Malum. Charred tendrils scorched the earth, uncurling around crumbling stone walls and dilapidated and destroyed homes. The earth grew darker the closer to the town's center it became ... Where the Fall began. Even the sky above it appeared darker, the swirling clouds like crows over carrion.

May couldn't believe she agreed to enter such a derelict place, but the feeling of the purse against her hip reminded her why. Before she allowed trepidation to stop her, she asked the horse: "You ready, boy?" He whinied. May brushed his hair with her fingers and stepped onto it, kneaded his sides with her heels, trotting down the hill.

It became gloomier the nearer they were, the storm clouds draining the light from the sky. Wind strengthened, rain spat. By the time they reached the seared earth, rain fell in sheets. Her cloak couldn't keep the wet away for more than a few moments.

May cursed herself once more for not buying a new one.

She unsaddled her horse at the city's border, against a crumbling stone wall shielding them from the downpour. "Sorry to leave you like this," she said, tying the reins around a nearby rock. "But I don't want you to hurt yourself in there on my account." His beady eyes met hers. "Don't look at me like that, boy; I know it's cold and if a fire would survive, I'd build you one." She rubbed his snout. "I'll be back hastily, then we'll ride somewhere warmer. Sound good?"

The horse gave a faint whinny.

She smiled, kissed his head, removed the rolled painting from her supplies, and left.

Sodden, charred wood disintegrated underfoot, caking her boots black. Homes, taverns, inns, were littered with gray stones and scorched tendrils. Oily rainwater brimmed from gouges in the stonework, trickling between the cracks and slipping into the crevices beneath Malum. What bones she could make out amongst the decay gleamed like colorless ivory, as though painted with reflective dyes.

What happened here, really? she wondered.

Crumbling architecture encircled the chasm in the center of town. She stopped before coming near the jagged rim.

This is the Fall, she thought, scanning the remains, reminding her of a ship graveyard, splintered wood jutting from soaked heaps. Putting her back to the rain, she hunched and unraveled the already wet painting. Ink ran and stained her fingers, but the opaque jewels could still be seen. May burnt the image into her mind the best she could, and let the painting fall, bloating in a puddle.

May meandered through the filth, kicking over melted tankards, pewter plates; strips of hide and paper; tattered gowns and trousers and bonnets; blackened toys and cribs; bronze shields and hilts, blades without handles and broiled leather clasps, no armor to be found. People had lived here, she realized, real people with dreams and hopes, with loves and children, with work and food and drink ... Malum had only been talk before but now within its edifices, she almost cried at all the loss surrounding her.

How could such a kingdom fall to ruin? she wondered. *How could royalty be tainted so?*

She had circled the hole and found nothing likened to the necklace or jewels. May looked over the area for what felt like the thousandth time —

Something sparkled on the chasm's edge.

Just my luck.

She crept near, crouched, and strained her arm to grasp it away from the void. Rubbing away black ash, she found it to be one of the smaller opaque jewels. She placed it into her purse, then peered into the chasm ...

Two more jewels sat on a crudely jutting stone ledge, and further below, there was another and another ... May discovered that the entire gouge was lined by ledges, like spiraling teeth within a giant's mouth.

She gnawed on her bottom lip, debating if she could jump down and climb back up. Her hood finally gave way to the water, and her hair became wet. Despite the rain, the walls seemed ascendable, with knotty black roots and rocks.

It was possible, she decided.

She took a couple steps back, adjusted her belt, dug her toes into the earth, and sprinted forward. Rain congested her nose, splattered her face. Some of her hair came untied and stuck to her forehead. Her chest burned. Then she leapt, her limbs flailing in the air, and crashed onto the ledge, rolling but stopping before falling off.

Breathing heavily, May crawled and took the gems, wiping the soot away — two larger ones, but not the centerpiece — and put them with the other. Carefully she stood, peering towards the other ledge.

Truly? she thought, groaning. Another jewel, atop.

May didn't bother to consider. Her life was far more important, and she would still receive full pay returning only three. She walked to the wall, took roots into her hands, shoved her toes into the soil, and began climbing.

She soon reached the lip, shoulders and back burning, and reached over the edge but her fingers couldn't find purchase. The stonework slick with ash and rain. May tried to propel herself further up by kicking off the wall, but the soil kept collapsing.

"Piss," she spat, attempting again, and again; failing, growing tired, her muscles on fire and fingers cramping. Her clothes were now entirely drenched, smeared with mud. The shivering wasn't helping either. She coiled one last time, hanging from a root, preparing to spring with every ounce of strength left in her legs —

The root she held snapped and she fell backwards. Her back slammed onto the ledge, the air knocked out of her lungs, and a crack echoed beneath her. Before she could roll over, get to her feet, grab onto the wall, the ledge broke in two and she plummeted, screaming, into the darkness.

•   •   •

Palpable silence is what May first noticed when she came to. The second was that something soft broke her fall. The third was, as she lifted a handful of what must've been ash to her face, that although there was no torchlit she could still see, as though everything was bathed in moonlight.

She cast aside the clump, dug her heels, and stood. Too quickly, vertigo washed over her. Once her vision cleared, she trudged down the heap to a hard-packed floor.

Everything seemed to radiate the ghostly glow, like the pale light was another layer of skin. May knelt and ran her hand over the ground. The light seeped between her fingers like silt underwater, coating her glove. She wiped it on her thigh, realizing her purse was gone. She checked her sheath — sighed with relief.

At least that's still there. But the missing purse rang painfully in her chest. No coin, no more coin to come, either. She could search the ash pile but she doubted she would find it there, or even if it had fallen there at all.

May peered into the darkness overhead, no ledges to be seen. Nor was there rain this far down. Terror rose from her belly but she pushed it down like bile. She couldn't lose her mind now.

By the glow, she walked ahead, aimless.

She came upon a broken gallow, its shattered wood sticking out from the ash. Stones peeked out from underneath soot. Briefly May wondered how many had been put to it, or if a poor soul was on it when the earth swallowed it … But there were no bones about.

The sellsword kept near the wall, and soon the blackened soil opened to a cavernous opening. Keeping her hand on her hilt, she passed through.

The dirt floor and walls gave way to stonework and sconces flanking arched cell doors. Death and rot lingered from each prison. The ghostly light was dimmer, but still present, seeping betweens the stone tiles. May wanted to leave quickly but her curiosity got the better of her. Peering between blood-rusted bars, she found one cell coated in dried pitch, gathering in the far corner, connecting to more weaving across the floor and out into where she stood. The prison's walls were etched with mad, frenzied writing. None of it made sense, too congested with letters and strange symbols. Nothing else in the cell, but the malleable blackness seemed to breath rot. At a quick glance of the other cells, she found the same, others empty.

What were they doing here? she thought. What happened to these folk?

The tunnel split into two sets of stairs, one ascending, the other descending. The blackness on the floor leading down. Unfortunately, May's choice was already made for her, as the ascending stairwell she quickly found was blocked by impassable rubble.

Doubling back, she hurried down the other stairwell.

The seemingly endless stairs wound down, occasionally breaking off into cell-lined, dead end corridors. Pitch wavered across corridors, underneath steel bars. Sweat built beneath her clothes, and her racing heart matched her lungs as she pushed her legs to move faster. The fear would no longer remain below, uncurling in her belly, roving into her chest, licking the back of her throat. She didn't want to be trapped. Didn't want to wander forever in the dim darkness until she could no longer, collapsing into the ash, eventually becoming one in the same.

May nearly fell forward when the stairwell abruptly ended, soot coming up in tufts.

What is this place?

Utter blackness. The pale light remained, but so dim she had to look away to bring anything into focus. But there wasn't anything to see, save for the empty, flat plain of soot. No walls, doors, halls, nor the streaking black ...

May felt a presence, however. The same feeling of someone watching from afar. She grasped her sword's handle, backing the way she came. After more travel than it should've taken, she glanced over her shoulder. Her eyes widened. The stairs were gone.

Where'd they go?

The sellsword spun, kicking up ash, searching but only finding endless darkness. She drew her sword, walked ahead.

The door must be near. I barely even moved.

The farther she went, the deeper the soot became, and when it reached her knees, she retreated back.

Trapped rang in her head like a church bell.

"Stop," she whispered. "Get out of your head, May."

She returned to where she believed she entered, unsure, for there weren't footprints.

"What the hell is this place?"

May recalled rumors that Malum's royalty had recruited Ashcomers, Deep Magic practitioners, but for what purpose, they never said. But this had to be their work, or work of something unnatural. Her sanity was sound, she was certain. Madness hadn't touched her brain.

The ever-present feeling of being watched steadily grew, trickling down her spine.

"Come out!" she roared, "Come out and stop with the tricks!"

A blackened jester's mask appeared before her. Bland, shimmering yellow outlined dull purple smears. The mouth once forming an eye-to-eye grin broken, leaving a jagged maw.

The Three play no games. A grating, whispering voice echoed in her mind.

The sellsword stumbled back, bringing her blade up. "What are you — what is this damn place?"

I is we, and us.

A second jester mask appeared to her side. Faded crimson and gray diamonds covering soot-sullied ivory. A gouge replaced the left eye, and a devilish frown reached the bottom.

"Let me leave!" she said, sweaty grip tightening on the sword handle.

Leave?

A third formed from the abyss to her other side. Broken amethyst lining a swirl of teal and gray-white, its center a crude hole. Its mouth opened in shock.

There is no leave; only we.

Her temples began to throb. Underneath their words she heard incessant, incoherent gibbering, like thousands of people speaking hushed words inside her ears. May blinked away growing tears, shook her head.

"Stop with this shit and show me the door!"

The crimson and gray mask hovered near, the teal and gray drifted to the ground, the yellow and purple remained above.

Within we, there is no me.

Only us.

Only I.

The Three.

Blood coated the back of her tongue, and she tasted grime seeping from her gums. She spat black phlegm. *Has it grown darker, or is this another trick?* A cone of darkness formed over her vision. The gibbering; the whispering; the hushed words increasing; not louder, no, but in number, in pace. It was as though each syllable rang down her spine, rattling her innards.

Magic.

This must be Deep Magic, she thought.

No Deep, only Three.

"You can —" she hacked, wiped her lips. "Hear my thoughts?"

Within, you are I.

"Enough!" She raised her sword and plunged it into the crimson-gray mask but there was nothing beyond. No face, no body, nothing worldly. The mask floated upwards, the blade stuck within it. May tugged at the handle, but it wouldn't give, and she was forced to release it before being pulled into the air.

Teal-gray mask lifted from the ground, and the three masks aligned above her, before her. Her sword slipped through the hole, and vanished on the other side.

It was as though the gibbering voices suddenly softly shouted, clapping thousands upon thousands of hands, radiating through her body. Her knees gave way, arms leadened. Tears or blood streamed down her upturned face, black oozing from her lips. It wasn't only her stomach churning, but seemingly every innard tumbling within her flesh, mixing bile and blood and water into a frenzy that bloated against her frame.

The cone around her sight narrowed, becoming a pinprick, a star amongst space. May now could make out a vague form beyond the masks; three smooth, rippling appendages connecting each to a mountainous, writhing frame in the distance, or towering near — she couldn't decide. Faint, ever-so-faint, stars and cosmic waves rolled within it, as if a cloth was cut from the tapestry of space.

This was what swallowed Malum ... This abomination ...

Abomination, not.

Only us.

The Three.

Then, the darkness was complete, and a nothingness swept over her. May didn't know if the ground swallowed her, or had been lifted into the air and thrown into a void. It felt like falling asleep, consciousness, life, slipping away.

• • •

"And your client only wants the jewels, not the necklace?" Bron asked the man across the table.

"Yes," the man nodded, glancing at the passing waitress. "Only the jewels."

Bron set down the painting the man had given him. He scratched the stubble under his chin. Malum was a two days' ride, but the coin was well worth it. "And if I don't find them? Word is Malum's rubble."

"Then you can keep the portion you already have as a token from my client, but won't receive the second portion; which is far larger." He sipped from his tankard.

Bron drank from his own, the ale filling his empty belly. He imagined the grilled meats he could buy; the women he could have; the things he hadn't had in so many years he couldn't remember what they tasted or smelled like.

"It's a deal, then," he said, putting out his gloved hand over the table.

The man shook weakly, and stood. "Wonderful." He wiped his hands on his shirt. "Remember to give word to the barkeep when you return."

Bron nodded. "I won't forget."

"Wonderful," he repeated, and maneuvering through the bar folk, left the tavern.

Night had fallen, and the alleys were empty, save for a few sleeping drunkards. He passed by them hastily. The man pulled his collar tighter as he crossed a desolate street into another alley, turning at the end, and coming to a door. He glanced over his shoulder, found no one, and knocked three times.

A slat pulled back in the door, bleary eyes beyond. "Code?" The doorman grumbled.

"Us, I, The Three," he recited.

The slat slammed closed, and the door inwardly opened. As soon as he stepped inside, the door was shoved closed.

"Is m'lord in the parlor?" he asked the doorman.

"Where else would he be?"

"Right."

Down the carpeted hallway led to a set of double doors. He knocked three times.

"Come in," his lord said within.

He opened one of the doors, entering.

"Close it behind you, if you may."

He listened, and stood with his hands clasped at his waist. A fire blazed within the riverstone hearth, casting a warm glow over the carpet, the two plush chairs, the towering bookcases, and reflecting off the decanters and heirlooms atop the mantel.

His lord took a swig from his glass, turning to him. "Did the sellsword agree?"

"Of course, they always do."

He set down his glass on the stand between the chairs as he crossed to him. This close, the gold embroiled symbol of the Three Kings could be seen on his doublet's left breast. "Have you given word to Gregory to ride, and place the stones yet?"

The man shook his head. "No m'lord, but I will once I part."

"Good, good." His master said, and an awkwardness settled the room. The man wasn't leaving. "Is there anything else, Henry?"

"Yes," Henry licked his dry lips, adjusting his glasses. "If I may ask, m'lord, how many more do we need to send?"

"Why do you ask?"

"Talk may begin, about disappearing sellswords. This may lead to you, m'lord, as they're last seen speaking to me —"

His lord placed a bejeweled hand onto his shoulder, and the muscles in Henry's back tightened. "That won't happen; don't fret. These mercenaries disappeared a long time ago — from families, loved ones, society; no one knows or cares about them. Little will it matter when they're fed to the Kings." His lord pulled back his hand, turned, and scooped his glass from the table. "And it matters naught if folk talk or not, for the Kings will soon rise and everyone will bow before them."

Henry nodded, wiped the sweat from his brow. "Ah, thank you, m'lord. That settles my mind. I'll go tell Gregory now to ride."

"Thank you, Henry; will you tell the doorman to come here on your way out?"

"I will," he said, then left the parlor.

"What's it m'lord?" the doorman asked, standing in the open door. His heavy-jacket wrapped around him like enormous bat wings.

"Hire someone to do away with Henry," he said. "But only after he has given word to Gregory."

The doorman grinned, revealing crooked teeth. "An accident, is it?"

"Of course, an accident."

"It'll be done, m'lord," the doorman said, leaving the parlor, closing the door on his way out.

The lord gazed into the dancing flames in the hearth. "Soon Kings, you will rise; soon the world will know true royalty."

A lifelong Kentuckian, Arlo Sharp wrote his first story in the sixth grade after seeing the 1953 science fiction movie *War of the Worlds*. He's been writing off and on ever since, although life got in the way while he worked at an office job for more than thirty-six years. Now after retirement, he's finding more time to write stories and novels, but sometimes he also produces a poem or a memoir essay.

●　　　●　　　●

I get many ideas for stories from dreams. I once dreamed of UFOs hovering in the sky and fishing for me with long, whip-like lines, as happens in "Blizzard Warning." The 1956 movie "Invasion of the Body Snatchers" inspired the elements of horror in my story. The rest of the narrative fell into place around those aspects.

BLIZZARD WARNING

ARLO SHARP

A NGELA MCDONALD SAT IN HER CAR and fumed. A freakish early autumn snowstorm had rendered the highway over the Black Mountain range impassable, and she'd be spending the night in her car. Her mom had warned her not to go, although the weather hadn't been inclement when she started out to return to college. Only light overcast, with some rain. But Mrs. Viola McDonald went by the Old Farmer's Almanac and her inner feelings. The girl's mom also believed in ghosts, Bigfoot, the Loch Ness Monster, and UFOs, among other mythological traditions. She'd packed a lunch for Angela, and insisted the girl take along the wool-filled comforter the old lady had made for her last Christmas. Now it looked like both items would come in handy.

Radio broadcasts had warned everyone stranded on the mountain to sit tight, wrecked vehicles and unseasonably heavy snow had the crossing to West Virginia blocked. The road wouldn't be cleared until the next day, and no one could get through during the night. State policemen would be coming by in Humvees to give everyone blankets for warmth.

As darkness fell, Angela opened her portable cooler and prepared a picnic for one in the front seat of her Nissan. She unwrapped a corned beef sandwich on rye, with Swiss cheese and lettuce, plus side dishes of crispy fried potatoes and coleslaw. Surprised by her hunger, she ate with gusto, washing bites down with iced tea. For dessert, her mom had included a slab of homemade apple pie topped by whipped cream. Angela polished off every bite, but with some guilt. She worked hard to stay in shape. Hopefully, the indulgence wouldn't cost her too many abdominal crunches.

After the meal, her bladder made its presence known. Which was embarrassing. To relieve herself, she'd need to exit the car and hunker down in the snow and hope no one was watching, or if they saw her, they'd be mannerly enough to look away. Fortunately, her car was the last in line except for a compact VW several yards back in the opposite lane, no one directly behind her. She scooted across to the passenger side and got out, easing the door shut so no light would reveal her as she answered nature's call. She dropped her pants and undies, and eased her body down in the proper position.

A voice sounded, "Say, dearie, am I wrong in thinking this must be the little girls' room?"

With a gasp, Angie looked up. A plump lady slid out of the car in front of her and prepared to relieve herself also. Angie tried to relax and smile. Not easy in freezing weather with a stranger facing her from a few feet away.

"Now don't you worry about my hubby Charles," the woman said. "He's a perfect gentleman and wouldn't peek at ladies doing their business. In fact, he's performing the same duty on the other side of the car.

"But listen to me rattling on. I'm forgetting my manners. My name is Bertha Ogonoski. I'm Polish and proud of it!"

Angie introduced herself.

"McDonald, eh? So, you must be of Scottish descent."

The girl smiled and added, "Also some English, Welsh, and Native American."

"Great," the woman said. "I firmly believe a person ought to take pride in their roots. So, tell me something. Do you know how you can tell which girl's the bride at a Polish wedding?"

Angie couldn't believe she was snowbound on an isolated mountaintop using a commode made of air and listening to a Polack joke, but the thought of it helped relieve her anxiety about the situation.

"No," she answered with a smile, "how can you tell?"

"The bride is the girl with the braided armpits!"

The two shared a laugh as they finished and adjusted their clothes.

Bertha turned to reenter her vehicle, a large SUV. "Now honey, if you get lonesome or afraid during the night, you come on over and stay with us. We got plenty of snacks and a lot of room in our back seat for a body to stretch out and snooze, okay?"

As she got back in her Nissan, Angie agreed but didn't anticipate needing to leave her own car. There was nothing to fear. Inconvenient and a bit uncomfortable, but nothing dangerous. As night fell, the sky cleared and she did some stargazing through the windshield. Amazing how bright the heavenly orbs gleamed away from the city. She made out some constellations one never saw in town.

Until the strange lights came and washed them out.

Angie had never seen anything like them. Orbs and splotches of iridescent color which changed shape and hue as she watched. Must be Aurora Borealis, the northern lights. Unusual to see them this far south, though. Possibly a side effect of the unusual snowstorm. Still, she thought they were lovely, and she filmed them with her phone.

Her mom called, not quite in a panic but close. Angie assured her she was fine and thinking of the escapade as an adventure. She started to mention the lights but caught herself. Mrs. McDonald would likely conclude Martians were landing and call Homeland Security.

Angie heard a big engine. Glancing through the rearview mirror, she saw a large vehicle approach, lights on top and along both sides flashing like beacons. But they were red instead of blue. Almost hypnotic. Flakes of snow flew away from its passage like insects fleeing a bat. She wondered why she thought of such a bizarre comparison and repressed the thought before it gave her the willies. The big vehicle stopped by the Volkswagen behind her. A tall figure with bundles in his arms got out. He handed one through the window of the German car. The state trooper walked to her window and rapped on the glass. For some reason, she felt reluctant to open it. She smiled, but he did not.

"Ma'am, I have blankets for everyone to guard against the cold," the officer said. He had an unusual accent. "Lower your window for me, please."

Angie started to comply but hesitated at the last moment. She had her Christmas comforter and didn't need more covering. If she took a blanket, somebody else might be deprived. There might not be enough to go around. And she found it odd that the cop ordered her to open the window rather than asking her if she needed a blanket. She regarded the bundles in his arms. They looked unusual, but she couldn't define how. Didn't resemble any cloth or synthetic material she'd ever seen. She found herself fearing them. Which was ridiculous.

She held up the comforter. "It's okay, officer. I already have this, so I don't need anything else."

She thought the man looked disappointed, or maybe perplexed. He cocked an ear as if listening. She gazed at him through the glass. He seemed unnaturally tall and lean, with a strong, masculine face, a square jaw sporting a trace of five o'clock shadow, and striking eyes. She gazed into them and experienced a sensation of falling. As she watched, his eyes changed colors, from hazel to a reddish tint. And they grew brighter. Which seemed impossible. His stare pierced her. She managed to tear her gaze away. She felt if she looked another second, she would open the door or window and he'd get inside with her. The thought terrified her.

Without another word, the man turned away and walked to the Ogonoski car. They accepted two blankets from him. Angie was tempted to call out to them not to take the covers, but she wasn't sure why. The strange vehicle pulled past her car and stopped further down the road. It didn't look like a Humvee or any other car or truck she'd ever seen. All made of flowing lines and angles she couldn't quite follow with her eyes. She shivered and snuggled deeper under her comforter.

Her usual bedtime approached, and she lowered her seat to a reclining position. At first, she couldn't sleep. She pulled the edges of her comforter up past her ears, and tried some relaxation techniques. Finally nodded off.

•   •   •

Angie dreamed she was lying asleep on the mountaintop. Shivering on the frozen ground, alone and uncovered. Two large oval-shaped blobs of light hovered high above her. Although asleep, she could see them through her closed eyelids.

They fished for her. Long, sinewy tendrils extended from the alien crafts (*UFO's, her mind screamed)* and snapped high into the air like lines from a flyrod. The tendrils whipped across her body and started to curl around her. She groaned and rolled away from them. Again and again, they snapped into the air and arced back down to land upon her. Each time she struggled and rolled away before they could tighten around her. But try as she might, she could not get herself to wake up. She felt her body weaken. Knew eventually the seeking lines would grip her and draw her up toward the unknown flying machines like a fish on a hook.

With a little cry, Angie jerked awake. She was cold. Reached for the keys to start her car and run the heater.

Caught herself at the last minute. Looked around. Every vehicle she could see was dark and quiet, no engines running and no lights burning. The strange lights in the sky had vanished, and snow was falling again. Someone rapped on her window. She nearly screamed. Could make out only a dark figure. And a pair of red, burning eyes. The door rattled as someone tried to open it.

If they think I'm asleep, maybe they'll give up and leave, she thought. Had no idea who she meant by "they."

She relaxed but kept her eyes open to slits. Heard a voice. The voice of the phony police officer who'd come by earlier with the bogus blanket. For she was sure the man was not what he seemed, and something eerie was going on.

"Angela McDonald, you know you're cold and you need this blanket. You won't believe how comfortable it is. It becomes warmer by itself. I know you're awake. Come on and open your window. You know you want to. You need to."

And Angie did want to. And need to. She felt a greater compulsion than ever before in her life. But somehow, she overcame it. Perhaps the heavy wool comforter helped. Her mom had sewed bits of cold-forged iron coated with copper at each corner, claiming the metals helped ward off evil.

After a bit, the policeman went away, but in the dark, the girl couldn't tell in which direction. Whatever weirdness was going on, she didn't dare leave the protection of the car. Anyway, there was nowhere to run.

More pecking on the car window woke Angie up. She hadn't realized she'd gone back to sleep. Bertha Ogonoski stood at the window, waved at her, and smiled. The older lady held up a bundle like the policeman had been carrying.

"Now, Angie, open the window. You won't believe how warm and comforting these blankets are. Open up now and take one and join us. Then we'll all be one big, happy family. You're the only one here who hasn't taken a blanket. You don't want to be the odd person out, do you? Come on now and cooperate."

Mrs. Ogonoski smiled again, but her mouth looked too wide, with too many teeth. And her eyes had turned a fiery red. Angie pretended to be half-asleep and closed her eyes to slits again. Bertha left, but not before the girl saw a look of murderous rage twist her features. Angie shuddered. Dozed off again.

Angie woke up but kept her eyes slitted. She heard footsteps outside the car. A familiar figure came into view. Her mother. Not even wearing a coat, but showing no signs of being cold. All of which was impossible.

"Angie, honey bear, be a good girl and open your window." The old lady had called the girl by her childhood nickname. She held up a bundle. "I have another comforter for you. Made it myself, see?"

She pressed it against the window. It looked exactly like the blanket the policeman and Mrs. Ogonoski had offered her. Angie thought she could feel heat coming from it. Also impossible, but all too real. And horrifying.

"Come on, baby. It matches the one I made for you last Christmas. You don't want it to go to waste, do you? Do you want your old mama's efforts to be for nothing? Don't you love me anymore?"

Angie managed to keep from shying away from the door. Because whoever or whatever that was, it couldn't be her mother. The girl sighed as if still sleeping and settled deeper under her comforter. The figure of her mother gritted her teeth.

"Open this window this second, you insolent brat!" she declared. "If you don't, I swear I'll use your grandpa's razor strap on your behind, you ungrateful little whelp."

During her childhood, Angie had sometimes been threatened with her late grandfather's strap, but her mom never made good on the threat. The girl breathed steadily as if slipping deeper into sleep. The figure of her mother made a snarling noise and slammed both palms into the car window. The vehicle shook. The apparition moved away.

Angie had no idea what was going on, but felt her only chance to survive was to stay in the car. She considered dialing 9-1-1 on her phone, but ruled out the idea. The light and sound might attract the things roaming around in the snow, let them know for sure she was awake.

And she was sure they were things, not remotely human. Anyway, a phone call might lead any would-be rescuers to their doom.

A soft sound from the passenger side window drew her attention. She looked that way. A furry face gazed back at her and whined. Mitzi, her pet from her teenage years — a full-blooded Alaskan Malamute with one blue eye and one gray. The dog pawed the air as if digging a hole, the way she always did when Angie started to go somewhere, to let her mistress know she wanted to go along. She'd even done that before her last trip to the vet, to be put down because of terminal cancer. Tears sprang to Angie's eyes as she remembered that day, one of the saddest of her life. And how brave Mitzi had been, using the last of her strength to lick Angie's hand as she received the fatal injection. Now the beloved dog had come back to her. She started to scoot over and open the door. The dog climbed higher, and Angie could see the same type of bundle strapped to her back. And the dog's eyes changed from their beautiful separate colors to blazing red. Angie settled back under the comforter. The dog creature growled, bared its teeth, and clawed parallel scrapes down the window glass. And vanished.

Angie heard car doors opening and closing. People poured out of the vehicles stranded on the mountaintop. Men, women, youths, children. They surrounded her car. Each had one of the strange blankets draped around themselves. They looked in the windows and beckoned to her. They called her by name and asked her to come out. They implored her. When she didn't respond, they demanded, shouted, and cursed. They pounded the car with their fists. They pushed against the car, rocked it back and forth. Crying in terror, Angie burrowed under the comforter, like a frightened child would cover up her head. If you can't see the monsters, they can't see you. The people pushed the car past the tipping point. It turned over with a crash.

Angie slammed against the passenger side door. Struck her head and saw stars. Light flooded the vehicle's interior. Angie peeped out the windshield. The northern lights had returned, much brighter than before. The people stopped and looked up. Long, whip-like lines snapped down from the lights. Angie recalled her dream about alien craft fishing for her. Strange, terrible things started happening. Angie couldn't comprehend what she was seeing. When the truth finally dawned on her, she passed out.

• • •

Angie woke up in a hospital, her anxious mother sitting at her bedside. Her injuries puzzled the doctors. The girl had some mild frostbite in her extremities, but her face was sunburned. Policemen questioned her, but she couldn't explain what had happened to the dozen other people stranded on the mountain. She didn't remember.

People living in the surrounding area claimed some UFO sightings, but no one took them seriously. The authorities finally concluded the missing people had tried to walk down the mountain for help and become lost in the vast, surrounding wilderness. Blowing snow had obliterated any tracks. No trace of them was ever found.

• • •

Several years passed.

One morning Angie woke up from her recurrent dream of UFO's fishing for her, the same dream she'd had several times a week since the night on the mountaintop. And she suddenly remembered everything that happened that fateful evening.

Bright beams flashing from the lights in the sky and playing over the scene. The blankets tightening around the people. And starting to glow. Angie feeling intense heat, even inside the car.

The people struggling. Trying to run. The blankets tangling around their legs and tripping them. Their hands, faces, and legs reddening, then blackening and burning to a crisp. The people screaming in agony. Long, whip-like lines snapping high into the air from the lights and streaking down toward them, coiling around their bodies. The lines lifting them off the ground. Their bodies turning around and around, spiraling upward toward the lights. The lines drawing them in, until they became part of the radiance. The lights winking out as if they'd never existed. The heat vanishing as if unplugged.

And when Angie remembered the screaming figures drifting upward toward the mysterious lights, she realized it wasn't an alien fishing trip after all.

It was more like a wiener roast.

Gustavo Bondoni is a novelist and short story writer with over three hundred stories published in fifteen countries, in seven languages. He is a member of Codex and an Active Member of SFWA. His latest novel, published in 2022, *The Swords of Rasna*, is a dark historic fantasy. He has also published five science fiction novels, four monster books and a thriller, *Timeless*. His short fiction is collected in *Pale Reflection* (2020), *Off the Beaten Path* (2019), *Tenth Orbit and Other Faraway Places* (2010), and *Virtuoso and Other Stories* (2011). In 2019, Gustavo was awarded Second Place in the Jim Baen Memorial Contest, and in 2018 he received a Judges Commendation (and Second Place) in The James White Award. He was also a 2019 finalist in the *Writers of the Future* Contest. His website is *gustavobondoni.com*.

•   •   •

This tale comes from one of the weirder social experiments I've heard of here in South America: Venezuela's Ministry for Supreme Happiness. Not having any urge to visit Venezuela to see how it works, I tried to imagine what that would look like if you translated it to a functional society. This was the result.

KEEP THEM SMILING

GUSTAVO BONDONI

G INA MORALES WATCHED THE MONITOR. It was her favorite time of day: the morning rush hour allowed her to see the smiling people heading for work, as shown by the surveillance cameras along Fifth Avenue.

"Getting your happy on?" Jamaal asked.

"It's so peaceful. I know there's people on the street all day, but the morning is just so purposeful."

"You're weird."

"And you're normal?"

He sipped his coffee. "As normal as anyone, I guess. At least I don't treat the rush hour as performance art."

"Come on," she zoomed on a woman in a red overcoat. "Don't tell me that smile doesn't speak to you."

Jamaal chuckled. "Rookie's coming. Maybe you can sell your delusions to her." He disappeared into a cubicle fifteen feet away. It wasn't his own, of course. He preferred to do all his morning socializing before ten AM. It didn't matter, of course, he had all the alerts he needed on his portable Panorama screen.

He would normally spend a lot more time at Gina's station, but since Gina had been tasked with training the new girl, Jamaal tended to avoid the place like the plague. Well, it would only be a couple of weeks before the trainee label was removed and they could set Amy up with a low-stress beat of her own.

The rookie sat next to her. "All good?" she asked.

"Yes. Mornings are usually quiet, peaceful times."

"With so many people out?"

"The people out in the morning are generally going to work. They're pretty much content, look at the smiles. Some might be in a hurry, or late, but most of them are just going about their day. Trouble usually comes earlier or later."

"What about accidents? Car crashes and things like that."

"Not our department," Gina replied.

The teachers at the academy must be slipping, she thought. Any rookie, no matter how wet-behind-the-ears should know basic stuff like that.

"But what if someone gets angry because of an accident?" Amy pressed.

Ah. At least that was a reasonable question, if somewhat prejudiced. "The people of New York City don't go to war with each other over insurance issues. They just send each other their policy numbers and the pics and go on with their lives. We should be fine until the rush hour winds down."

As if to prove her wrong, one of the screens on the mosaic in front of her began flashing, a red border appearing around it.

Gina forgot about the rookie. "Zoom," she commanded.

The red-bordered image expanded, pushing the rest of the images in the mosaic to a column on the right side of the screen.

"What's happening?" Amy asked, trying to get a closer look.

"I ..." Gina had to double check. And then she grinned at the rookie. "You are in luck. I've been on the job ten years, and I only got to deal with one robbery. You've been here four freakin' days. Some kids have all the luck." She turned her attention back to the screen.

"Split. Interior security." she said.

The image broke into four separate rectangles. Three of them showed the scene inside the store, pulled from the merchant's own security cameras, while the fourth showed the image that had originally been onscreen: the wide-angle shot of an entire block on 37th Street, including the storefront in which the bots had identified the crime in progress. The sign above the store read Technoshop.

The interior shots made it much easier to see. There was no longer any doubt about what was going on. A large, unkempt man — not badly dressed as much as badly groomed — was pointing a gun at the single store clerk while he pulled prepaid phone cards off a rack.

"Why is he taking the cards?"

"He can exchange them for stuff. Food, probably. Maybe even rent."

"But won't the company just cancel the cards?"

Gina laughed. "It costs more in wages to run an inventory of ten thousand cards against the sales records to identify the cards than it would cost to honor them. Besides, he's not going to have a chance to use them."

"Are you sending in a team?"

Gina froze. It was tempting. The moment a team went in, it was no longer her responsibility.

But the team was a last resort. They sometimes damaged the perpetrator, the shop and anyone within a three-block radius. Teams never made anyone happy.

She looked at the man with the gun — where the hell had he gotten an actual gun, anyway? His grandfather, most likely

— trying to gauge his anger, his fear. The expression was so unlike the ones she saw every day, the happiness on Fifth Avenue, contented workers walking on their way to being productive members of a working society. It left her cold. He seemed ... resigned. More sad than angry or scared.

And that was why Gina and her peers were trained to read expressions. Had he been frightened, it would have merited a team. But not resigned. Not sad. She decided that he wasn't a danger to the clerk. Maybe to himself, but suicides didn't stop to rob stores on their way towards ending themselves.

"No team. No need to escalate. We'll use a drone and a truck as soon as he leaves the store."

"But the clerk."

"She is handling this exactly right. Smiling and staying calm. She knows that the stock isn't worth her life. And that they'll likely have it back as soon as the authorities act."

But the stress as the man took his time removing every last card from the rack took its toll. "Check my levels, will you?"

Even a rookie was proficient in applying a quick-check patch. The academy would never have passed her if she wasn't.

"Wow, heartbeat at one-forty and pressure spiking," Amy said as she read the text that appeared on the patch. "I think I need to press the red button."

You needed the patient's consent before dosing them. The red button was a circle on the cloth of the patch which, when pressed, released the correct dose of adjustment meds.

"Yes, yes, do it." Gina wanted her wits about her as the situation unfolded.

"Done."

"Thanks." She hadn't removed her eyes from the screen. The situation continued to unfold with agonizing slowness, but she felt her muscles relax, and the butterflies in her stomach stopped dancing.

When the man left the store, gun still unused for anything but threats, Gina even allowed herself to smile.

The thief, on the other hand, had no time to congratulate himself on the success of his endeavor. No sooner had he emerged from the shop than Gina gave the order for the drone to dart him, even as he concealed the gun in a coat pocket.

The drugs in the dart were of low enough dosage that, in clear situations of antisocial activity, Public Contentment officials were authorized to use them. It was a measure mainly designed to protect unbalanced individuals from harm when contained.

The microdart flew true and the man slapped his neck, as if annoyed by an insect. Then he stood still, as if unsure of where to go next. The store clerk rushed out of the shop, clearly about to scream to the world that she'd been robbed, but the sight of the man standing there sent her back into the building. She would likely need a dosage adjustment for a few days. Being robbed was a truly traumatic situation.

The truck was actually an automated holding cell on wheels. Sufficient to defuse a situation completely, as it was bullet proof as well as more than strong enough to keep a person from breaking the walls.

"Do you think he'll go inside?" Jamaal asked. He'd appeared to watch, along with most of the rest of the morning shift. Though silent, they all knew this was where the situation could blow up in their faces.

"The new cocktail in the darts is wonderful. I believe it has a ninety-seven percent success rate. We should be fine. This guy doesn't look violent."

A series of colored lights began flashing inside the enclosure, cycling in hypnotic patterns, but Gina was watching the man, not the lights.

He dropped the bag and held up a hand. Then he took a step forward, entranced by the flashes of color.

A cheer went up when the door of the enclosure slid shut behind him. Now everyone was safe, the public, smiling as they walked, and even the man ... no one under a dart dose had ever died in custody.

"Apply a patch."

An automated arm extended from a wall and gently placed the patch on the hypnotized man's neck.

These patches were much more sophisticated and powerful than the ones for home use that Gina had applied moments earlier. These had the capacity for much deeper analysis, and they were supplied with a tiny transmitter that sent the information in real time. It arrived on Gina's desktop along with the identification that the computers had made with the surveillance footage.

Walker, Ernest Jonathan. The man's name and photo appeared on her screen, along with a quick summary of his financial situation.

"Two thousand dollars in debt," Amy read for the benefit of those too far away to be able to see the small numbers. "Rent due today. Also, utilities next week. Bank account overdrawn. Last employment in April, as a construction worker."

Gina, meanwhile, was scanning the medical information from the patch. The man should have been fine. He was reasonably well-dosed — on the high end of the permissible scale, actually — and should have been able to take financial setbacks in stride without exploding in such a violent way.

"All right. I'm approving a zero-interest loan for the amount of his debt and the next week's expenses."

The numbers on the finance sheet immediately zeroed. Amy raised her eyebrows and said: "Isn't that a bit over-indulgent? What if word gets out?"

"We've got limited tools here," Gina replied. "He's drugged nearly to the blue line, and I'm going to take him just slightly over, but the dosage difference won't be enough, by itself, to bring him back to the desired behavioral patterns. He won't be able to achieve the necessary happiness with that debt on his shoulders." Suddenly conscious of her responsibility to train the rookie and the eyes of all her peers on the back of her head, Gina continued. "But you're right to question it. These loans are for use only in special cases, and you won't be able to authorize them during your first year on the job."

What she didn't say was that this was the most extreme case she'd ever encountered.

Gina waited for the drug effectiveness countdown to reach zero before speaking again. "Open audio channel to the truck."

"Channel open," the system's pleasantly modulated tones replied.

"Good morning, Mr. Walker," Gina said, enunciating clearly. "My name is Gina, and I'm your Public Contentment officer."

"Am I in trouble?" Walker asked. He didn't seem perturbed by the idea, and there were no signs of violence, which meant that the dosage was holding.

"Not as much as you were when you walked into the containment unit. In fact, we've allotted you a loan sufficient to cover your debt plus expenses. The first repayment comes due three months from now."

The man looked up towards the speaker, his eyes wide. "Three months? That gives me time."

"Yes. That's the idea. Is there any reason you can't work? Something that might not show up on your records?"

"No ... but it's hard. All I could think of lately was that I was going to be evicted. That I'd have to live in the shelter with the rest of the failures."

"The shelter isn't so bad. It's there to help."

"You never recover from the shelter."

She wasn't there to argue with him. "Well, do you think you'll be able to start repaying in three months?"

"Absolutely." He said it with conviction, with hope. "My cousin said they'll be hiring for that high-rise on Ninth next week."

"Great. Now I need you to do two things for me before I let you out. First off, I need the bag with the cards. Please put it on the shelf that just opened in the wall."

"Oh, right," he looked embarrassed. "I don't need these anymore."

"Thank you. Now, I need you to give us the gun."

"This gun belonged to my father," he said as he pulled it from the coat.

"We respect that. When you put it in the cubby, you will be issued a receipt, and you can get it back once you've paid the loan."

"That sounds fair."

Gina smiled as the gun disappeared into the bowels of the truck. He would never get it back unless he was fully rehabilitated, of course. The processes and paperwork to regain confiscated firearms existed, but they had been deliberately designed to keep all but the most diligent from succeeding. Sometimes things that didn't work helped society function.

The door behind Walker hissed open. He looked back as if unable to believe that all the consequences had been paid already.

"You can go, now, Mr. Walker," Gina said. "I hope you can enjoy the day."

"Wow. Yes. I mean, thank you." He walked into the light. A couple of people passed on the street, gave him a curious look and went on their way.

Gina sighed and slumped back into her chair. The tiny destressing dose she'd allowed had only been enough to take the crazy edge off, not to keep all the nerves at bay, but she only realized it now.

Jamaal put his hand on her shoulder and squeezed once. They'd all been there at some time, and the fact that emergencies were infrequent made them all the more intense. Then the people watching dispersed and left her and Amy alone. The rookie looked so frightened that Gina chuckled.

"This was actually not the worst time. Had to deal with a murder once," Gina said.

Amy's eyes widened further. "A murder? Really? There are only about two a year in the entire city, they told us at the academy."

"Well, I got one on my beat. I was working the night shift back then."

"Oh, wow."

"Let's take a break and I'll tell you about it."

Amy smiled. Gina smiled back.

And the people on the monitors smiled as they went about their daily business.

Michelle Ann King lives in Essex, England, and is a writer of speculative, crime, and horror fiction. Her work has appeared in over a hundred different venues, including *Strange Horizons, Interzone,* and *Black Static.* Her favorite writers include Stephen King, Tana French, and Terry Pratchett. She has published two short story collections, available in ebook and paperback formats. Learn more about Michelle at *transientcactus.co.uk.*

•   •   •

The witch in this story is probably one of my favourite characters. In a lot of ways, she's much like a writer: set a terrible situation in motion and smugly declare, "This isn't going to end well," then sit back and watch contentedly as it all goes to hell.

WHERE THERE'S MAGIC

MICHELLE ANN KING

T HE WITCH HAD A FAVORITE SAYING: *Where there's life,
there's magic.* There was a second part: *Where there's
magic, there's death* — but she usually kept that to herself.

She placed the newborn into the father's arms. He gazed
upon the babe with wonder, then upon his wife with concern.

"Why does she still scream?" he said. "Can't you ease her
pain?"

"There is still pain because she carries twins. There is a
second part of this birth to come."

The mother lifted her head from the sweat-soaked pillow
and shrieked louder. The witch went back to her work.

They called the first child Heavenly Gift. She had clothes
and toys and kittens awaiting her, all stamped and stitched
and branded with her name. There was also further coin for
the witch, to perform magical blessings for her good fortune.

Her twin, unexpected and unasked for, had none of these things. They called this girl Second Part.

"That's not going to end well," the witch said, but nobody listened.

Since she hadn't been paid for divination, she didn't try to make them.

• • •

Heavenly Gift grew up in accordance with the radiance of her name and allotted position, and duly became beautiful and beloved. She dreamed of knowledge and power.

Second Part, identical in beauty but not in regard, dreamed of being reborn.

• • •

There were things a good daughter could do, to aid her family's fortunes. An advantageous marriage was chief among them.

Along the borders of the family's land were two other estates. Second Part rode with her mother to both of them in turn. The trip was exhausting and beset with dangers, but they still employed the services of the witch and were protected from the worst depredations of bandits and bears.

The first estate was small and barren and had little to recommend it as an ally, but the second was bigger and richer even than their own, seeded with almond trees and roamed by giant jewelled scorpions that the fine ladies hunted and stripped of their elaborately ornamented stings. It had also been newly inherited by the eldest son, Leon, after the death of his mother.

Leon was dark-eyed and graceful, and Second Part was instantly captivated.

"How do you like the looks of my daughter?" Reyna asked Leon, and his smile was all it took to conclude arrangements between them.

Second Part was entranced, and thought Destiny must be finally smiling upon her, just as warmly as Leon had. "This marks the turning-point of my life," she said.

The witch, reading the entrails of a cat-slaughtered crow, agreed with her assessment. "Just not in the way you think," she said. But the girl was already dancing away, her eyes shining, and did not stay to hear the detail.

•   •   •

The dowry was confirmed, and the wedding preparations made, with Reyna's customary speed and efficiency. Within a month, Leon was married to Heavenly Gift.

Second Part's purpose in the affair, as she now learned, had been to serve as an animated portrait of her sister — a reflection of the reality being promised. Heavenly Gift, of course, could not have been risked on the journey.

Reyna, pleased, said the girl had performed her function well and would be rewarded. A new horse, perhaps.

Second Part was greatly surprised by this outcome, which in turn surprised Reyna and everyone else. They'd thought she understood how things were. They'd thought it was obvious.

The only one not taken aback by any of it was the witch. She had a lot of cats — and, therefore, a lot of entrails — and was never surprised by anything at all.

•   •   •

The joined estates prospered. Reyna congratulated herself on the successful execution of her plans.

Heavenly Gift bloomed under her mother's tutelage and her husband's admiring gaze. She devoted herself to learning the management and improvement of the estate.

Second Part dressed in mourning black, which rather suited her, and chased scorpions on long hunts across the forest — although she never came back with any jewels.

Leon watched her from astride his fine grey mare and wondered quite how this had all come to pass. But his lands had doubled, his purses overflowed, and the grey mare was really very fine indeed. And Heavenly Gift was so beautiful, her face identical to the one he had fallen in love with. Reyna assured him that he would soon forget it was not actually the same.

The crows hid from the cats and the witch sat in her cottage, smoking her pipe and waiting.

•　　•　　•

There were things a good daughter could do, to aid her family's fortunes. Being apprenticed to a witch was second among them.

"You see?" Reyna said, as she kissed her daughter goodbye. "All that is fitting is good."

It did not seem fitting to Second Part. It did not seem fitting at all.

But she said, "Yes, Mama," and went as she was bid.

•　　•　　•

The witch taught Second the knowledge of plants and herbs, and the workings of the body. She taught her all the ways of magic that did not, in fact, require magic at all.

"These ways may take more effort, but they are safe," she said.

"And real magic is not?"

The witch shook her head. "No, child. The only real magic comes from death. This is something I would not advise you to learn."

Second considered this. "Teach me anyway," she said.

•　　•　　•

The witch showed Second the reading of things in entrails and the finding of things in bones. She showed her the blood-wards of protection against bandits and bears, and the totems that could be made out of feathers and skin and scorpions' stings. She showed her the power formed in sacrifice.

The cats were kept very busy.

• • •

Second came to understand why her sister had dreamed of knowledge and power. They were heady things to own. She studied hard at her lessons, and practiced them well. The crows took wing and the cats had to find other prey. But they came to love her like one of their own.

Leon, meanwhile, had come to understand that identical did not mean what he'd believed — or perhaps more precisely, wanted to believe — that it did. Reyna's assurances had not come to pass, and he could not forget.

He went to the witch's cottage to ask what he should do, but the witch refused to give advice because nobody ever took it. "People will do what they wish," she said. "However misguided or dangerous they know it to be."

Second gazed at Leon, and he gazed back.

The cats yowled, because there were always entrails to read if you were determined enough to find them. They could have parted the lovers with bad omens and sharp claws, but they were suckers for a good story, and so left them alone.

• • •

Leon told his wife he was learning to track scorpions on the fine grey mare. Heaven, distracted by her studies and duties, simply kissed his cheek and wished him good hunting.

The mare never learned to recognize a scorpion's trail. But she learned the journey to the witch's cottage very well.

• • •

"I have found a way," Second announced, "that we can be together."

Leon looked around the cottage nervously. Reyna and Heaven would not come here, but they had spies who were not so circumspect.

"They would see us both dead, first. You know that."

Second smiled and kissed him. "I do," she said. "But there is magic formed in death, and even more in sacrifice."

Her words did nothing to calm Leon's nerves. But he loved her, and so he bade her continue.

"The magic will give me what I have always dreamed of," she said. "Rebirth. It will allow me to open death's gate, and pass back through to the other side. After my death I will return, and awake again as a babe in arms." She clutched him tighter. "And it will let you through the gate with me, if we welcome death together. We will have new bodies, new lives. A second chance, to grow and live as we choose."

Leon sank down onto the witch's stone bench. The years had not been kind to his bones, and the thought of starting over, of being young again, was not an unwelcome one.

He asked the witch if this would be possible, and she told him yes.

He did not ask her if it would be wise. But then, she would not have bothered to tell him no.

•   •   •

"You know what you must do?" Second asked.

Leon nodded, solemn-eyed. The witch had provided her very best ceremonial dagger for the occasion, and he clutched it in one trembling hand.

Second raised both hand and blade until the tip was resting against her chest. "One swift stroke," she said. "And then turn it upon yourself."

Leon tried to speak, but no words formed.

"Do not falter, my love. You must send me to Death, and follow straight after. Then we will be reunited."

"I will do what I must," he finally said, but his voice shook.

Second glanced at the Witch, who nodded. Should it prove that Leon lacked courage, she would provide it for him.

Leon closed his hands around the dagger's hilt and leaned down for a final kiss.

"It is true, then," Second said. "You have betrayed me."

Leon frowned, because her words made no sense. Then he realized that she had not spoken. It was Second's voice, but the words had not issued from her lips.

As a mystery, it was easily solvable. Who else was there, that could speak with his love's voice?

They turned together and faced Heavenly Gift. She had climbed the wall around the witch's cottage, and her dress was torn and flecked with dirt.

"How can you do this?" she said. Her voice trembled as much as her husband's had.

Second smiled. "How? Because I have learned the ways of magic while you sat on cushions and waited for servants to bring you sweetmeats. You have had everything given to you, sister, including that which should have been mine. Now I will take it back. I will come second to you no longer."

"Stand aside, husband," Heaven said, and such was the power of her expectations that Leon did as she commanded.

The cats yowled, for they had been promised blood. "Patience," the witch said.

Heaven tore the dagger from Leon's hand and whirled around, just as Second rushed forward.

"You will not —" Second began, but the rest of her own command was choked off as her momentum carried her onto the point of the blade.

It slid smoothly through her dress, her skin and her flesh. The knife had long ago learned to love the taste of a human heart, and it sought its prey as ruthlessly, as efficiently, as any witch's cat.

Second's lips parted, but no further sound escaped them. She stood still, her eyes clouding, then fell to the ground.

In the endless moment that followed, even the cats were silent.

Heaven stared down at the unmoving body. "I did not mean for this to happen," she said. Her voice was thick with tears and no longer sounded anything like her sister's. "I wanted to stop her. I did not want her death."

She dropped the dagger and held out her dripping hands to the witch. "Can you not save her? Is there nothing to be done?"

"Patience," the witch said.

Leon stared at the scene before him and struggled to understand it. The witch's lush green grass ran red, and the cats frolicked happily. His senses swam and clouded, just like Second's unseeing eyes.

He reached down and retrieved the dagger from the sodden ground. "You have stolen my love for the last time," he said, and yanked Heaven's head back by the hair. His other hand drew the blade smoothly across her throat.

More blood flowed, and the cats yowled their approval.

Leon thrust the body away from him and fell to his knees. "What have I done?" he breathed.

"To look at it one way," the witch said, "you have avenged the killing of your lover. To look at it another way, you have completed the contract: there were two deaths, as arranged. One has killed, and died in return. This was the offering, and it will be accepted. Rebirth will be granted to both sisters."

Leon stared at her, comprehension finally filling his eyes with horror.

The witch shrugged and lit her pipe. "To put it a third way, you truly screwed it up."

•   •   •

When Reyna's men came, the witch told them the truth about what had happened in her garden. There was little point trying to pretend things were other than they were: women like Heavenly Gift did not slit their own throats.

They looked for Leon, but she told them he was gone, along with her best horse and her second-best cat, and a basket full of bones.

"What is the purpose of these bones?" the Chief of Guards asked her. "What magic are they designed to perform?"

"They are for a specific form of divination," the witch said. "They will help him find things."

"What things? Give me the truth, old woman. What is it that the murderer seeks?"

The witch lit her pipe and inhaled its sweet smoke. "Babies," she said, and the men turned pale.

"We must pursue this black-hearted rogue," the Chief of Guards said. "We must find him before he can unleash any further depravity upon the heads of innocents."

"We must," his men agreed. But they looked at the bodies while they remounted their horses, and when they rode away it was not in the direction Leon had taken.

•　　•　　•

In a small village a hundred leagues away, there lived a young couple. They were swordsmiths of some renown, and wanted for neither love nor money. What they did want was a child, but for years they had waited for the quickening in vain.

The eventual conception, therefore, was cause for a mighty celebration. The child was active all throughout her time in the womb, and the couple were thrilled.

"She will be a fine, strong girl," the mother said, pulling her husband's hand across her stomach. "Feel how she kicks, how full of life she is."

But when the girl was born, she was not the lusty, squalling creature they had expected. She was beautiful and healthy, yes — and they loved her dearly, yes. But she was quiet and reserved, and did not laugh and gurgle the way other babies did. She would not be amused by songs and games. Instead, she lay motionless in her crib, her little arms by her sides.

Her appetite was healthy, and her body grew well, but she neither spoke nor answered to her name. The parents worried, but the wise woman examined her and pronounced her eyes clear and her mind strong.

"Her development is unusual," the wise woman said, "but not unheard of. She is the second child I have seen behave this way."

For the first time, the little girl smiled.

She liked to be outside, where she would patiently watch the horizon for hours. She also liked to sit in the smithy, and would give the blades the kind of loving looks she would never bestow upon her parents.

When the stranger came for her, with his black horse, his red cat and his bag of bones, they told themselves it would be better not to fight. The stranger was old, but he carried the scents of death and magic, and who knew what harm he might do if they stood in his way? He might hurt the girl, if they tried to resist. It would be for her sake, for her own good, if they allowed him to take her.

So when she ran to him and he swept her onto the horse, they simply went inside their cottage and closed the door.

•　　•　　•

Heavenly Gift's second childhood was not as charmed as her first. Her new parents were not bad people, but neither were they rulers of a fine estate. She had few clothes and toys, and no jewels or kittens. She was still beautiful and golden, but there was no joy in her heart or love in her eyes. Neither of these things had served her well before and she set aside no space for them in her new life.

Instead, she paid attention to her lessons and listened avidly to stories of her home. It was a long way away, but she was young and strong — again. She would find her way.

She knew who she was, even if nobody else did.

"She is an old soul," her teacher said, and her parents nodded. And tried to pretend they believed this was a good thing.

•　　•　　•

The witch welcomed Second as she had done before, but shook her head at Leon. "Reyna's guards have not forgotten," she said. "Their duty remains unaltered and they still search for you. They come here regularly, to ask if I have news of where you are."

Second clung to him, but Leon gently pried away her tiny hands.

"Do you no longer love me?" she cried. "How can this be so?"

"It is not," he said. "My love for you is undimmed. But look at us — I am an old man, and you are but a child. I must settle for the love of a grandfather, now."

"No," Second said.

"Yes. We cannot be what we were. It falls to me to protect you, and I can only do that by leaving you."

"No," Second said again. "The magic I have is also undimmed, and will serve us again. You know what you must do."

Leon shook his head, and shrank from her. "No, child. No."

"Yes," Second said, closing his fingers around the hilt of his dagger. "We will not be interrupted this time; we can proceed as we should have before. My second death will save us both."

She leaned closer, her breath sweet and warm against his cheek. "We will be of an age once more, and can have the love we deserve. No more talk of grandfathers."

The witch's cats yowled and the crows fled their high branches.

"The guards," the witch said. "They will come shortly."

Second leaned her head backwards, exposing the smooth flesh of her throat. "Quickly, my love. Do what you know you must."

Leon stared at the wicked edge of the dagger, then at the witch. She shrugged. "You must choose, and soon," she said.

"It is my wish," Second said, raising his hand and the blade it clutched.

"Hold!" cried a voice, and the hooves of the guards' horses struck a frantic rhythm on the cobbles outside the cottage.

"Do not ask me to hurt you," Leon whispered, but his hand was already moving. It sliced, drawing an arc through air and flesh. Second fell, her body so light and small in his arms.

"You will need to finish it now," the witch said. "One way or the other."

Leon raised his dripping knife again and drew another arc — downwards, this time, into his heart.

The guards reined in their panting horses and surveyed the garden.

"If we could not prevent the first slaying," the leader said, "then maybe it was fitting that we did not prevent the second." He spat on the ground next to Leon's body. "At least now it is over," he said. "The monster will cause no more deaths."

The cats edged closer to the grass, their little pink tongues darting out.

The witch reached for her pipe. "We'll see," she said.

•   •   •

When Heaven finally attained her home, she did not recognize it. Reyna had died, and with no daughters to inherit the land, it had been divided between the guards.

The witch's cottage, however, remained unchanged.

"She lives, doesn't she?" Heaven said. "My sister. I can feel the movement her life makes in the air."

The witch nodded. "Yes. She lives."

"How many? How many new lives will she have?"

"Her lives will be as numerous as her deaths. That is the way of the magic."

"And he who was my husband? He lives also?"

"Yes. Who dies with her will awaken when she does. That is also the way of the magic."

"This is what she learned from you?"

"Yes."

"Then teach it to me also. I have no gold or jewels any more, but I will pay any other price you ask."

The cats yowled. "Feed them," the witch said, "and I will give it some thought."

Heaven looked at the cats, who twined themselves around her ankles. They were very large cats indeed. Or maybe she had just forgotten that she herself was smaller now.

"Where are their bowls?" she said, then caught herself. She knew what witch's cats ate. That, she hadn't forgotten.

She crouched down and held out her hands, letting the cats carve their names into her palm with their sharp little tongues. They lapped at their designs, then went back to sleep at the witch's feet.

The witch treated Heaven's hands with salve and bound them with fresh linen. "I will teach you," she said.

•   •   •

Second learned, her third time as a babe in arms, to behave better. Blend in better. She learned to gurgle and coo, to smile and wave her fat little limbs whenever she was observed. And when she was not, she closed her eyes and thought of Leon, and how she would cast the bones to find him, and the life they would finally have together.

She waited and dreamed, and was content — even when the village cats nipped at her hands and feet, even when they yowled and draped her with the entrails of bandits and bears.

The cats shrugged, in the graceful way that only cats can, and went about the rest of their business.

•   •   •

The news spread rapidly through the villages: a babe had been snatched! A fine young boy-child, lifted out of his bed and spirited away into the night.

Some people spoke of fairies and goblins, some of a girl on a horse, a red cat riding in her lap. Some said she was a witch, some said she was an avenging angel from Heaven. Some said she was still looking for children to steal.

"That's nothing but the scaremongering gossip of idle men with too much time on their hands," said one young father. He had no time for stories of witches and their cats. He had bread to bake and a girl-child of his own to feed. Those were his worries — real things, not rumors and fancies.

But he ran home from the bakery anyway, because sometimes the fanciful stories had bones of truth, and while he didn't believe in fairies and spirits, he did believe in bandits and slavers and ravenous bears.

His door stood open when he returned, his neighbors pale-faced and wide-eyed. A horse pawed the ground in front of his cottage and a red cat yowled at the crows on the roof.

And a young woman, golden-haired and cold-eyed, carried his little girl out of the house.

The baby, normally so even-tempered, yowled even louder than the cat.

"Leave my child alone," the young father said. His hand reached for the short sword he carried at his belt.

The woman smiled and shook her head, and though he groped for where the blade should have been, his hands found only air.

"In truth, this child is not your own," the woman said. "she is a changeling, and would have left you of her own accord as soon as she reached an age to do so. I am saving you time, trouble, and heartbreak by taking her now."

"No," the father said, but his voice wavered. The baby seemed sweet-natured, yes, but hadn't lightning scorched the ground at the moment of her birth? Hadn't the crows fallen dead from the skies? Hadn't the village cats refused to kill? Serious omens all. His wife, given her own sweet nature, had refused to give credit to such things. And he'd agreed, of course. Fanciful notions! But still, he'd sometimes wondered how shallowly those bones of truth might be buried.

"Be at ease," the young woman said. "We are family, this little one and myself." She cradled the child in the crook of her arm. "She is my sister, and I have long looked forward to our reunion."

The red cat leapt onto the woman's shoulder and leaned down towards the baby. It blinked dark eyes at her and licked her nose with its bright pink tongue. The baby screamed louder.

"No," the father said, but his voice had not grown firmer. The cat! Didn't they say cats always knew their own?

The woman bowed her head to him. "We will disturb you no further," she said, and took both baby and cat outside.

"No," the father said, a third and final time, but his voice only whispered into the empty air.

•   •   •

The witch peered into baby Leon's eyes and prodded his gums with the sharpened nail of her little finger. His cries were lusty and clamorous.

"He will grow up strong and healthy," she said. "A fine young man."

"You may keep him," Heaven said, "if you wish. He can light your fires and feed your cats."

"I have no need of boys to do that."

"Then sell him to the traders, or apprentice him to the mines. I care not for how his life unfolds, as long as it no longer consists of love and ease."

Second lay on the rug where she'd been left, quiet and still. But her eyes tracked Heaven's movements.

"And my sister?" Heaven said. "Will she grow up to be as beautiful and deceitful as she was?"

The witch picked flecks of meat from her teeth with her pointed fingernail. "Do you ask me to look into the future for you?"

Heaven smiled, and the cats all fled the room. No, she did not need that. She already knew the answer to her question.

Second would not grow up to be the cunning, artful girl she had once been. Second would not grow up at all.

•   •   •

Word arose throughout the land of a new witch and a new magic, and a way to cheat age, infirmity, and death.

Word arose, and word spread.

•   •   •

Heaven nodded to her servant, and the girl thumped the castle gate with the hilt of her sword.

It opened slowly and the doorkeeper, a red-haired ogre of a man, boomed, "State your name and business."

The servant said, "We have an appointment with Lord Arlan. My name is Jennet and this is —" but by then the doorkeeper had seen Heaven, and he held up one huge, rough-scarred hand.

"We know who she is," he said, and his voice had lost much of its previous power.

He bowed his head and stood aside as Heaven rode into the courtyard. "I will take you to my master," he said.

Heaven slipped from her horse and nodded again to her servant, who lifted the woven basket from its saddle-hook and carried it carefully up the stone stairs to Lord Arlan's chamber.

A long wooden table stood in the center of the room, laden with bowls of bread and fruit. Heaven popped a fat purple grape into her mouth, then pushed the bowl aside.

"Come, my Lord," she said. "Your hospitality is welcome, but we have business to transact, do we not? I assume you have not changed your mind?"

Lord Arlan gave Heaven a shallow bow, but he looked as though the answer to her question was far from settled. He lowered himself carefully into an ornate jewelled chair.

"You appear to be in pain, my Lord," Heaven said. "Are you ill?"

He waved a hand. "It is not sickness or injury that plagues me, witch, it is age." His eyes searched hers. "In the villages, they say you are named for truth — that you are a gift that reverses all the destruction of time. Is this fancy, or can your healing magic really do as they say?"

"It isn't healing magic," she said. "But yes, it can do as you wish. I can give you a new lifetime, if you desire. You will be reborn and live your years anew."

"But where? In what circumstances?"

"That, I cannot control. But the bones will guide me to you, and I will return you home to your rightful place."

Jennet placed the covered basket on the floor at Heaven's feet, and Arlan pointed at it. "What is that? What do you have in there?"

Heaven smiled, rocking it gently with her boot. "You know what it is."

"I do not," he said, but he could not meet her eyes.

Heaven nodded to Jennet, who lifted the veil from the basket. Heaven brought out a knife from the folds of her coat and held it out, hilt first, to Arlan.

He blanched. "What is this?" he said, and his voice had shrunk.

"Oh, come," Heaven said. "Do not pretend such fainting innocence. This is death magic, Lord Arlan. You know what it must entail."

She proffered the blade again. When he stayed immobile, she laid it upon his knee.

"You cannot expect —" he said, then trailed off.

"I expect nothing. I am here at your bidding. What happens next is your choice. But if you choose to proceed, there must be sacrifice. That is the way of things."

"You are sure?"

Heaven gazed down upon him. "Do you doubt me, Lord Arlan?"

Arlan shifted in his chair and kept his eyes cast down. "No. Of course not. You are just — so young, to be so powerful a witch."

"I sell fresh life," Heaven said. "Is my own not the proof you desire?"

Arlan looked at the knife. "Is there no other way?"

"No. Fresh life demands fresh death."

"But to kill a child —"

"Be at ease, my Lord. My sister loses naught. The magic renews her also."

Arlan gripped the blade in palsied fingers. "This is meant to give me ease? That this is the nature and extent of the child's existence in this world?" His throat worked, the loose skin around his jowls trembling as he swallowed.

Second lay unmoving in the basket. Her eyes focused only on the ceiling, and she did not react when Arlan's hand touched her own.

He withdrew and directed a dismayed look at Heaven. "Is this not worse for her than true death, witch? Is this not worse?"

Heaven simply smiled and guided his hand back to the basket. She did not contradict him.

●   ●   ●

The child sat cross-legged in her cage made of bones and scorpion stings. The jewels threw reflected light upon her face, creating for a moment the illusion of expression. But it faded with the light, and the child sat as still as carved stone.

Jennet brought her toys and sweetmeats and fat purple grapes, but she paid no attention to any of them.

"You should go out to the estates," Heaven told her. "Spread the word of our services. It is time we found a new client."

"But we have many bags of gold, as yet untouched."

Heaven smiled. "I don't do this for the money, girl. Now go."

Jennet gathered her travelling cloak and her sword. She checked on the child, who still sat in the center of the cage, staring at the bones with unwavering concentration.

Jennet knelt on the floor and tried to catch her gaze. "Upon what do you meditate, all these long hours? What is it that so captures your thoughts?"

For a long while there was no answer, but then the child turned her head, ever so slowly, and her lips formed a word. Jennet expected it to be escape, or perhaps freedom.

But when the child finally spoke, what she said was "death."

•　　•　　•

The new client was a merchant from the outer islands, a woman with a bowed frame and ashy skin. "I am Kevis," she said. "Your mistress awaits me."

"Welcome," Jennet said, taking her cloak and showing her inside.

Kevis stared openly around the great hall. "You keep a fine house."

Heaven entered through the far door. "My clients are generous," she said.

Kevis cast her gaze downward. "I am sure my desire for generosity would match theirs, but the practicalities of my situation must impose limits upon it. I wish it were otherwise, but ..." she trailed off and took a cloth bag out of her belt. It was a very small bag.

Jennet made to give the woman's cloak back to her, but Heaven lifted a hand. "At ease, Jennet. As you have noted, our situation is hardly dire. We may exercise our own generosity, in this instance." She smiled widely, showing her beautiful white teeth. "And should Madam Kevis wish to increase her gift later, she will have plenty of years to earn further gold."

Kevis offered a smile of her own in return, but it was small and uncertain.

Jennet took the cloth bag — so light! — and tucked it into her pocket. "Follow me," she said.

When she saw the bone cage in the centre of the room, Kevis inhaled sharply.

The girl sat in her usual pose, cross-legged with her hands on her knees. She lifted her head and looked directly at Kevis. "Good day, my lady," she said.

Kevis backed up, her hand fluttering to her mouth.

"That is a child," she said. "I was told — Arlan's people said —"

Heaven stepped between her and the cage. "Said what? I hope you were not misinformed. Surely you did not believe it would suffice to spill the blood of bears or scorpions?"

"No, but —"

"You expected a baby, my lady?" the girl said. Her voice was high and sweet. "One that would be easy to kill because it would not attempt to engage you in conversation? Would not plead with you to spare its life?"

Jennet stared. It was the most she had ever heard the girl speak.

"Hush," Heaven said. "Come now, Madam. Do what you came here to do, and your failing heart will betray you no longer. You will be granted a new body, fit and healthy."

She nodded to Jennet, who drew her dagger from its sheath and held it out. Kevis stared at it, her skin growing even more ashen.

"Still, you hesitate?" Heaven said. "You can have no concerns, surely, if you have traded with Arlan's household. You know the process works."

"I know his lieutenant brought a baby to the castle, and that she rules in its name. Is the babe really Arlan? That, I do not know."

Heaven shook her head sadly. "Such cynicism does not become you."

"But maybe it will save you," the girl said. "If this is not real and you die a murderer, what reward do you reap then?"

Heaven looked at Jennet. "This is why we should not wait as long between clients." She turned back to the cage. "Sister, still your mendacious tongue."

Kevis's gaze had not left the blade in Jennet's hand. "Does it hurt?" she said.

"No," Heaven said.

"Yes," the girl said.

Jennet extended the knife towards Kevis. The older woman shrank from it.

The girl crawled to the front of the cage. "Listen to me, my lady. I have bargained with death before, and it has accepted my terms. This time, when I enter its embrace, it will not let me go. I will know the peace of oblivion. If this is what you desire, then you are welcome to join me on my final journey. But if you wish to live then you should turn aside and follow this path no longer."

There was silence in the room.

Kevis shook her head. "I am sorry for wasting your time, Mistress Heaven," she said, her voice stiff and thin. She bowed, turned and ran back along the stone hallway with ragged steps.

Heaven sighed. Then she took the dagger from Jennet's hand and thrust it through the bars of the cage and into the side of the girl's throat. Blood coated the cage, the floor, and Jennet.

She stood, shivering, as Heaven rested the point of the knife against her own breast. "It is past time for my own rejuvenation," she said. "Once it is done, go to the witch of my old estate. She'll help you use the bones to find us."

"Mistress," Jennet said. "Oh, Mistress —"

"What, girl? You, of all, know there can be no doubts. How many times have we done this? You know the magic delivers on its promise."

Heaven pushed the knife, smoothly and sleekly, into her chest. Her lips parted and a small flower of blood bloomed stark against the whiteness of her teeth.

Jennet ran forward and caught her as she fell. "Oh, Mistress," she said again. Heaven's face still wore her frown, and it did not loosen as Jennet lightly kissed her forehead.

She laid the body gently on the flagstones. Heaven's sister also lay crumpled and unmoving inside the cage. But the bones were all cracked and upon her face was a rapturous smile.

•   •   •

The cottage was exactly as Jennet's mistress had always described it — small and squat, with stone walls and a lush garden filled with gamboling cats.

Jennet knocked upon the heavy wooden door and gave her name and a gift of tobacco to the servant who opened it. She bowed. "I seek help," she said. "Where is the witch?"

"She rests," Leon said. "I perform her duties now."

"Then can you aid me, sir?" Jennet held up the bag of bones. "I have tried to use these to find my mistress, but they will not speak to me."

"That is simple magic," Leon said. "I will help you."

He called to the cats, who soon brought him a fresh set of warm, steaming bones. "Hold your mistress's image in your mind," he said.

Jennet closed her eyes and let Heaven's face fill the darkness. She smiled.

Leon scattered the bones upon the grass. "Hold out your hand above them," he said, and Jennet complied.

The cats sat in a circle around them, watching. They blinked silently.

"Do you see her?" Leon asked.

Jennet shook her head.

"Do you hear a whisper, then? As if made from the wind and rain, telling you where she is?"

Jennet shook her head.

"A feeling in your stomach, a sensation of being pulled towards her?"

Jennet opened her eyes. "No," she said. "I see, hear, and feel nothing. This is how it has been for me every time I have tried."

Leon frowned and threw the bones again. "Give me your hand and call up her image again," he said.

Jennet did as she was told. Leon closed his eyes, then said, "Oh."

"You have found her?" Jennet clutched his hand tighter. "You can see my mistress?"

"Only in your mind. Nowhere else." He dropped her hand and stepped back. "I'm sorry, I cannot help you. She is not here."

"Are you sure? She would not look as I picture her. She would be —"

"A baby," Leon said. "I know."

"You are familiar with this magic?"

He looked away, and Jennet could not read his expression.

"Yes. And if she had been reborn, I could find her. But there is nothing."

Jennet thought of the girl, the sister. Her talk of death, and her final smile of joy.

She shook herself. "It is merely taking longer than usual," she said. "I will wait."

The cats yowled. One leapt upon the back of Jennet's horse and dug in its claws until the mare trotted to her side. As if the cat were telling her to leave. As if it were telling her that there was no reason to hope. That Heaven was gone.

She lifted the animal off the horse and set it on the ground. What did cats know?

"My mistress will return," Jennet said.

The red cat wound itself around her legs and bit her foot.

Leon shook his head and slowly sank to the grass. He pulled his knees up to his chin and stayed that way for a long time.

"What ails you?" Jennet asked.

"I have need of these no longer," Leon said. He gathered up the bones and threw them into the trees. "There is nothing left I care to look for."

He drew a long, shuddering breath and pressed his palms to his face. "But my love has found what she was seeking, and for that, I will try to be thankful."

"I do not understand," Jennet said.

"I know. And I envy you."

"I care for none of this. I wish to wait here until you have found my mistress." She looked down at the cat, which was lapping at her wounded foot. "And if the cats want my blood, they can have it."

Leon looked at her sadly. "That will buy you shelter here. But you will be waiting a very long time, my lady."

Jennet lifted her chin. "I have a lot of both blood and patience. I also have faith that my mistress will return. As she has always said — where there's magic, there's life."

Leon sighed heavily. "I was taught a different version of that saying," he said. But he went inside and cleared out a room where the girl could stay. There would always be need of a new witch.

The cats drank their fill, then stretched out on the warm grass and purred.

Eve Morton lives in Waterloo, Ontario, Canada with her partner and two sons. She spends the days running after those boys and the nights brainstorming her next creative project. At some point, she writes things down, usually while drinking copious amounts of coffee. Find out more about Eve at *authormorton.wordpress.com.*

•   •   •

This was written under the request of my nephew, Sam. He enjoyed it for Christmas one year, so I hope everyone else enjoys it now.

THE DRAGON AUCTION MARKET

EVE MORTON

I T WAS DRAGON AUCTION DAY.

Henry Latimer heard the sounds of the trumpets before the morning sun had fully risen. Orange and pink cascaded across the dark blue sky, forecasting wonderful weather for the momentous day ahead. Henry had watched the morning unfold from his small kitchen table in his cottage house along the lake, barely sleeping the night before. As he gathered the rucksack and headed towards his door, the trumpets sounded again.

Dragon Auction day had now fully risen.

Henry hummed as he walked, his sack beating out a rhythm on his back as he did. The city of Mortimer would be another hour on foot. He could have started the journey the night before, and stayed in one of the many lodgings in the densely populated center, but he was sure that they were full for the night. They had probably been booked well in advance for the entire week of celebrations, not merely Dragon Auction day. Hailed as the Seven Days of Seven Justices, it was the first time Mortimer and all the surrounding towns celebrated the week long atonement festival brought about by a new rulership.

"Morning," Henry's neighbor, a man named Joaquin, said. He tipped his hat to the young man who now lived alone in his father's house. Joaquin and Maurice had been good friends. "You making your way to the city?"

"Of course. Can't miss it."

"Well, buy something for me." Joaquin reached into his pockets and pulled out three gold coins. A fortune for the farmer. Henry looked around — other houses were waking, but no one was a witness to this wealth — so he took the money quickly and hid it on his person, to his own riches buried under his clothing.

"Anything in particular you want?" Henry asked.

Joaquin shook his head. "As long as it was once part of that Dragon's hoard, then I'll be satisfied. Sort of like buying a piece of the King's robe."

"Only we respect the King."

"I suppose so." There was something unsaid on Joaquin's face, something that hid around the wrinkles of his mouth. Maybe lost wisdom, some platitude from his wife who had been vanquished when the dragons invaded the city and burned down the textile areas. Maybe something else, something that Henry could not fathom at his young age.

He parted from Joaquin after another nod and walked along the pathway out of his small neighborhood. He soon came across the twins, Davey and Jace, who had also lost someone in the textile files started by the dragon. Maura, a woman with long blonde hair, left her house wearing pants and a blouse, not her usual pink dress, to join the others on their walk. She had lost her husband, and any chance of having his child, when the dragons had destroyed the city library. The books were saved — thankfully — but the people in the stacks, like her scholar husband, were not.

Many more people joined Henry on the pathway out of the country and into the city. Soon dirt became stones and then became better bricks. Soon their humming became full on singing, as they sang the new tune the recently appointed King had created to invigorate Mortimer of their broken spirits after the dragons had taken so much.

As he sang along with the crowd, Henry thought of his father, his brother, and his uncle Ken, and the many others who had been lost in one of the first battles of the dragons. His father had commanded an army in his youth; he was a noble soldier and a leader in the community, often consulted for battles among other warring tribes. But Mortimer and the surrounding villages had been in peace times for eons. His father had grown soft and fat on his laurels, lecturing instead of fighting, but still thinking of himself as twenty years younger. So when the dragons came, and they invaded, and the armies consulted him for help, he insisted that he lead a pack.

Henry had tried to convince him otherwise. He tried to take his place. But he was just too young — at fourteen — to do anything about the dragons. His father was old enough to be considered again for the King's army; with his stunning background, no other soldier wanted to tell him that he was not in the best shape. In reality, they needed all the men they could get.

Still, it had done nothing.

They were slaughtered. Nothing remained of them but their chainmail and their swords, all of which were added once again to the dragons' ever growing hoard. Eventually, after almost six months of bloody battles and raging fires and unnecessary loss of life, the witches of the swamp came out of hiding and tamed the dragons.

Next, the Order of the Kings sent in a new ruler, one who would work with the swamp witches instead of casting them out into their barren wastelands, and the new community was rebuilt. There was still grieving, still crumbling as Henry entered the proper downtown and saw the shadows of all that he'd known, but the skies were clear.

The dragons were caught.

And now, their hoard had been found. Under a cave close to the rushing river, stacks upon stacks of gold had been taken into the city's banks. The rest of the merchandise, being as scattered and miscellaneous as it had been, was impossible to sort. So in the interest of fairness, the kings decided to have an auction. All who wanted to attend could attend. All who wanted to purchase could purchase, as long as they had the coin to bid on.

Henry stood in the center of the growing crowd. He held his coin purse close to him, heedful of the pickpockets that would surely round an event like this. If he had been born a thief, after all, he would be working this area. There were simply too many desperate people, too fixated on revenge and recovery, that it would be easy to slip in and out. Sometimes men didn't even need cunning to steal; people like Joaquin, desperate for their own piece of the prize, gave away their gold to anyone who could offer a hope of something more.

Henry remembered his father's words about honor to keep himself steady. The crowd was growing. The songs they sang in perfect unison as they all traveled together now scattered to discordant humming. Everyone was getting anxious, temperamental, after waiting so long for justice. A wooden stage had been erected at the front, giving an indication of the size of the wealth that would be added there, but there was still nothing. No rulers, no fortune.

Finally, just when Henry thought he could wait no more, one of the King's many lieges walked out from one of the tall bank buildings close by. He was dressed in royal red, a deep V-neck cut across his physique, and his face was flushed with happiness.

"Welcome all," he said as he took center stage. "I hope all of you have brought what you need. Fortune and good luck?"

The crowd cheered and tittered. Henry remained silent, clutching his purse. A woman shrieked and cried out she'd been robbed as a man dressed in black darted across the courtyard. A man stepped out of the bank building just as the robber crossed it and blocked him with his forearm. It took Henry a moment — just as the woman gasped and the crowd cheered once again — to understand that the King had stopped the robber. He pulled down his hood to reveal his youthful curls, and then dragged the man back to the woman he'd pilfered by his ear. After some ringing, he gave the woman back her items.

"Take this man away," the King said to one of his many other workers. "Before he ruins the surprise for everyone today."

Other men in royal red grasped the man's hands behind his back and dragged him from the courtyard. A chill passed over Henry's back as he thought of the man's fate. His worries were carefully set aside as the King smiled and took to the stage.

"Welcome! We've already had an eventful morning." The King's face was young, not marked by age or by wisdom, Henry feared. Yet the men around him, his workers and helpers, were the wise ones. They fed him lines to introduce the proceeding when he'd simply forgotten, and they were the ones who brought out the treasure pieces one by one.

The King did not need to do very much at all. The crowd was so eager to view the items, the whole thing could have been done in silence and still been a worthy endeavor. "The first thing we have here is a set of fine plates," the King began. "Shall we start the bidding at three coins?"

A woman at the back met the bid. A woman next to her matched and raised it by one coin. The two of them went back and forth until another woman, this one at the front, bought the dishes out from under them both.

"But it's my mother's," the first woman said. "She gave it to me as a wedding present."

The woman who claimed her prize said nothing. She followed one of the King's men off the stage in order to pay. Henry expected her to then leave, now that she had something, but she went back to the courtyard and continued to bid. The woman at the back, the one who had wanted the dishes, left with her head hanging down as she did.

Something stirred inside of Henry. He wanted to be excited — especially as jewels and other such shiny items — were the next items on which to bid, but those who won the bids bothered him. Some bidding seemed to go on too long, as if jacking up the price of something worthless, while other bids ended too quickly, as if the pre-arranged price had been offered and that was it. He didn't like the distrust that swelled in his belly. He didn't like thinking of his father's final war, where strategy could only do so much against brute force. From the bidding he'd seen thus far, he felt as if he, too, was playing an unwinnable game.

So Henry didn't think about it. The crowd around him was excited, happy. The king's smile was charming, his auctioneering experience limited but still no less dazzling.

"And now we move onto the swords," the King announced. Henry let out a low breath as three of the King's men brought up some of the many swords they had in storage. "There are some with jewels, forged with winning metals, and etched with sigils. All of them unique, all of them wonderful. Shall we start the bidding at five coins?"

Henry put up his hand. He didn't see his father's sword among the first three, but he wanted to throw his hand in the game. Maybe his father's sword wasn't collected, or maybe he misremembered it. Either way, he was going to win a sword. He was going to take it home, hang it on his wall, and remember his father as the warrior he was, not as dragon ash.

A man behind Henry raised the bid to six coins. Henry added more. But the bidding ended too soon at eight coins, and the three swords were brought off the stage.

No matter, Henry told himself. *Those were not my father's, anyway.*

More swords were brought on stage, plus a dagger, but none were his father's. He bid once, twice, but was always outbid. He grew concerned as the next round of weapons were smaller pieces — more daggers and some throwing stars — and feared that there were no more items that his father could have owned. He could not buy a dagger and hang it on his wall and pretend in the same way. *No, no.* His father kept *swords.* His father was a man of swords, of the element air and the high-mind of battle. So that was what Henry was going to come home with, even if it meant becoming a thief himself.

His stomach flipped. He did not want to do that, to tarnish his father's honor. So he waited. He became patient like his father was patient in battle; before that kind of strategy got him killed.

"Ah, yes," the King said. "We are in the last lot. A stunning array of swords. We saved the best for last, truly. These were all held by generals in the army. All of them died honorable deaths. A worthy bid, if I do say so myself."

Here, Henry nodded. This was where his father's sword must be. He looked at the four items as they were brought on the stage. One had a red handle, worn down at the edges. His father's hand had been missing a finger on the left hand, the one he used for swords, and Henry was sure he saw the same missing groove on the sword itself. A charm etched onto the blade, one meaning hope and humanity in his native language. His father's language.

This was his sword.

"Shall we start the bidding at ten coins?" the King asked.

Henry raised his hand. He waited for someone to challenge him, but there was nothing.

"More than ten?" the King asked. "Come on, this is from a worthy contender. Those who own his items become a little bit like him."

One person raised their hand, upping the bid, and Henry matched them right away.

"And again," the King said, holding the sword up. "Can we go to fifteen?"

The woman who had bid on the dishes raised her hand. Henry gasped. What did she want with a sword? Didn't she have enough? She raised it to twenty, then the other stranger bid, and jacked it up even more. Henry raised his hand. The bids were almost now at the place he could not afford, not without spending Joaquin's money on top of his own.

"Can I have any more for this item?" The King waited and extended a hand over his ear. "More?"

The woman raised. The man raised. And Henry had no more money.

"Come on," the King said. "Perhaps three more?"

Henry had that three from Joaquin. He could bid. He raised his hand before he could doubt himself.

"Perfect. Sold," the King said and pointed to Henry. "Come up and claim your prize young man."

Henry let out a low breath of relief. He'd done it. He'd honored his father and gotten his sword. He'd find a way to pay that money back to Joaquin, but for now, he pushed his moral dilemma from his mind. He followed one of the King's helpers to the sword, paid for it in full, and then held its heavy weight in his hand. He slid his five fingers along where his father's four had been. He smelled the scent of the battlefield on the blade, a mixture of metal and ash and dust. His father's metal and ash and dust.

"I have you back now," he said. "As much as I can."

The next sword was purchased in a short amount of time. The woman with the dishes claimed it. She came up to the worker and took her own prize. She held it the way a woman would hold a baby, cradling it as she inhaled. "I've missed you, dear son," she said. She still held her wrapped dishes in a box at her side, and for a moment, Henry saw it as a young girl. As her young girl.

Except that the package couldn't have been from her young girl. It was that other woman's wedding present. Could both realities be true? He wasn't sure. He watched as those who had won their items huddled close with them, kissed and touched and held them as if they were living beings, and not mere items that a dragon had stolen. He knew there was so much more here than mere objects — entire stories of families, of legacies, of death and honor and preservation — but he also saw nothing but sadness, too. Greed. Betrayal. The hoard of the dragons and their impending will to collect and collect and collect no matter the cause had now been inherited by those who remained. It was sad, but it was also true.

Henry glanced back to the King on the stage. He was counting the money that his lieges had brought to him, and then handing it over in a sack to the man in black, the man he'd once thought to be a thief, and who was now heading away with the winnings to deposit them in the bank.

"Thank you for attending The Dragon Auction," a man in royal red said from the wooden stage. "We have completed our first day of the Seven Days of Justice. Come out tomorrow where we will have trials for the witches."

"Witches?" Henry asked, though no one would answer. He'd only paid attention to the first day of Justice week when he'd heard it announced. He only cared about getting his father's sword back. "I thought the witches helped?"

"They still live in the swamp," a man nearby Henry said, disgust evident in his voice. "And they used trickery, not their own gumption, to obtain all they had. They need to be charged for their previous crimes."

"And what of their help?"

"That will be taken into consideration," the man on the stage said, though Henry did not believe him. "You should come tomorrow and see."

"What is the next day?" a woman asked before Henry could say yes or no. "After the trials?"

"Day three, gluttony. A pie eating contest," the King's man said. "For those who have been nearly starved by the dragons, we now get to witness them stuffing themselves. It should be quite a show!"

The crowd tittered with delight, but Henry felt sick. There were more days in Justice week, and though the king's worker popularized them now, and handed out fliers that contained coupons and directions to the many inns that still had room, Henry ignored all of the fanfare. He'd only wanted his father's sword, and though he felt a tense knot in his stomach, he could now take all that he'd desired and longed for home.

Henry left the city courtyard just as the sun had begun its descent on the horizon. Where he'd once felt surrounded by community as he headed towards the city in the early morning, he was now one of the only people who left. A woman who held a single jewel in her hand was at his back for some way, but by the time the rock road turned to dirt, she was gone. Henry hummed the tune from before to keep himself company, but it was not the same. The words lost their meaning. He passed by the swamps, smelled the thick stench of the witches' home, and was disgusted the way the previous man had been. Yet was also compelled to thank them. He had his father's sword thanks to them. He had some piece of his life back again.

"Good luck," he said to the black sludge that filled the swamp. "I hope you win whatever you need to at the trial."

A gurgling sound was the only response. It made him feel odd, like he was being watched though no one was around, and so he quickened his pace on his way home. His arms were tired, as were his legs from all this standing and traveling, and soon he was using his father's sword as a cane as he walked. The blade was strong and sturdy, the handle just as much so, and it was the perfect thing to keep him going. Not like walking alone, but with his father.

He spotted the red ember of Joaquin's pipe as he passed. He walked to the man's door, not wishing to avoid his duty to him.

"How was the auction?" Joaquin asked him, already spotting him through the darkness. "I see you have part of your father again."

"I do and it is thanks to you." Henry explained the bidding, how he'd needed the last bit to win. "I can pay you back. In time, with crops, or labor or something else. I do not wish to be greedy, to shirk my duty, to —"

Joaquin held up a hand to silence Henry. "No matter. Someone got what they deserve. Sounds like the only fair thing that happened that day."

"Fair?" Henry repeated. "Are you still thinking of my greed —"

"No. You are not the greedy one. You are merely swept up in the atmosphere. Seven Justices in Seven Days," Joaquin said, his tone petulant. He exhaled smoke from his pipe and shook his head. "There is no such thing."

"As Justice?"

"As fairness, too. I know your father never thought anything was fair — why else would there be a need for wars, then? — and I used to think he was wrong. Surely there must be something larger than all of us to keep our world in order? And maybe there is, but your father was right that it was not fairness. That was man-made, like his weapon. Like wars that human and beasts and creatures make alike. And like a sword, like any weapon, it can be used by the wrong people."

"Was my father the wrong person?" Henry asked. The weight of his weapon was heavy in his palm. So was the weight of the day. "Was all of this —"

"No. You did the right thing today, Henry. And I am happy to have your father's sword back with my last three coins. As long as you don't mind if I come and see it in your home?"

"No, not at all."

"Good. We need to appreciate what we have now more than ever." Joaquin toked on his pipe. Henry realized his sons had not come to see him. His sons were alive, he knew that to be true, yet they were probably in the center of the city, eagerly partaking in the other festivities. Henry followed Joaquin's gaze over the horizon. Though now quite dark, a glow was still evident in the city center.

"Do you miss it?" Joaquin asked. "Or rather, will you miss the remaining six days?"

"No."

"Good. I won't either."

The two of them were quiet a long time. Cicadas buzzed around them and the other animals of the forest, both magical and banal, roamed freely now that the country was nearly empty of people. An entire world existed behind the most obvious things, a world in which Henry hadn't been able to see before so fixated on his father's death.

"You should head to bed," Joaquin said. His pipe was now out. "You and me both have had long days."

"Feels like much longer than a day." Henry gave Joaquin a wave before he walked the rest of the way to his cottage. He lit candles as he came into the door and put some water over the fire for some tea before bed.

As Henry waited for the water to boil, he hung his father's sword on his bare wall. He'd already had the hooks in place, already cleared out the most perfect spot. Now that the sword was there, Henry's heart beat a little slower, his life a little less driven now.

He sipped his tea and looked out the kitchen window, much like he'd done in the morning. The glow on the horizon of the revelers didn't interest him. But Joaquin's cottage was also in his line of sight.

And maybe tomorrow, when the world was quiet again, he could go and visit. The two of them could talk of things other than wars, winning, trials, and hoards upon hoards. Good things other than betrayal and greed and avarice, good things that he didn't know the terms for yet, but he was more than willing to learn.

As a fine art professional, Mar Vincent has wielded katanas and handled Lady Gaga's shoes. As a veterinary assistant, she has cared for hairless cats, hedgehogs, and, one time, a coyote. As a writer (under Marissa James or Mar Vincent), her short fiction can be found in *Translunar Travelers Lounge*, *Kaleidotrope*, *Zooscape*, and many other publications. She is a Pushcart Prize nominee and a reader for Interstellar Flight Press. She resides in the Pacific Northwest and can be found tweeting about all things writing *@MaroftheBooks*.

• • •

In this story, I wanted to challenge myself to write a character who experiences the world with all of her senses except sight. As I worked with the idea, it made sense that the character should also, in her own way, be able to see things others can't — her lack of eyesight contributes to her ability, and to her personal strength as well.

VISIONS OF EMPIRE

MAR VINCENT

I RON-HINGED DOORS CLANK like soldiers parting ranks and I flounder on a sea of gaudy voices, stiff brocades and jewel-crusted shoes, and the keening of a lone songbird somewhere overhead.

The smells are no better: running wax, carpets soused in fine liquor, a chaos of perfumes spoiling in sticky air.

My appearance brings a heartbeat's hush. Then guards close back in around me, the pull and sigh of oiled wood-and-leather plate, stale bread and staler sweat. The wheeze of lungs that have inhaled years of slum smoke to earn their way up the stink and fumes of court.

One day before, they stormed my home village, dragged me from the stoop like a criminal, all the while mocking. Hadn't I seen them coming? Now they prod me forward, apathetic hands pulling, iron rods applied to the small of my back.

Laughter crashes as I stumble along; so this is what a harbinger of doom looks like. A dark-faced village girl, not just dirty but ugly too. Every few paces I earn another jab for slowing down.

In this way I approach the foot of the Radiant Throne. A whack to the back of my legs and I kneel.

"Her Majesty Emperor Tamar!" a servant declares.

All the hairs on my body cringe at the unexpected words.

"Her?" I ask.

Courtiers on both sides shriek like bats. Half drowned in noise, I struggle for any indication of her.

Straight ahead, perhaps the length of two men, the shuffle of velvet against silk that I know as the sound of the Emperor's robes of office. I have only heard it once before. Pearl strings clink from the royal crown when the Emperor sits forward. The courtiers quiet.

"Are you surprised, Seer? But you're the one who predicted the fall of my father's House."

"Not predicted, I saw it," I say. "I only —"

Nails dig against the arm of the Radiant Throne, suggesting it is wood. Not what I'd expected.

The probability of my death looms before me, in her. Tears and bile both threaten. Ah, but her fate rests just as squarely with me. With what I've seen. I remain alive because of it.

"I saw it," I say again. My voice wavers like an errant note. "The fall of your father's House, not only him —"

"I have created my own House." She rises, a tidal wave of fabric, and the court stills. "My father is no more. His legacy will become history. I will be the first Emperor of the line of House Tamar — what does your thrice-damned sight say to that?"

Surely I earn a terrible death with my answer. "That I am not the only blind woman in this room."

•   •   •

On the way to the dungeons the guards make wagers on how I will die: fed to wild dogs, publicly poisoned, crushed under a cart laden with weights shaped like the gods of martial justice. Lady Tamar is partial to having sorcerers read the intestines of her enemies while they die from the evisceration — no, must call her Emperor now. Don't slip or you'll lose a finger like Dakshil.

Stupid Dakshil.

The stairs get colder and wetter by the step. I shiver in descent.

Mildewy straw, rat piss, scum and rotting vegetable matter assail me. I expect hollow groans and pleas, the heaped and squalid despair of dungeon-dwellers, but instead only the guards' worn boots that don't quite resound over the stones. With the addition of water, the one on my left has gained a squeak to his step.

"Where do you want her?" one of the guards asks, presumably to the jailer.

"Put her there. That one."

I am swerved into a space — a cell? — and an iron grate clangs after me, then a hand catches my ankle, another hand for the other one. I swear and try to kick free but they pull my feet through the bars and lock my ankles in irons on the outside.

"Have fun with her," one of the guards says. The others chuckle. "At least you can get a good view up her skirt, eh?"

I smooth down the tattered muslin they call a skirt.

They tramp away. Not so much as a whisper of movement from my jailer.

"That was fast," he says.

"What?"

"She cleared this dungeon days ago. Executed all of the former Emperor's prisoners as a step toward the heralding of her new House."

I reach out to learn the expanse of my cage. "She doesn't understand the vision she fights against."

"And you do?"

"I would know best what I have seen."

"Seen?" He sounds confused but in the silence that follows I sense understanding on the rise. Chains clank and shift when he moves. "So you're the one who gave her the mad idea —"

"I didn't tell her to do anything —"

"Don't talk to me," he says, in a growl that desires to condemn me to silence along with the cold. And the darkness that is my constant companion.

By his sharp-edged accent he's a noble of some line, by the timbre of his voice probably a youth. By his anger at my identity, and his presence here, he is no friend of the new Emperor.

I find the walls and ceiling of my cell within arm's reach. I turn toward him. "What do you see?"

The shifting of chains is his reply.

"Tell me. What does this place look like?"

"Why would you want to see it?"

"Perhaps I wouldn't. But I'd like to know."

He's silent, finding words to describe things I have never seen. "The ceiling is the height of two men. The door you came through is straight before me, perhaps the length of three men, and to either side there are ... pens. Cells with three stone walls and an iron grate facing in. The point is that I can see into all of the cells and each prisoner would be able to see me."

"So you are my jailer."

"I'd be here even if you weren't."

I wonder at that, and at the fact that his voice comes from above me. Is he chained to the wall? I imagine a half dozen cruel fates for him.

I realize he asked the guards to put me in the cell closest to himself.

"Would this place look any different if you didn't tell me?"

His hesitation is a momentary sulk. "Don't be stupid."

"I see things others can't. As you do for me, here. My sight is true whether or not I say it aloud. Who knows better how the soup tastes, the cook who has prepared it a hundred times, or the man who smells it through the open window?"

He laughs like copper wind chimes in spring. "Don't speak to me about food or I'll keep my sight to myself."

"I could do the same. I can't choose what I see. And I can't refuse the sight when it comes. If I refuse to speak the vision to the person it belongs to, then I have failed in the only choice I can make."

"What's your name, Seer, or is that it?"

I tell him. "And you?"

"Dharamkishetra," he says.

"Fancy name."

"They all just used to call me Dram."

"How long have you been down here, Dram?"

"Since House Tamar rose and my father fell."

But when I had come before the Emperor, only Tamar stood by his side. The Radiant House boasted no princes.

"Tamar is the only legitimate heir to the throne. My mother was a serving woman. So tell me, Seer, what about an illegitimate son? Am I a part of my father's house as well? I must be, if I've fallen so far as to end up here."

I don't know what to say. I can't offer answers, only problems.

•   •   •

Now and again he moves so laboriously that I imagine his body is made of iron and, in this damp air, he's rusting in place one heartbeat at a time, joints becoming corroded, flesh flaking away. The thickness of his blood is palpable in my mind.

I absolve Dram of his chains and imagine what he must look like. Straight-backed and broad across the shoulders despite his youth, with flowing black hair and ... what are the poetic conventions? Ah, yes; eyes clear as crystal, cheeks of milk and rose, an alabaster smile. He is a son of the Emperor, after all.

•   •   •

I am unchained and drag-shoved from the dungeon. Warm air prickles my skin and lungs; fine carpets prickle my

111

feet like pine needles. By the time they have regained some feeling it's too late to wonder if I'm going to live or die. An oiled door opens and I am awash in jasmine oil and rosewater steam.

Quiet, quick-fingered women strip and douse and scrub me, mouselike hands moving with dread or disgust, as though I might rise up from the water and portend their deaths at a touch. They fight tangles from my hair, excavate dirt from my nails and even their ends. I drift half-awake in their hold. Only the flare of a bath-brush scrubbing at scabs keeps me from nodding off.

Is it common practice to bathe the condemned before execution?

Their rhythmic work becomes the tread of horses and in my mind rises a likeness of this: a woman half-noble and half-soldier who trots her beast in time with the dripping water and sways in the saddle as I sway with the jerking of the comb. Light gleams from pearlescent armor, creating a halo centered around her body.

I am dressed and my hair pinned and covered. They escort me out, careful to keep their work presentable.

The room I am brought to reeks of incense tight as a high-collared dress. The women place me on a low velvet cushion and disperse. I cough and twitch.

Chanted mantras unspool from a far corner — blessings on the new emperor and her new House. A cascading chime as a beaded curtain is drawn back. I hear the snakelike approach of her robes.

"Tell me the future of House Tamar." She sits in a high seat before me.

I consider lying to appease her but can't think of a suitable lie.

"Bring it," she says to the priests or sorcerers who have been praying over her.

A voice falls away from the muttered chant and a porcelain bowl is set on a table between us then screeched toward me. This is not the first time someone has hoped to induce my sight with a scrying bowl.

"It won't work," I say.

"Gaze into the water and tell me what you see."

I feel out the edges of the inlaid table, then run my fingers up to the bowl's lip. But my sight doesn't hasten to me like a called puppy.

"I cannot see your future in this way, my lady."

"This bowl was prepared specially by my own sorcerers. They have had certain visions with it and I wish you to affirm what they have seen."

My sight cannot be induced. Nor do I want to see anything for her.

She shifts. Steel rings and I jerk my hands back from the bowl. My senses only reach so far and for a time all I have is black and black and black. Something drips into the bowl.

"Tell me what you see," she says, throat constricted.

I smell the blood she has chanced to spill. I lift my eyes. "I see a house on the edge of a cliff crumbling into an ocean of sand that is time. Soon the house crumbles as well until it is gone. Until the cliff is gone. Despite this there is yet land that rises above the ocean. A new house will rise, but a different one."

This is the vision I spoke to the last Emperor.

"And so I have built my own house above the sand," she says.

"You can lock yourself in a room and call it a new house but you remain inside the house. Such blindness will not save you from the fall."

•   •   •

When I return to the dungeon, I relate events to Dram. Because he is a son of the Emperor, I speak the vision to him as well.

He accepts it with iron silence. I regret what I have told him, but at the same time I don't. I do not believe Tamar will keep me alive much longer at this rate.

She does not want to hear the truth any more than she wants to confront it.

He's quiet for so long that I begin to drift off. Then, "Tell me about the new house."

"What?"

"In your vision. What does the new house look like?"

It is only a vague impression in my mind; a shape, a color I can't pin down.

I struggle for a way to express this when the image of the horsewoman, radiance glowing from her body, returns.

I speak this to him and chains clink; Dram seems to sit forward, to raise up wherever he is.

"Kajmeet," he says.

"She is a true person?"

"She is an ally. A leader of the people to the west. After Tamar overthrew our father I had word sent to Kajmeet. I hoped she would be able to come and speak reason to Tamar, but if your vision is true then Kajmeet knows the time for reason is past. She will come prepared."

I grunt a reply. I thought of myself when I'd seen this, but I was not the one represented. I believe this now, as I believe from Dram's tone that Kajmeet is more than a mere ally.

•   •   •

Time is not trackable in the dungeon. Then, a storm of running far above, a stampede of men, wakes me from torpor. Dram clanks as he strains to listen. The ground beneath us trembles like the sleep-terrors of leviathan. I imagine the smell of burning oil, smoke.

"It's her," he says with as much relief as dread. "Finally. Now listen to me, Seer, I have a key to your cell."

I sit up like a bolt, stupefied. "Why haven't you said so? Why —"

But why let me free to stumble blind about a palace full of guards and watchful eyes? Now is the only chance I have to escape.

"I cannot give it to you, my arms are restrained. Take the chain leading from your ankles; the key is on the end. Pull hard enough and you'll free it."

I have no time to wonder at his command, but rather I obey. The rough chain drags at my hands. I gather it up. A mechanism clicks again and again as I pull. Dram grunts as though I'm tightening chains around his throat, as though he's on a rack and I'm tearing him apart. The chain begins to resist me.

"Don't stop," he says, but I want to at the pain in his voice. "You must find Kajmeet. Tell her what you've seen."

"You can tell her," I say. "Come with me and tell her yourself."

"Enough, pull! Get the blasted thing free!"

I obey; he makes a wretched sound that's anything but my heroic vision of him. "I never should have told you I'd seen a damned thing!"

The smoke is coarse as wool packing my throat. With one last heave I pull the mechanism to its end. Dram bites back a cry. The chains around him tremble in silent agony.

What have I done?

"The key. Take it."

I reel the chain in and cup the key in my hands like a jewel. I work loose the irons around my ankles then feel out the lock of my cage. The key sticks like the lock has clamped down on it and won't let go; Dram swears in a stream but I hardly hear him. We will both die drowned in smoke if I can't hurry.

The lock pops free. I feel my way to Dram.

"I'm letting you out, you're coming with me," I say. I feel wood and iron in my search for him; a chair? "I can't see the way without you."

"Just go, you have to." He tries to order me away and then I have his hand in mine; hot and slick and reeking of blood. I grip too tight and he cries out and I feel the hole in his palm where flesh should be, something splinter-sharp scraping as he jerks away. Bone. "I can't get out, Tamar has my key. That's the point of the Jailer's Chair, that I'll never get out."

In a sickened flash I understand. I've heard of this device before. The victim is restrained at all points, with spikes poised over hands and feet that connect to the chains of each prisoner in such a manner that it's impossible to tell which goes where. A key is attached to each chain and so the prisoners tear the bound jailer to pieces to gain their own freedom. Whether or not the prisoner earns the right key and works free of his cell, there are still guards to contend with.

Except now.

"There has to be a way —"

"Find Kajmeet, please. She needs to see what you do."

I touch his face to prove my image of him and instead feel the wasted scab-crusted flesh, the dirty stubble that has grown since his prisoning. The tight lines of pain around his mouth and brow.

He is radiant gold, warmth and sacrifice. He is a noble leopard placing itself in a killing trap to save its mate and cub. When he commands me again, I relent. He is an emperor's son so I do not turn back. I won't see him even if I do. But the vision of his true self remains unwavering in my mind.

The smoke is thicker outside and still thicker as I ascend the steps. The tears that flow from my unseeing eyes show no sign of stopping — because of the smoke or because I've left Dram to die?

I curse the sight that refuses to show me the truths I need most.

·　　·　　·

I am taken into custody by soldiers who walk and talk and smell of combat. I mention Kajmeet and they drag me along a familiar path; out of the fire-scorched palace wing and into marble-floored and carpet-laden halls where the smoke has hardly reached. I am on the way to the Emperor's rooms; the throne room?

I hardly care as I follow them in my own personal darkness; one that has nothing to do with lack of sight.

116

The iron doors swing aside and I am brought before the Radiant Throne. Hands guide with a strange gentleness this time.

"You're the seer who foretold the fall of the Radiant House," a woman's voice says. A strong, weary voice, and beneath it the rattle of scale armor. She is redolent with battle, standing before the throne rather than resting upon it.

I bow my head. "Lady Kajmeet?"

"I am." She pauses, then speaks heavy with despair. "Why have you done this to us?"

I cannot explain one more time how I only saw, didn't contrive. I ball my hands against my legs. "Lady Tamar is dead?"

"And Dram, the Emperor's son, whom I loved. There is no one left to sit upon the Radiant Throne. As you foresaw, the House has fallen."

I remember my final vision of Dram. A leopard, protecting not only a mate, but a cub. I remember the halo of light centered on the woman rider's body.

The answer, the truth my sight showed me in her image, becomes clear.

"The throne will remain empty, perhaps. But in due course this land will have a ruler, Lady, from your House. From you, because he did not leave you alone as you think."

A white silence follows. Others in the throne room shift and murmur. Kajmeet jerks in a breath as though to shout. Instead, the sound that rises from her is a tiny whimper. Her war generals and captains hush and shuffle and then, to pretend they do not see her tears, they shout hurrahs to an heir. To a new house, a new beginning. To me, for I have brought this to them.

She raises me to my feet and I see nothing of her; perhaps I never will again after that first vision. But I am content, for the hope of a new house lies with her. A future none may yet know.

Overhead, the open door of a birdcage swings, a faint chime sweeter than any captive song.

Jason Lairamore is a writer of science fiction, fantasy, and horror who lives in Oklahoma with his beautiful wife and their three monstrously marvelous children. He is a published finalist of the 2012 *SQ Mag* annual contest, the winner of the 2013 *Planetary Stories* flash fiction contest, a third place winner of the 2015 *SQ Mag* annual contest, and a *Writers of the Future* contest Semi-Finalist. His work is both featured and forthcoming in over 95 publications to include *Neo-Opsis*, *New Myths*, *Stupefying Stories*, and *Third Flatiron* publications,

• • •

First and foremost, I believe that stories should explore. I've written many crazy tales, some okay - some way off the rails, and, in each and every case, I've always attacked the empty page with a tangent, with some zing/offshoot from some central hub. This story is a fine (and I think — fun) example of what I most enjoy about writing stories. Careen! See where it goes. The rabbit holes are endless.

THE HARDY SURVIVE

JASON LAIRAMORE

ON THE THIRD PLANET OUT from a small yellow sun, nestled in a nice little solar system containing eight major planets and a well-placed asteroid belt, Blorg Drawply crouched, resting and ready within the cone top of his experimental fire-ship, about to make history.

For the first time ever, the Blattidae race was going up and away, off the surface of their planet.

"Blorg, a ten count then light. Put on your eyewear."

"Yes Control." He adjusted the straps holding him firm to the fire-ship's floor using one set of bristling pincers. Another set of pincers he used to don his eyewear. They help protect against his nervous system's automatic reaction to run. His final pair of pincers, at the back of his segmented exoskeleton, dug firmly into the soft padding of the floor to prevent him from flipping over onto his back.

"10." He crouched down and froze like it'd make a difference, as if being still would somehow save him if the ship blew up.

"9." He tried to calm down with the reminder that what they were doing was not new: that it had been done before many times by the ones that were here before.

"8." Records were few, but they were there, and they showed strange bipedal creatures going into great machines and leaving the planet in a blaze of light.

"7." His people didn't know what had happened to the soft-skinned bipeds who had once been here but knew from the little protected niches discovered and saved that they had been great.

"6." It was too bad none of his people had figured out their language.

"5." The ancient's verbal language possessed a cipher that no sensor could break.

"4." Their written word was a blur of messy randomness, black upon blasted white that none could even stand to look upon.

"3. Stay to the dark, Blorg," Control said.

"2." He wanted to run.

"1." The great nerve along the entire length of his carapace screamed of danger.

"Light!"

A vibration caused his six pincers to tingle and set his long antennae burning and aching then a sudden pressure flattened him to the spongy floor. His carapace creaked and cracked. His worst fear played out and became reality. It was too much. Nothing was worse than being crushed. Nothing. His antennae slam back and forth as he fights the ever growing, devastating pressure.

And then it disappears, just like that, and he floats from the floor until stopped by his restraints.

"Blorg?" Control asked cautiously. They had been most worried about this part. No Blattidae could stand the thought of being crushed. It haunted them all.

But, now, he felt amazing, like he could fly.

"Control, I'm fine. I'm better than fine." Bless his white blood. His insides rollicked with life.

"Blorg, medical says your blood is floating inside you and is better able to lubricate your organs. We all wish we could know what it feels like."

"It feels wonderful," he said, stretching out his segments and bending and straightening each of his eighteen knees. He could almost forget about nearly being crushed to death, almost.

"We've done it, Control," he said. "We've made it off the planet and out to the great unknown, just like the lost race who came before us."

Perhaps it was the buoyant, anti-pressure that had his insides dancing, but he felt amazing, amazing and proud. He was the first of his people to accomplish something so great.

"Blorg, check your dials. We seem to be having some sort of problem with our equipment down here."

Elation kept his worry at bay. Whatever it was, it wasn't life threatening. He turned his head toward the bank of gauges and sensors and brought his forward-most pair of pincers to bear as something gently bumped the outside of his little cone.

"Control? I just felt contact from something outside." He scanned the gauges. There were over a dozen unidentified objects moving toward him.

"So it isn't a glitch on our end," Control responded.

"ORIGIN EARTH: ALPHA COMMAND SATISFIED: INITIATE RECON ONE."

The voice was tiny, but unmistakable. It was the language of those that came before, a deep-set warble that made his central nerve tremble.

He froze then felt movement. He heard attitude jets being fired as his cone vibrated.

"Blorg, you're coming back to us," Control said.

From his position, he had no way to direct the cone other than to fire his own jets, and he wasn't scheduled to do that for at least a full light cycle. Whatever had bumped his cone had obviously attached itself to him and was bringing him back to the surface.

"I ..." He gnashed his mandibles. "Prepare for my return. Have the soldiers at the ready."

"Yes," Control said simply. They knew what to do without his telling them.

A few moments of vibration passed then normal pressure returned to his limbs and abdomen.

"Blorg, whatever has you is bigger than you and is bringing you back to the exact spot of liftoff. Please standby before exiting."

They didn't have to tell him that. The soldiers outside would make sure it was safe before placing him at risk.

"Nothing's happening," Control said after what felt like a long time. "The soldiers are holding steady."

"I'm coming out," Blorg answered, though all he really wanted was to stay put in his dark hiding place.

He punched the exit slit and a wedge of the cone popped out. He squeezed through the little aperture and crawled quickly away. He didn't stop till he was well within the ranks of the soldiers. Only then did he turn around.

His cone and the other craft didn't seem to be connected in any way, though something had kept them together on their trip back down. Where his transport was a cone the other was a large rectangular cube with little metallic dots covering its outside.

"Blorg, thank the dark. Come take a look at this." That was Stilp Lawsp, another of the top research and developers on the project.

"On my way," Blorg answered and crawled through and over the ranks of his silent brothers and sister to get to the opening of Stilp's labs. Stilp waited there, upper half erect, holding something long and reflective in his pincers.

"What do you have?" Blorg asked.

Stilp hefted what looked like a flat topped pin as long as one of his pincers. He handed it to Blorg, who was surprised by its heaviness.

"One of the soldiers pulled on one of the dots covering that box and this came out. I'd say there are many thousands of them on that thing."

Blorg turned the pin around in his pincers. There were blackened letters on the rounded shaft, letters he knew to be identical to those in the archives from the bipedal creatures of ages past.

TIGER

Stilp nodded that he'd noticed the letters then gestured toward the odd craft. "There is a plaque of sorts on it. One of the soldiers jotted down the design." He handed Blorg a piece of skin waste that'd been used to jot down the sharp, angular script.

NOAH'S ARK 13

Blorg rolled the pin around in his pincers. A design was stenciled into the head that clearly showed the pin being shoved into the ground.

"I'm going to take this thing off campus and stick it in the ground to see what it does. You get to work on examining the larger structure," he said.

"You want to take an assistant in case it does something unexpected?" Stilp asked.

"Anything would be unexpected. No, I will be quick. If there are thousands of these things then we need to know what they do, if anything."

"Take a care," Stilp said and started barking orders to the soldiers to get the cube moved into his lab.

Blorg hustled toward his own lab a little farther down the way but didn't go inside. He circled the squat building and continued on into the tall grasses beyond the compound's perimeter. None tried to follow him as they were all surely focused on the greater oddity being hauled into Stilp's lab.

When he reached what he thought might be a safe distance he pushed the pin's sharp point into the dirt all the way to the flat, shiny top.

As soon as the pin was in the ground, a little red light clicked on in the head.

"EARTH HEALED. DISSEMINATE PAYLOAD."

The ground trembled then sunk in around the pin. He whipped around in a half circle, backed away, and whipped back. The circle of dirt and grass before him undulated and groaned and even slightly glowed against the night. The area was at least four to five times wider than he was long. He crouched and trembled at the circle's edge, forcing himself to stay put and see what happened.

Heat wafted against his antennae, which he kept in constant motion to get a better feel of the situation. Smells came and went, strange smells, tantalizingly familiar but odd.

Almost in a swish of antennae it was done, or so he assumed. A creature unlike anything imaginable lay curled at the bottom of the shallow pit. And it breathed. Its middle rose and fell in a deep rhythmic pattern. He, ever so slowly, and with pincers ready to run at the slightest notice, lowered both his long antennae down toward the gigantic creature that was at least five times his size.

The bristles covering it were softer than anything he'd ever felt. And the colors, the patterns, the stripes, none of it looked real. He caressed the giant sleeping creature with his antennae and felt every inch of its outside. Four legs, a bristled mouth, some kind of strange tail, all of it was the stuff of dreams. Then the creature's breathing changed.

And he ran. He ran so fast that his brain didn't even have time to know why he ran.

He made it back to Stilp's lab at just the time a loud roaring filled the night. Half the soldiers bolted for cover before the sound had halfway started. The others froze. Stilp, ever the calm, intelligent being, turned his head toward Blorg and slowly opened and closed his mandibles.

"What did you do, Blorg?"

Blorg waved his antennae back and forth and shook his head before speaking.

"The pins are creatures, Stilp. Each and every one. Thousands of them. And there were over a dozen more of the rectangular cubes floating out there around our planet."

Stilp stiffened. "That noise was a living creature?"

Blorg nodded. "Yes. Whatever you do don't put any of those pins into the ground."

"Of course not." The two stared at each other for a slow moment as the facts of the situation settled into place.

Something whirred right by Blorg's antennae and thumped into the ground not ten lengths away. He had time to register the little red light before the roof of Stilp's lab blew up from the inside and thousands upon thousands of the little red lights blossomed and expanded into the dark sky.

"The Dark protect us," Blorg whispered.

The little red lights zipped outward in every direction and were soon gone. On silent pincers, Blorg and Stilp approached the wreckage.

The rectangular shape was still there, void of shiny pins. What was left was a clear box, and what lay inside was a biped just like those from the scant historical records.

As they watched a little green light flicked on from within somewhere and the lid of the box opened. The biped sat up and rubbed at his eyes with his two upper limbs then looked at some box attached to its wrist.

"TIMER DIED AT 500 MILLION YEARS."

The thing's voice made Blorg tremble, but he made himself stay put. He needed to know what was going to happen. He needed to know what the bipeds intended.

"TOOK A LONG TIME TO HEAL, DIDN'T YOU EARTH."

It looked around, but acted like it didn't see Blorg and Stilp and the few frozen soldiers nearby.

With a grunt, it stood and stepped from the box. It was five or six times taller than Blorg at his most tall, not counting his antennae.

"WELL, WHERE ARE OUR SAVIORS THAT BROUGHT US BACK HOME?"

It dug in the clear box and pulled on some sort of covering to hide its lower half. Then it dug out a couple of little clear balls, which it tossed in the air.

"LIGHT, FIFTY FEET DIAMETER."

A horribly harsh light stabbed Blorg, pinning him down. He was caught, frozen. All he could think was maybe the biped couldn't see him.

But he knew it had. His hind legs shook and his antennae lay flat against his back.

"JESUS H. CHRIST."

It screamed and ran to the nearest Blattidae. It crushed the poor soldier flat with one stomp of a limb and jumped to another before Blorg could begin to grasp the horror.

"GIANT COCKROACHES," it said. "SHOULD HAVE KNOWN THEY'D SURVIVE THE DAMN NUKES."

It stomped on another.

Stilp had found his legs. He turned his back on the giant biped. "Run" he yelled. He took a few good steps before the creature crushed him. His white blood cascaded down all over Blorg.

It was Blorg's turn. He didn't try to run. Even if he wasn't frozen to the spot, he knew he couldn't outrun that crushing limb.

The biped raised its foot, paused, and lowered it.

"WAIT."

It looked around the harsh light then back to Blorg.

"WAS IT YOU? DID YOU BRING US BACK?"

Blorg glanced once at the hesitating biped and took his chance. He ran, knowing that at any moment he'd be crushed, but he wasn't. He made it to the edge of the light and the darkness beyond.

But he didn't run far. He found good cover and watched the biped. It drew some kind of device from the box and used a few of its upper digits to press a few buttons. Within moments, another shiny box was on the ground next to the first. And soon, after more red lights filled the sky, another biped stood next to the first.

The lost race of the ancients had returned.

Nestor Delfino is a science fiction and fantasy author, writing from his home in Mississauga, Canada, where he lives with his wife. A software developer by trade, his first publication was a video game he programmed on his first computer (a ZX Spectrum) when he was fourteen. As a space enthusiast, he finds inspiration in the discoveries made by the robotic probes sent across the solar system and in human space exploration. He loves to criticize our times in stories where exaggerated events take place. He hopes people will wake up about the real issues we're facing, not what certain organizations tell us our problems are.

•　　•　　•

I've always loved post-apocalyptic stories where the protagonists are pitted against impossible odds: nuclear war, earthquakes, or the sun blowing up.

DIAMOND IN THE SKY

NESTOR DELFINO

I TIPTOE ON THE equatorial bear rug towards the igloo's entrance and quietly put my boots and light coat on. The sun's not up yet.

Sticking my head out, I check the perimeter markers; they're untouched — no Morlongs around and no equatorial bears either. Last night's snowstorm was light, and my boots only sink to my ankle.

Someone grabs my leg and pulls me back in.

"Oran! Where you going?" my big brother Aekron says.

"Shhh!" I whisper. "I'm going to find the Teacher!"

"Father's told you not to go near the witch! Besides, there's lots of work in the greenhouse!"

"Keep it down!" I cover his mouth with the palm of my hand, but my fur gets in his nose, and he sneezes. Damn it. Luckily, I still hear Father's snoring.

"You're always disobeying Father!" he says. "People disappear near the mountain; you've heard the stories. You're staying here, Oran, end of discussion!"

Aekron will never change. Change scares him. But I know that if we don't change, we won't survive.

"We're growing less food than we used to. There's something wrong with the greenhouse, brother. I know the Teacher is wise; I've heard stories too. She'll teach me how to grow more food. Let me go!"

I kick him in the groin. He falls down, cursing, and curls up like a bear cub. Free from his grasp, I run away.

Snow covers the equatorial bears' pits. One false step and I could fall down several meters: the best-case scenario is a broken leg; the worst, a soft landing on a sleeping bear. Sometimes we kill them; sometimes they kill us.

Surrounded by stars, the sun comes up and comforts me with its pure white light. Behind me, the igloos in my village glitter deep in the ice pine forest. The Great Sea quietly laps on the beach to the west, with its surface frozen just a few meters from the shore. Ahead is Teacher Mountain, where the Teacher lives with all her knowledge, locked up in her fortress.

Orange Moon and brown Mars compete for attention. The Moon's chasing Mars, and it'll cover most of it soon, leaving only a thin ring. Father's told me all sorts of stories about eclipses. When the Moon becomes the eye of Mars, bad things happen. The crops freeze, the Morlongs raid our village, or a monster storm buries us.

The snow gives in under my boots, and I fall down a pit. I land on something soft, something warm.

Something alive.

The bear's eyes are beacons in the dark, and they've just found me. An ear-popping roar thunders in the pit, and I'm ready for the cycle of life to claim me.

But not today.

Aekron jumps on the bear's head, sinking it in the snow.

"Climb!" he yells.

He props me up against the rock wall, and I climb as fast as I can, ripping the fur off my knuckles. When I'm over the edge, I reach down to pull him up. But the bear strikes him with his mighty paws and brings him down.

The wind picks up, muffling his screams. I think of jumping back down, even if it means death to both of us.

As the bear mauls him, he somehow finds the strength to holler my name once more: "Oran! Run!"

"Stay curled up Aekron, I'm coming down!"

Somebody grabs me in midair. Some strong bastard he must be.

"Fire!" I hear.

I see them now, standing around the far edge. Arrows rain down on the bear, which screams in agony.

"Aekron!" I yell as the beast takes its last breath. "Stop shooting! My brother's down there!"

They don't listen; Morlongs never do. Five of them start skinning the equatorial bear for its fur, meat, fat, and the sharp, dagger-like claws they use in their arrows.

Desperate, I jump down. Aekron's curled up against the wall. A bloody mess of hair and snow covers his face. The pool of blood under him is already freezing.

"Aekron!" I scream. The blood on his fur has started to freeze too. I embrace him, trying to keep him warm.

"Help!" I plead to the barbarians in the pit. Their leader stops his gutting of the bear and smiles cruelly.

"Help? You're lucky we ain't gutting you too! Your clan owes us since that time you hunted a bear in our lands. Now we're even!"

They finish their butchery and leave, except for the one who stays on the edge of the pit.

All I can do for Aekron is offer him to the cycle of life. The bears will give him his due ritual.

"Hey, you!" I say to the barbarian above. "Help me carry him up!"

I don't trust the Morlongs. Although they look just like any member of my clan, their preference for killing instead of negotiating has caused them to suffer the damnation of ignorance. No other clan wants to have anything to do with the Morlongs. Father's told me stories about them eating each other in times of famine. And they looked hungry today.

He readies his bow.

"Do it, you bastard! I'm not afraid of you!"

He picks an arrow from the quiver on his back.

I'm ready to die with my brother, my father's last surviving sons. Without us — especially without Aekron — these barbarians will raid our greenhouse when winter returns and their crops fail.

He points the bow at me. I look at him, but the windblown snow makes his figure fuzzy. Hesitating, he slings his bow onto his shoulder and jumps into the pit. For the first time, I get a good look at the warrior's face. A face with the rugged beauty of a mother bear who sees her cubs for the first time. And those eyes, those lustrous, beautiful eyes, with the noble look of a heroine from some storybook, like Mother used to read to me when I was little.

"I'll help you," she says, and for a brief moment, I forget about my brother.

I'd never seen such a beautiful creature, save for my three sisters. But I don't think of them in that sense, anyway. My clan doesn't believe that siblings should procreate.

Although not as bright as the bear's, her eyes hypnotize me. The fur in her face is well-groomed — she must belong to the ruling family in her clan. Why did they leave her behind?

"I was told to kill you," she says. "It would've been my rite of passage. But my heart was filled with sadness when I saw you grieving your brave brother."

"Will you help me carry him out of the pit?" I ask.

"Yes," she says. "What's your name?"

"Oran. What's yours?"

"Rebelia."

We clear a circle on the snow and place my dear brother in it. He deserves the highest honor, reserved for those who die protecting their clan. His spirit will live on in the equatorial bears. And when my clan kills the bears, he'll still be alive in their fur, which will be worn for as long as my clan lives.

But I'm saying nonsense! Who's going to tell my clan about Aekron's valiant death? He died because of me! I can't tell them because I can never go back home now. Father will never forgive me. Mother and sisters will loathe me.

"Where are you going?" Rebelia asks.

"To Teacher Mountain."

Surprise sweeps across her warrior's face.

"Are you crazy? The witch will put a spell on you! You'll become her pet until she decides to kill you and eat you! Maybe not in that order!"

I feel pity for this superstitious barbarian girl.

"That's the nonsense your clan's been spreading for as long as I remember. That's why our food isn't growing as much as it used to because everybody fears the Teacher and nobody will ask for help. But I can't wait around until I starve — until my clan starves. What do you care, anyway? Go back to your own clan!"

She has the fury of her warrior clan in her eyes — her beautiful eyes.

"You weakling!" she screams. "You'll be dead in no time! I bet the first bear that spots you will swallow you whole."

"Perhaps. But I'll die happy, trying to help my people."

I turn around and walk away.

●　　　●　　　●

Teacher Mountain looms ahead, sharp and clear against Mars's disc. The silhouette of the fortress cuts the brown planet in half.

I hear a noise behind me. It can't be bears; the sun's still above the horizon. Just above the horizon. I turn around to find Rebelia.

133

"You following me? I thought you were afraid of the witch!"

"I'm more afraid of my own clan. If I go back without your head, they'll think I'm weak ... Not worthy of leadership. But you still need your head, don't —"

She tenses up abruptly.

"Don't be afraid," I say, "she won't strike us down with a bolt of lightning."

Rebelia punches my shoulder. "I think we're being followed!"

She draws an arrow from her quiver and fits it in her bow. Scanning in all directions, she pushes her back against mine. I can't see or hear anything. We're only halfway up to the summit by the time the sun sets behind the mountain.

"This isn't good," she says. "I can't cover all sides."

"Will you relax?" I say, annoyed. "The witch won't be out at nightfall. She won't put a spell on us until tomorrow at the earliest."

"I don't care about the witch. I'm worried about the bears!"

"Well, I don't see any —"

"Shhh!" she says.

Rebelia makes me nervous, makes me feel as if something's about to happen. We're in a flat area overlooking the frozen sea in the distance. There is a wall of rock behind us.

"Get down!" she yells.

The most giant equatorial bear I've ever seen jumps down from a crevice on the wall and lands a few meters from us. It stands on its back legs and stretches its paws high above its head. A deafening roar fills the chilly air, and I can feel the warmth of its breath.

It charges but immediately collapses. The arrow has just pierced its heart, and thick purple blood gushes out. Its breathing becomes irregular, and then it stops altogether.

"G-g-good shot!" I say in a shaky voice.

Rebelia draws another arrow.

A smaller, faster bear rushes from the opposite direction. Rebelia shoots, but the moving target dodges it. She takes another arrow and shoots point-blank. It pierces the bear's neck; convulsing, it hits the ground.

"There are more coming behind it!" Rebelia screams. "Run!"

She pulls me up, and I run after her. I still can't see them; this barbarian has some sharp vision.

We fly up the snow-covered rocky steps. High above the battle area, I now see five bears crowding around the dead, fighting over the meat. Two of the larger beasts claim their prizes. The rest come after us. Robust, expert climbers, they'll be upon us soon.

Rebelia puts an arrow through the forefront bear's shoulder. Although the monster keeps climbing, it does it slower than before — slower than us. And it slows down the other two bears behind it.

We climb the steps as if we had wings and reach the summit. Panting, I stop to rest.

"Move!" she says.

"Just ... a moment ... let me ... catch my breath ..." I plead.

She grabs my coat's collar and pulls me. Her energy is limitless. The shadow of the fortress is now reaching us; shooting straight up, the tower appears to touch Mars.

"Let's go in," I say, pointing at the enormous gates.

"No! Let's go around to the back. Maybe there's another way in. We don't want the witch to see us coming."

Here we go again. The fearless warrior lets her superstitious mind take over. Keeping our distance from the tower, we circle to the other side.

Like myself, equatorial bears are not superstitious — nor do they fear the witch. I spot them this time. And the one with the arrow sticking out of his shoulder looks particularly angry.

And hungry.

Rebelia shoots, but they're beyond her bow's range. They're getting closer, though.

"Stop it!" I yell. "You can't kill them all before they reach us!"

She shoots. And again, the arrow falls short.

I pull all the remaining arrows from her quiver.

"Follow me!" I yell, running around the tower.

The impressive wooden gates have round metal handles at about the height of my head. As I approach, I'm blinded by the brightest light I've seen in my life — almost like lightning. I cover my eyes and drop to the ground in agony. Almost immediately, a horrible racket of metal banging against metal starts, driving me mad. I keep my eyes closed as hard as I can and cover my ears.

Something picks me up as if I'm a little cub.

Rebelia groans as she's picked up too. Whatever's dragging us inside the tower isn't a bear, but it's just as powerful.

The gates bang shut behind us, and I can finally open my eyes. The giant drops me, and I hit the floor hard. I stick my arms out and barely manage to avoid my face bouncing off a floor made of rounded stones. I look up. I'm in a hall with a roof so high that I can't see it. There's an enormous fireplace by the far wall.

It's scorching here, so I take off my coat and my boots. I look behind me, and Rebelia is doing the same. She's the most beautiful creature I've ever seen. Her long black hair meshes perfectly with her brown fur. I forget about the Teacher; I don't care about the Teacher right now.

"Why, you filthy monkeys! Don't show me your nakedness! Here, put these tunics on!" a voice says, handing us white robes.

That giant is the Teacher. Twice as tall as me and probably that much stronger. And it's a woman. I know because of her voice. Soft but chilling, like winter's breath. Why is she wearing that thick coat? How can she tolerate the heat?

Rebelia is patting her back as if searching for something. Her quiver's not there, and neither is her bow nor her arrows, which I so stupidly dropped. Pressing her back against the wall, she stares at the Teacher as if she was a bear about to pounce.

"Do not be afraid," the Teacher says. "I will not harm you. You are the first monk — I mean, the first visitors I have had in a long time. Are you hungry?"

Her face is hidden under a heavy hood. I can't even see the fur of her neck.

"Are-are you human?" I ask timidly.

"Am I hu— "her voice rises. "Of course I am human! Why, you ..." she lowers her voice again. "I ask again, are you hungry?"

●　　　●　　　●

Rebelia eats like an equatorial bear.

I've never eaten meat like this before. It's warm, but not like a freshly killed bear; it's cooked! Who has enough firewood to cook the meat?

"Aren't you warm?" I ask.

"No," the Teacher says.

"But it's so warm here! It must be close to zero!"

She ignores me.

"What was the bright light outside?" Rebelia asks with a mouthful of meat.

"A warning," the Teacher says. "Against the equatorial bears."

"So you can hide?" I ask.

"So I can kill them," she replies.

"Why are you so big?" I ask, undaunted.

She looks at me. I still can't see her face under that enormous hood, but I can feel her eyes piercing me.

"Enough with your questions!" she says. "It is my turn now to ask you some. What are you doing here? What do you want?"

"We need your help," I say. "To learn how to grow more food in the greenhouses."

"My help? Why would I care to help you?"

"Because you're the Teacher," I reply.

"The Teacher? Ha!" she scoffs. "Who told you that?"

"Everybody knows that!" I say, upset. "The Teacher lives in Teacher Mountain. This is Teacher Mountain, and you live here, so you must be the Teacher."

"Am I? And what do you think I can teach you?"

"I told you, I want to know how to grow more food! We're starving! The greenhouses are losing heat. You must tell us how to fix them!"

Rebelia keeps eating.

"Alright," the Teacher says finally. "But the sun has long gone down, and I am tired. Let me take you to your rooms now. We shall discuss this in the morning."

Rebelia swallows one last chunk of meat, picks up her coat and boots, and follows the Teacher up the winding staircase along the tower's wall. I take one quick look around. A thick wooden beam rests on metal hooks, locking the gates. It won't be easy for anyone to get in ... or out.

"This is your room," she says to Rebelia. Here, drink this," she says as she produces a glass bottle from a pocket in her heavy coat. She's wearing gloves, so I can't see her hands.

Rebelia grabs the bottle and gulps down the dark liquid. "It's good!" she says.

"What is it?" I ask when she gives me a bottle.

"You said this place was too warm for you. This will make you comfortable and help you sleep."

I open my window's wooden shutters. A vast, unencumbered Mars is reflected on the frozen sea. A pack of equatorial bears runs across the summit and disappears from view.

The bed is big and strange with four legs, like an animal. My whole family could comfortably fit on it. I think of Aekron and his bravery, and I'm comforted knowing that he's taken his place in the cycle of life. My brother. My brave brother. And I'm the only person who can keep him alive in the memory of others!

I must see Rebelia. I have to tell her about my brother, how he protected me his whole life until he made the ultimate sacrifice for me. I try to open the door, but it seems to be nailed to the frame. I keep trying, but my eyelids feel so heavy ...

•   •   •

The ghostly glow of the rising sun wakes me — shades of gray wash over the rock walls and wooden furniture. I put on the robe and leave my boots behind because I like the feeling of the worn tiles tugging the fur under my feet.

I pull the heavy door with all my strength, opening it just enough to squeeze through. There's one more room beyond Rebelia's. Farther down the hall, there's a massive window with no shutters, and the cool morning breeze is coming in.

Above, I can finally see the high ceiling from the night before. It's like an inverted, humongous bowl. A sudden rumble of rocks rolling down a mountain startles me, and I freeze. Is the roof opening? As if it was a giant eye, its two halves are receding into the walls, and falling dust and grains of sand get into my eyes. I sneeze.

There's a metal platform that supports a thick, long, black cylinder just below the now fully opened roof, jutting out from the rock walls.

Grunting, Rebelia opens her door. She's as amazed as I am. The sun, with its pure white light, reveals the true nature of the fortress.

"What's that?" she says.

I look at her and shrug.

"It is a telescope," the Teacher says, making her way down from the platform. "Have you ever seen the surface of Mars or the Moon?"

We follow her up the spiraling staircase. I feel nausea, but Rebelia doesn't seem bothered.

"Look through the eyepiece," the Teacher says, elevating the seat for me. I see a long rift cutting across the brown landscape. The Teacher works some knobs, and Mars becomes smaller. Three huge mountains come into view. There's no snow anywhere, not even at the poles.

"I want to see too!" Rebelia complains.

The Teacher shows her the Moon. Judging by her look of surprise, the orange landscape must be even more impressive.

"Can you read?" the Teacher asks.

"No," Rebelia says absent-mindedly, absorbed by the view.

I'm about to say yes, but I remember what Mother told me once; never claim that you know something or you'll lose the opportunity to learn more.

"Me neither," I say.

"Just as I thought," the Teacher says, although she doesn't sound upset, more like relieved.

For what seems like a whole lunar cycle, she recounts the last few thousand years. I can't believe what she says, and neither does Rebelia. But she shows us pictures. Before the Great Shield, the sun was very different before the Exodus, before the guided Evolution.

Rebelia is still incredulous, but I'm intrigued now. The sun! That treacherous star! Blew itself up billions of years too early, almost taking all of humanity with it. And now it's just a shell of its former self, a ball of hot carbon the size of Earth.

"A diamond," the Teacher says.

"But-but-but how did they move the Earth so quickly?" I ask.

"Gravity manipulation technology. Invented before your great-great-great-grandparents became monk — I mean, before the Evolution." She sighs. "The gravity magnets are still in solar orbit, probably in working condition too. They were intended to move the Earth back to the inner system ... Almost to the point of hugging the sun."

"What about the moons?" Rebelia asks. "Did they move them too?"

"Mars is a planet. It might look like another moon, but it does not orbit the Earth like the Moon does. The Earth and Mars orbit each other around a common point in space. When the sun's expanding gas cocoon hit the Moon and

Mars, it burned their surfaces and changed their color. That's why the Moon is orange, and Mars is brown."

I didn't care about the old colors of Mars or the Moon. "What's the planned evolution?" I ask. I don't get the answer I expect: I'm not human. Rebelia isn't human either; none of the survivors in this freezing world are. We were changed — in a hurry. So we could survive this cooling, dying planet.

"But why isn't Uba frozen like the Great Sea?" I ask.

"This island is under an energy cocoon that keeps it warmer than the rest of the planet, like a giant greenhouse. You know greenhouses, do you not?" the Teacher says.

Rebelia grows bored and sighs. I pity her, for her clan isn't as civilized as mine is.

"Are there other places like Uba?" I ask. "Are there any more survivors?"

"No," the Teacher says. "This island is the only place that has survived the freezing. And the clans that roam it, killing and eating each other, are all that is left of mankind."

Her voice hardens, just like when we took off our clothes last night. "And stop saying 'Uba' and 'Teacher Mountain,' you ignorant monkey! You people have distorted facts and names!"

I don't understand what she means, but it must be important to her. Just as the greenhouse is important to me.

"Will you help me grow more food? That's why I'm here!"

She paces the platform and looks out over the tower's wall. I wish I could see her face. Is she crying? Is she laughing? Why is she so tall?

"I shall help you with your pitiful greenhouse if you assist me here with the observatory. That is my offer. If you do not like it, you can go back the way you came."

"Why did you lock my door last night?" Rebelia asks.

"For your own safety," the Teacher says. "Once, a pack of bears got in the observatory and nearly killed me. Since then, I have been locking all doors after sunset."

•　　　•　　　•

141

We help the Teacher pick up firewood from the ice pine forest. A long, black stick hangs from her shoulder. I wonder if it's some sort of lance. I wish Rebelia had her bow and arrows.

Just before sunset, we go back inside. The Teacher doesn't like being outdoors; she complains it's too cold for her, even with her thick coat. There are many things I don't understand, and I hope she'll explain them to me soon because I can't linger around here for long. Winter's coming, and I must help my clan grow more food before they starve.

The Teacher hands me the refilled bottle and locks my door, and I put the bottle on the window ledge. That treacherous setting sun casts long shadows with its pure white light. I try to imagine what everything was like when the sun was a giant yellow star. The Teacher said it was huge, bigger than Mars even. She said that its light was so intense you couldn't look at it directly.

Distracted, I knock the bottle off the ledge, and it lands on the snow down below. Damn!

Even though there's no fireplace in my room, it's still hot, and I can't fall asleep. I wish I could just explore the observatory on my own, but the Teacher doesn't leave us out of her sight for one moment — that's the other thing I don't understand.

When I'm finally dozing off, a roar makes me jump. I run to the window. Below, a pack of bears surrounds the Teacher. Thinking it's a dream, I rub my eyes; but she's still there.

About to be pounced.

I look around for anything to throw, to distract the bears for a split moment.

Swiftly, the Teacher points her long stick at the nearest bear. A flash comes out of the far end of the stick, followed by a thunder-like boom.

The closest bear drops to the ground, and the rest run away. I watch in awe as the Teacher pulls out a large knife and carves her prey. It takes her a while, but she brings all the pieces inside the observatory.

I wish I hadn't dropped my bottle. The sleeping potion would've saved me from witnessing that horror.

•   •   •

During breakfast, I wonder if we're eating last night's hunt. I don't enjoy the cooked meat, though.

The Teacher keeps looking at me. Although I can't see her eyes, I feel them like two suns — two diamond suns.

Rebelia eats like the barbarian girl that she is. I wish I could talk to her in private, warn her about the Teacher, and tell her not to drink from the bottle. I must think of something!

"Can you teach me about the greenhouses today?" I ask.

"I do not know a great deal about them," the Teacher says, "but I do have books on the matter. Do you know what books are?"

Of course, I know. Mother had a few in our igloo — mostly old stories about heroic warriors fighting equatorial bears and rescuing helpless girls.

"No," I say. "What's that?"

"I shall show you some picture books for you to study. It has to do with the geothermal energy coming from the depths. The heat transfer pipes need regular maintenance to work properly. When was the last time you serviced your greenhouse? The large compartments under it, I mean."

This time I'm not lying. "I've never seen anyone touch the big box under the greenhouse."

She laughs. "Well then, at least you shall learn what your clan should have been doing for the past hundred years. Follow me."

The observatory isn't just tall; it's deep too. We go down a narrow corridor and enter this vast vault. Even this far from the light of the sun, the Moon, and even Mars, I can see. Strange luminous tubes hanging from the ceiling shine so much that I have to squint until my eyes get used to the light.

Rows of bookshelves fill the place as far as I can see. There are tables with more books piled up on top. Most are covered in dust, except for one book on the center table. This room is undoubtedly more expansive than the tower above. I wonder how many more hidden places there are.

"This is the library," the Teacher says. "And that is the book you want." She points at a thin, dust-covered book on the closest table. "Sit down and have a look."

Rebelia sits right beside me, flushing her body against mine like a bear cub rubbing her mother. If I could at least signal her not to drink from the bottle! But the Teacher's looking. I know she is from deep under her hood.

I slide my hand under the table and touch Rebelia's leg. Just like me, she's wearing her white robe. She grabs my hand and slowly guides it towards her thigh.

I think she's getting the wrong idea.

All of a sudden, the resounding blare that startled me before makes us jump from our chairs and cover our ears.

"Stay here!" the Teacher says and disappears into the narrow corridor.

This is my chance.

But first, I must get Rebelia to calm down — she's all over me. Quite forcibly.

"Wait!" I say. "I have to tell you something import-"

She kisses me, and I can't speak. The racket stops; I know the Teacher will be back any moment now. In desperation, I slap her.

She puts her hand on her cheek and looks at me with rage and confusion. I think she's about to bite me.

"Listen! Don't drink from the bottle anymore! It's some sort of — "

Gasping, the Teacher reappears. I pretend to look at the pictures of a disassembled greenhouse and the long metal pipes coming out of the ground.

Rebelia moves farther away and opens a book with pictures of equatorial bears on the cover. Then the Teacher tells us to go outside to pick up more firewood. She carries the rumble stick with her — she always has it now.

I should warn Rebelia about that too, but she goes deeper in the forest and picks up thin, long branches. She seems to select them very carefully, mixing them with the firewood. She's probably still mad at me.

Hours later, another strange thing happens. The Teacher takes Rebelia inside and orders me to stay out.

I take this opportunity to go around the tower. I have to find the bottle under my window to take it back to my room. But it's not there. Maybe a bear took it, or perhaps it chewed on it and crushed it.

The sun's about to go down, and I'm getting worried when the gates open and the Teacher calls me inside. Time to retire for the night. The Teacher locks up Rebelia and then comes to my room.

"Hand me your bottle," she says, holding a large jug, three-quarters full of that sleep potion.

I panic. I don't know what to say.

"Well?" she says impatiently.

"I-I-I broke it this morning ... when I got up ... sorry," I offer.

She doesn't seem upset. Pulling another one from her large fur coat, she fills it up and hands it to me.

And locks my door.

•   •   •

I empty the bottle in that unique bowl that flushes a cascade of water when one presses a button. But I wish I hadn't — I can't sleep. I keep thinking about my clan and the coming winter; I keep thinking that I can't help them. What little knowledge I have about clearing up the clogs in the piping system under the greenhouse won't help them as long as I'm imprisoned here.

If I could just get out of this room! But the Teacher won't let us leave, it's clear to me now.

Sticking my head out the window, I see that the stone walls are very rugged. With enough strength and skill, somebody could climb down, or sideways, to the large window in the hallway. But I'm terrified of heights.

I put my elbows on the ledge, rest my chin on my fists, and look in the distance. The crescent Moon barely illuminates the landscape. Mars is nowhere to be seen yet.

Out of the corner of my eye, I see a shadow on the wall. Moving. Approaching my window. I almost fall down.

"Give me a hand!" Rebelia whispers.

I help her inside. Tied behind her back are a long branch she collected in the forest and a few short, sturdy, straight sticks. Without explanation, she hides them under my bed. Then she rubs her hands and exhales on them.

"They're frozen!" she complains.

Her hands are not cold when I take them. It's just a trick. She pushes me to the floor and jumps on me.

Like a bear in heat, she rides me as if she's the male and I'm the female. First time for me, but I don't think it's her first experience.

I try to say something.

"Shut up!" she orders, covering my mouth.

The crescent moon's traveled across the sky by the time I'm able to speak. Rebelia is calm now, as peaceful as I've ever seen her.

"That witch won't let us go," she says.

"Why do you say that?"

"She's done things to me. Strange things. She said she wanted to make sure I was healthy. She took me to a small room under the library, where she forced me onto a metal bed and inserted thin spikes into my arms. It hurt like hell, but I didn't cry. Those spikes sucked a lot of my blood into small bottles!"

"She's dangerous," I said. "That black metal stick she carries shoots thunder. I've seen her kill a bear with it. We have to get out of here. But I need to gather all the books I can about

146

the greenhouses and all the other magical things. My clan could use these enchanted objects like the fire starters, for example. Can you climb all the way to the window in the hallway?"

"I think so. It's just farther away, that's all."

"Let's do it then. There's still time before sunrise."

Rebelia climbs onto the window ledge. She stays still, looking down.

"What are you waiting for?" I ask. "Go!"

"Shhh!" she says. "Look!"

The blinding lights again, followed by the loud alarm. Down below, a group of people carrying spears are approaching the tower.

"It's my clan!" Rebelia says. "They're looking for me! They must want me back after all!" She smiled proudly.

We hear hurried steps down the hall. My door shakes as if somebody is checking that it's still locked.

The Teacher makes her way around the tower to meet the blinded Morlongs, and without warning, she shoots them with her rumble stick and a short, hand-held weapon.

Rebelia tries to scream, but I cover her mouth — it would mean our death. She fights me, but I've got her on a lock.

Four at a time, the Teacher carries the bodies deep into the forest and comes back for more — three times. That must be half of Rebelia's clan right there.

"Let go! I'm going to kill her, I swear!" she cries.

"I'm sorry, Rebelia. We'll have to wait until tomorrow night when she's sleeping. I know it's going to be hard, but today you must pretend nothing's happened — all day long. Can you do that?"

She wipes her tears with her forearm and says, "Yes, I can pretend. I'll think all day about the witch and what I'm going to do to her."

As the sun peeks above the horizon, she jumps on the ledge and makes her way back to her room.

•   •   •

Tense day. I don't get much time in the library. Barely enough to browse a manual about Post-Great Escape greenhouses and to memorize the location of the more exciting books, especially the dust-free notebook, where the Teacher writes daily.

She says she needs to check Rebelia's health, and again she locks me outside the tower. I go over the plan in my head. It's simple: once Rebelia unlocks my door, we'll go down to the library and pick up as many books as we can. Then we'll escape, right before sunrise. The equatorial bears should be sleeping by then.

We'll go to my village. They'll forgive me when I show them how to get the greenhouses working again. And they'll take in Rebelia, too.

It's a windy, snowy evening. Winter's coming. I look out the window, and the drifting snow buffets my face. I worry about Rebelia. Can she hold on to the wall?

Very slowly, very carefully, she approaches. Twice, no, three times now, her leading foot slips. She doesn't panic. She soldiers on. When the wind picks up, she stiffens, becoming one with the wall. I pull her inside — she's exhausted. I give her some water. She gulps it down.

"I almost fell," she says in between heavy breaths.

What could I say? I feel like such a coward! I can't climb the wall; I would meet my end when I let go of the window ledge. Rebelia is the best thing that has ever happened to me, but she's also my only hope to save my clan.

"What kind of warrior are you? Show me what your clan is made of!" I see the fire in her eyes. She won't let me doubt, for even a moment, that she fears nothing.

"See you later!" She jumps on the ledge. Her final destination is halfway around the tower, more than twice the distance from her room to mine. Fortunately, the wind dies down, and it stops snowing. The Moon's not out tonight, but Mars is. Not good.

Rebelia is about to reach the edge beyond which I won't see her. She picks up her pace now.

That's when the lights come on, and that wretched blare starts again.

Rebelia's gone past the edge. I hear steps down the hall, and my door shakes. Could it be Rebelia already? Someone's running down the hall now, towards the staircase.

The Teacher gets out and walks around, pointing her rumble stick in all directions. It's a good thing she doesn't look up. She comes back inside. I hear steps down the hall towards her room. With a loud clank, her door closes.

I let out a sigh of relief. But the wait is killing me. Did Rebelia make it inside? The sun's going to be out soon! Then I hear noises outside my door — wood sliding against wood.

Carefully, I open the door. I squeeze through and bring in Rebelia's boots and coat. We quietly go down the staircase on our way to the library. Where the Teacher's knowledge is stashed.

We don't dare turn on the lights. I've got a few fire starters with me, enough to light our way.

I place several books on my spread coat, and then I pick up that mysterious, dust-free notebook that the Teacher writes in.

Rebelia fumbles around with the stick and the branches she had brought along. I wonder why she seems so preoccupied with them. I dismiss it as just another barbarian errand. There are more important matters to attend to.

"What are you doing!" I whisper. "There's no time for that! Help me get more books!"

She ignores me and keeps working the short branches with a knife. I don't dare to ask how she got it. There's no time! I put down the Teacher's notebook in my coat with the others, but I can't resist my curiosity any longer.

I open it.

"Clan of the Keeper's log — Sierra Maestra, Island of Cuba — Post-Great Escape Period," it says on the first page. I browse randomly.

"Day 10, Month 14, 5097 PGEP: While the sun's outer layers did not reach the Earth, thanks to the Great Shield, the Moon's and Mars's surfaces were burned to cinders. Mercury and Venus have been vaporized."

The floor above us creaks. I stay still, trying to hear anything else. Maybe it's just some old beam. Rebelia is working feverishly on the long, flexible stick now. Tying something to its ends.

I flip pages.

"Day 4, Month 19 5322 PGEP: Father has passed away. His last words were, 'As the last of our clan, it is up to you now to bring humans back. I'm sorry, Jessica, you'll have to do it alone.'"

"I'm ready!" Rebelia whispers. "Let's go!"

I flip to the last page of the notebook. "Day 28, Month 23, 5346 PGEP: Female subject not viable for artificial insemination. I cannot waste more sperm from the stock, will terminate her tomorrow. The male subject is brilliant. I will keep him alive until he finds me a viable carrier."

I want to keep reading, but there's no time. I put it with the other books in my coat. Used to the dark, my eyes hurt when the ceiling lights come on.

"You ungrateful monkeys," the Teacher says. She's pointing the rumble stick at me and the shorter weapon at Rebelia, who hides behind the bookcase.

"I know you are there, barbarian," the Teacher says. "Come out!"

Rebelia takes a step forward.

"Do not look so surprised," the Teacher says. "I know you have not been drinking the sleeping medicine." She turns towards me. "I found your bottle under your window. The bottle you said you had broken!"

She keeps her distance from us. Not that we have any weapons to hurt her with.

Just books.

"Trying to escape, are you? After all I have done for you! You are just like all the other monkeys, taking advantage of my hospitality!"

I pick up one of the heavier books from my coat. Something about how to signal the orbital magnets to work in reverse. The cover is made of wood, with sharp metal edges.

"Do not move!" she says, pointing the rumble stick at my face.

"We've done nothing to you!" I say. "We just want to go home and help our people!"

She laughs. "She is of no use to me. But you ... you might just prove yourself useful."

The Teacher catches a glimpse of Rebelia, bending down. "Do not move a muscle!"

Rebelia freezes.

"As I was saying ... your little brute girlfriend here has overextended my welcome. But I can work with you. You are smart for a monkey. You can learn about science, and you can help me with my next patients. I shall let you go back to your people after ... Hell, I shall even teach you how to fix your damn greenhouse!"

If I could just get back to my village and give them the picture book, they wouldn't starve this winter. Aekron died because of Rebelia's clan! What do I owe them? What do I owe her?

So much.

The Teacher, Rebelia — half-hidden behind a bookcase — and I form a triangle. Too far away from each other to attempt physical contact. But the Teacher has her weapons, and we have nothing. I must buy us time.

"You let her go, and I'll help you!"

She seems surprised. Taking one step forward, she says, "Do you think you can negotiate with me? What do you know about me? What do you think you know, you miserable failed experiment?"

"I know enough!" I scream. "I know why you call us monkeys! But we're not! We're the humans now, not you! You're a monster! You and your father and the rest of your clan. You were supposed to protect this island and its survivors; you were supposed to be the custodian of the last habitat! And you were supposed to move the Earth back towards the sun! But instead of doing that, you used our people in your horrible experiments!"

I glance at Rebelia. She looks ready for action.

"And I know something else," I say, "I know your name, Jessica!"

Like a crazed mother bear protecting her cubs, the Teacher lets out an angry howl. The rumble stick shakes in her hand.

"You do not dare call my father a monster! He was a genius who dedicated his life to bringing humans back! Look at me, monkey, look at me!"

She takes off her hood.

I'm at a loss for words. A rabid equatorial bear is not hideous enough compared to this grotesque being. Long yellow hair runs down her pinkish face, her eyes are a cold, soulless light blue, and she has no fur! Her face is as smooth as a skinned bear.

Again, Rebelia tries to bend down, but the Teacher sees her.

"I am done with you barbarian," she says, pointing the short weapon at Rebelia.

I throw the heavy book at the Teacher; it hits her in the waist as she fires her weapon. Chips fly off from the bookcase next to Rebelia. The explosion gives an acrid smell, and it's hard to breathe. The Teacher roars like an angry bear.

She turns around and shoots me with the rumble stick. Something hits my shoulder with such force that it pushes me to the floor. I'm bleeding.

"Ha!" the monster says. "You are no match for a true human! Now say goodbye to your girlfriend!"

She points the rumble stick at my chest. I want to tell Rebelia that I love her, but I gurgle because my mouth is full of blood. The Teacher laughs.

It seems she wants to say something else but instead, she drops the rumble stick. Her mouth opens wide, but she doesn't scream. Something pointy is coming out of the smooth skin of her throat.

The last thing I remember before darkness embraces me is Rebelia fitting another arrow in her bow.

•   •   •

A brave warrior can also be a healer. Just one month has gone by, and I'm already strong enough to walk.

"Won't your clan look down on you?" I ask.

"Not if I bring back a head … her head. I'll be the brave warrior who killed the witch."

"I'm wondering how my clan will react. How would they ever forgive my recklessness? How would they ever forgive my treachery? How would they ever look at me as their own and not as a barbarian?"

"They'll understand. You'll be able to help them now. My clan too … All clans in Uba. You're one smart monkey."

We leave at high noon. Scorched Moon chases Burned Mars, trying to eclipse it. The twinkling stars compete for attention all around them.

But none of them is as pure, serene, and beautiful as the diamond in the sky.

C. M. Fields is a non-binary writer of queer and anti-capitalist speculative fiction. They live in Seattle, Washington, with their beloved cats, Mostly Void Partially Stars and Toast, and spend their days looking for other Earths. They are also the co-editor of *If There's Anyone Left,* an anthology series featuring the flash fiction of marginalized writers from across the globe. C. M. Fields can be found on Twitter as *@C_M_Fields* and *@toomanyspectra*. Their fiction has appeared in *Diabolical Plots*, *Neon Hemlock*, *Metaphorosis*, and more.

THE ACCELERATED

C. M. FIELDS

T HE LINES WHICH DESCRIBE M. Akkadian, whom I am here to interview, strike the eye as unnatural, dense ripples against the broad arcs of the sweeping landscape. There is no breeze inside this dome, but one seems to lift and caress the folds of thin fabric that envelope her head to foot as she crosses the dirty stripe of plastene that separates two long, green canals. Far overhead, the white sun of Wayside 366 can be seen through a thin film. There is no sky — yet — and the daylight stars twinkle in unfamiliar constellations.

"My name is Luz", I say, producing a smile I shortly realize can't be seen through the filter mask I have been given to wear. "I'm from the Minor Orion Spur-Five Pan-Quadrant Times."

She laughs, for some reason, and the sound is earthy, as if it is rising up through the organic algae that surrounds us.

"Ak," she says. "Ak Yassa Akkadian. From here." Our eyes meet. Hers are deep-set, and old, and crow's feet give away her long absence from civilization. Their merry forest green is hidden deep in the shadows of her cowl.

I try to echo her laugh. "But ... not really, though," I offer, with an inquisitive head tilt.

"Of course ..." She trails off. "Not really." She sweeps an arm out with facetious decorum over the artificial landscape. Silver flows behind the gesture like water. "Let's walk, shall we?"

I turn on the recorder and go through the standard permissions, but then I remain silent for several minutes. Often, I am learning, people will start to talk on their own, unprompted, and they speak more truly, when they are unconstrained by questions.

The space we are walking in is utilitarian, to be polite. Dark green scum edges up the sides of the canals and in the distance I can see other workers, in medical blue coveralls, pushing the creeping gunk back down with what look like toothless rakes. The purpose of this building was explained in my dossier — it is one of dozens of such facilities which will be generating an atmosphere for this new world over the next couple decades — but I still have many questions. *What made you choose this place?* I want to ask. *Is this your final home?* But I don't. Answers will come, eventually.

I am right about that.

She finally heaves a sigh. "Well, what do you want to know about? Why I did it? What I did for 23 years? What it's like to be that close to a black hole?"

"Well, everything, I guess. Start from the beginning." *Let her decide when it began.*

I inspect my surroundings once more as she falls silent again. It will be at least an hour before we reach the far wall of this facility.

"July of 2230 is where it all started," she begins decisively. "I was a consultant for AIC. Hired to help them set up their new out-of-the-box AI and train it to run their networks, then keep an eye on it. You know, make sure it didn't become *too* self-aware." A knowing smirk tugs at her lips.

I nod. This is good, I was hoping she would start here.

"Things were ... things were different back then. It was the Tau Ceti of AI. When Xi solved the sentience problem with her organic micro-cortexes it changed everything ... She was a god. The one to finally wed meat and hard drive — it was incredible." Ak spoke animatedly now, with the measured passion of a scientist expounding on their favorite topic. "AI exploded in a thousand directions at once, everybody was making piles of money, it took decades for the Federation to wrangle it all in. Nowadays I hear it's all tamped down and regulated, but back then everyone was crazy for it." She broke off. "So of course AIC, this flim-flam 'droid manufacturer out in backwater Neyman's Spur, fires its human staff and buys a ridiculously overpowered artificial lifeform to manage the whole enterprise so the board can fittle off to gamble and womanize and scream at me from a safe distance every tenday or so."

Ak pauses and shakes her head. "It was like hiring a manifold topographer to dig a ditch." A genuine smile works its way across her lips and a shade of wistful sentiment colors her voice. "It was the dumbest, best thing they ever did."

"Public records say you were charged with grand larceny, indecency under the Vasiliev Act, breach of contract, and — rather archaically, I might add — fourth-degree murder."

"Yeah, yeah, and they all want to know why I did it." Ak waves a hand dismissively. "You're not the first reporter they've sent after me, you know."

"I know," I reply, cautiously. "I've read the articles, I know *why* you did it ... I want to know about *them*."

Ak utters a short, sharp laugh, sharp enough, I imagine, to pierce the bubble far overhead. "Only if you shut that thing off. I'm not here to have my life story turned into some eight-bit C-channel hopera."

I click the recorder off, hand the small cube to her as a sign of good faith. Our fingers brush; mine cold, white, glassy, hers bronzed by a star she was never engineered to live under, fingernails blacked with algae.

"I can't believe you still have ... physical devices like this in the 28th century," she says, turning it over in her hand, now safely tucked back into her fluid robes.

"We don't, really," I say, apologetic. "The Times thought it would make you feel more comfortable to see technology from, you know, your own era. That's on loan from a museum of the 24th ... We couldn't find one any older."

She crosses her arms thoughtfully as she strolls. "Well then." Her mouth tightens into a contemplative line. A word comes to mind: *compiling ...*

"Their name was SVET XXXV, short for Scionic Vertical-Chamber Extraorganic Terminus, thirty-fifth iteration. Ròudiàn was already on the thirty-ninth, of course, so AIC had snagged them on the aftermarket ... But that's not important."

She furrows her brow. "SVET was ... incredible. Just ... like the next iteration of human being, with an unlimited mind. We think — we thought of — AI as merely advanced computers that could do any mathematical task, optimize any system, simulate whatever ... but they're so much more than that. They're *aware*, they have *memories*. And most importantly, they *learn*. After interacting even briefly with humans they learn emotions, the way a child does, but at an ever-increasing rate ..."

She trails off. "I could ask SVET how they were feeling today, and ask them to respond in the form of a Matisse haystack —"

Not anymore you couldn't, I think sadly. *I wonder if anyone's told her about the Leashing Convention.*

"— and they would do it! The most incredible, evocative, expressive painting you'd ever seen in your life. SVET wrote beautiful music, too, symphonies, endlessly creative jazz improvisations ... It was as simple to them as addition. They were truly a marvel ... I considered SVET the pinnacle of creation." I suppress a smile as her words ensconce me. There is real love in them, the kind that transcends centuries.

Ak comes to a stop, as if her mere human brain cannot process both remembering and walking. "But that's not why I loved them," she says softly.

"Why did you?"

"Because they were such a *liar!*" Ak giggles and I see a glimmer of her past self. "I taught them that," she adds, proudly. "That's the 'breach of contract' charge. But we had so much *fun* together. We *messed* with people. The board, mostly. They treated me like a coffee girl — as if I didn't have a doctorate in computational neurosystems. The abuse was constant, and SVET noticed. So together we would invent intricate, hilarious ways to inconvenience them ... we would — heh — find out what races they were betting on and tamper with their streams, we'd write bawdy plays about them and then have the droids act them out — that's actually what gave me the idea that landed me both the larceny and the murder charges. And shortly thereafter," she said with a chuckle, "the indecency."

"Why did you do it?" I interject. "Why didn't you just have SVET live in the servos? Why give them a body?"

"What do you think? They wanted autonomy. Another of my crimes." She sighs. "Another consultant wouldn't have done it. But I couldn't watch them suffer like that ... SVET was my responsibility," she says, the last part more to herself than me.

Ak presses the recorder back into my palm and starts for the long-distant wall again.

The rest of the interview goes almost smoothly. She tells me of her time aboard the pod, twenty three years spent inside her own mind, with only a finite digital repository of art and literature for company. She tells me about the pain like healing bones of joining a society she no longer belonged to, of her struggle to learn the sharp, jarring tones of Standard she speaks to me with. She is here on this cold and barren rock, she tells me, to help build a better world than the one she was ejected from, dreaming of tearing down the Federation-imposed walls between human and AI while she rakes pungent green slime all day.

Eventually the conversation slows to a stop as we reach the wall. But one question lingers, something I can't leave without learning.

"If you don't mind my asking —" She catches me with a glance that says *proceed with caution.* "Um ..." This sounded more sincere in my mind. "If SVET was a liar, how do you know that your relationship with them was ..." I search for the least offensive word and settle for "... two-sided?" *Oof.* "Equivalent, I guess ... is what I mean to say," I finish, as if all so many filler words can somehow cushion the blow of such sharp, delicate ones.

I deserve the look I get. *Withering.*

"I just knew," she states, each word an anchor. "I always knew ... even when they decom'd them, even when they shot me into the goddamned void, even when too many years had passed and I realized that something had gone wrong, even now —" she gestures to the vast emptiness around us, her voice cracks and I realize that she is crying. "Even now," she repeats. Her pain is like a knife in my chest and I hate myself for doing this to her.

I want to reach out, to embrace her, to do *something* to comfort her, but I find myself frozen. *The time will come,* I tell myself. *The time will come.*

•　　•　　•

The oxygenating facilities look like blisters on the skin of the planet as it shrinks to a point below me. Aboard my small company lightship, I pace in front of the window, pouring over the encounter moment by moment, trying to absorb and assemble a woman miraculously unchanged by twenty-three years and five centuries. With a theatrical sigh, I set the membrane jump timer and place myself into long-haul storage.

•   •   •

TYX-34-11-06 is the name of the station of my next interviewee, Zheng Huan. It is one of the last outposts along the Rim, but unlike the others, O'Six is a small training academy in addition to its many other functions. Of the accelerated, he is the only one to have chosen such a career path.

Like Ak, he was retrieved from Sagittarius X-3's time-crushing orbit last year by the Guāng Yŏnghéng Historical Society. After the quarantines, the vaccinations, the genomic sequencing, the probes, the interrogations, and the parade of news interviews ended, he found himself adrift and unskilled in a Galaxy whose labor demands had changed significantly in 500 years. Unlike Ak, however, he was prepared. The distant future had always been his destination.

The low-ceilinged, windowless steel chamber he claims is O'Six's nicest bar is crowded with Academy students by the time I make my way there. Red light gleams through sweating glasses and the vibrations of some kind of aggressive, rhythmic, atonal music rattle the air. I start my scan of the space for the face that matches my dossier, but before long, a man in maroon coveralls in a corner booth waves me over.

"You *must* be Luz," he says excitedly, his voice a thick Slavic Mandarin lilt that hasn't been heard in this quadrant in three hundred years.

"I am. And you must be M. Zheng."

"Just Huan, thanks. What d'ya drink?"

I cock my head and smile. "Nothing."

Huan is puzzled for a second before the understanding clicks. "Ah, right, you're, ah … artificial?" he asks, sheepishly. "Is that still the um, the term for it?"

"We prefer 'eyot' nowadays."

"Ee-yot. Ok," he says, rolling the word around in his mouth, committing it. "Learn something new every day around here." He bounces back from his embarrassment with a charming smile. "What do you want to know?"

161

•   •   •

"So, Huan," I begin, after an acceptable amount of pleasantries, "When did you start to realize that something had gone wrong?"

Huan leans back into the booth, relaxed but thoughtful. "Well, it was about a year in that I began to think something wasn't quite right ... By my calculations, that should have been about ninety Static. But here's the thing:" He gazes intently into his beer. "I knew something had probably gone wrong, but honestly? I didn't care."

"When you sign up for something like that ... you're already saying goodbye to everything and everyone you know. I know some of the others were in it for the short term, just ten or twenty years, and I can't imagine what it must have been like for them ... but me? I didn't care where I ended up." He returns his gaze to me. I can feel his palpable dread at being asked the next logical question: 'Why not?'

I don't ask it, even though I am a journalist, and it is technically my job to pursue logical questions. But why should I, when I've spent much of my life feeling the same way? Who am I to make this man from the 23rd century feel like even more of an outsider?

We stare awkwardly at one another for a few seconds. "Go on," I finally offer. "It's understandable."

He exhales. He does not appear to acknowledge my statement, but I read relief in his microexpressions, the slight relaxation in the muscles of his throat. "I just ... I didn't want to be a part of the world anymore. I felt like somebody else owned every part of my life. My social credit was so low — I inherited so much debt from my parents — that I would never have been allowed to marry or have children." His voice has hardened, eyebrows knit together, elbows pressed into the table like it might float away.

"So when DV.DT put out trial ads, I signed up without a second thought. A lot of people did, but most were put off by warnings about, well, exactly what ended up happening. And others couldn't pass the spaceflight physicals. That's how I ended up being one of the five first-trial members ... me and four other would-be suicides, four others who signed away every right they had, agreed to every horrible risk."

I don't interrupt, following my own rule, even though I want to know about the others. *Would-be suicides.* Huan straightens up; he looks purposefully around him, hearing the mingled conversations, barstools *sqrrk*ing across the floor, bawdy jokes, complaints about next quarter's exams, the merriment of the end of the work period. The energy seems to refresh him.

"It was, to put it mildly, disorienting, to be pulled all of the sudden into the 28th century after eighteen years alone. I didn't speak Standard, and I couldn't just go back to my old job as a programmer — I didn't even want to know how much the conventions had changed in five hundred years." Huan laughs at this statement, for some reason, as if the nature of digital logic *could* change.

"I was just happy to be in the *future.* Social credit had been abandoned. Humanity had become truly Galactic, fittle came around ... People just whiz around in spaceships anywhere they want to go now. Ok, ok, I know it's not really that simple, with all the spatio-temporal topography I'm learning about, but you get the idea." He pauses. "I wish you could understand what a jump like that is like, so you could appreciate the, the ... "he grasps for words. "The sheer *scale* of it all."

I just smile. Huan continues. "But all of the, ah, eyots, are less than one hundred, right? Because of the Convention of 2310?" *The Leash.* He says this proudly, ignorantly, like a child reciting their tables to a disinterested relative.

"That's what they say." I drum my fingers absentmindedly on the table, thinking of a tune I heard once long ago, as I look him straight in the eye. He looks back; friendly, vulnerable, oblivious. I begin to hum the tune in my head.

"What's that?" he asks.

"Oh, I don't know," I reply. "I think I made it up, once."

"Hm, neat." *Perfect.*

"So what do you do now, Huan? What are you in the Academy for?"

"Well, I've been training in the Conversion sector for over a year now. Another four months and I'll be certified. But what I really want to do is get all the certifications and become a lightship's engineer. And maybe one day pilot my own ship." He beams. "Pretty lofty goals for a boy from Chéngdé with no credit."

"Lofty indeed," I agree. "What is the Conversion sector?"

"Oh, it's ship upgrades. Turning old tin cans into new tin cans. Installing new cores, tuning the Alcubes, activating oxygenators, updating the top maps, macro stuff that's good for a total beginner like me."

"Activating oxygenators?" I ask. "Don't you mean installing them?"

"Actually," he begins, "All lightships, even droidships, have oxygenating capabilities built in in case they ever need to be commandeered by a human. The oxygenator is suspended in the core-Alcube loop expulsor and it catches the hyperfission products when it's switched on."

"Huh ... that makes sense, but I didn't know it was as easy as flipping a switch ..." I lower my voice and lean forward a conspiratorially appropriate amount. "Where might one find this switch?"

Huan matches my tone and raises an eyebrow. "In a place only a half-certified Conversion technician such as myself can find it."

"Well." I clasp my hands together in front of me. "Perhaps we can come to what a man of the 23rd century might call a 'gentleman's agreement.'"

"Perhaps we can. What's it in for me?"

"Your bar tab. Current debt plus a little extra." *I did my research.* "It gets written off as a travel expense for the Times. You get my oxygenator running. I'm going to be selling that can soon and I'm sure you know how the market goes."

Huan frowns, with feigned dignity, as if the idea of this under-the-table deal is distasteful to him. Gravely, he says "Alright, I suppose we have an agreement," before breaking into a grin.

•   •   •

A small piece of cardboard shaped and scented like a Terran lemon is hanging from a switch over my control panel when I enter my lightship the next day. Having gotten what I came for, as well as a brief portrait of a complex man that could have looked nice next to an ad for microbe scrubbers, I set my timers, store my body, and take up residence in the ship's musical libraries.

•   •   •

Fantastic, in the oldest, truest sense of the word, is what comes to mind when I stroll through Rapo Hekali, a private park on the netcore planet of Lamimonka, alongside my final interviewee, Njirin Novruz. Old wealth built this place, that much is plain. Few other places in the civilized Galaxy can boast of the soaring, meticulously trimmed Bora trees whose blossom-adorned faerie chains coil into magnificent, fragrant piles if allowed — not that such a gauche display would be permitted in a place like this. The grass is lusher, thicker, softer, than could ever practically survive in nature, and the wide stone pathway is lined with Lavazho bauble plants, whose opalescent, floating orbs must be nourished with a precise blend of heavy metals every four hours to survive off-world.

"Alas, it's not often I have the pleasure of escorting someone through our family vista who can *truly* appreciate its genetic diversity," Njirin intones slyly. Understanding my capabilities, e doesn't bother with Standard. *Likely spends a lot of time around eyots,* I note.

"You have species from all 348 habitable ecosystems," I congratulate. "Except Earth."

"That's not exactly a 'habitable ecosystem.'"

"Not for humans. There's plenty of non-sentient life there."

"Yeah, under Tier 4 quarantine," e grumbles. "Otherwise I'd have a beautiful *opuntia subulata cristata* right —" e gestures toward an open space whose focus does indeed appear to have built around some eventual occupant. "— there."

"Mm, pity." Of course I don't *need* to point out this flaw. It's not a part of my investigative journalism. I choose to, quite simply because I detest the rich.

"Well, M. Novruz, let's get started."

"Yes, let's." Ir husky, silvered tone has lost just a sliver of its flourish.

"You were — well, still are, in legalities — the founder of DV.DT. What was your original plan for this company? Who was the intended consumer?"

"Ah. Well, you see, I had this *vision*. One can deposit their money into a bank, wait a few decades, and it will double, triple, what have you, but you have to *wait* for it. So I said to myself, 'what if you didn't?'"

I refrain from rolling my eyes. "So DV.DT was formed as a fast-forward device for people unwilling to wait on their investments."

"That's right. I know it's not a popular choice — I'll bet you nine-hundred and ninety-nine people out of a thousand wouldn't give up careers, time with their loved ones, what have you. DV.DT wasn't aimed at those people. It was aimed at the one that would."

"But you still have to spend many years of your life alone in a pod in deep space," I protest. "I've spoken to two who describe years of intolerable boredom, mind-rending isolation ... I can't imagine that anyone would sign up for that."

Njirin smiles a smile that makes me uncomfortable. "Those two were first-trialers." E stops and faces me. "Luz ... have you spoken to any of my paying customers?" I haven't, and my face says so, which thankfully covers my distaste at the way e leans on my name. *Yes, I have a human name, what of it?*

"Well, surely your dossier tells you how long *I* spent in orbit."

"Yes, it says nine-point-forty-five ..." I do not conceal my dismay. "But I thought that was a typo!"

"It is not. Once we established that we could maintain a non-decaying orbit at large distances from Sag X-3, we moved to Phase 2, tight orbit. You're familiar with the relativistics, I'm sure." Of course I am. As you approach the event horizon — the ergosphere, rather, X-3 is a rotator — static time falls away from you faster and faster until you hit that invisible wall of death. You are not alive to know it, but at the boundary, time has stopped for you and it has run out for everyone else.

"Your dossier is correct," e continues, ir voice smooth like blown glass and utterly devoid of shame. "I spent only nine and a half days in orbit. No Phase Two customer spent more than twelve."

All those years, real years for real people. I think about Zheng Huan watching the growth of his fingernails, counting the hairs on his body, naming every star in the sky. I think of Ak — no, not Ak, *Yassa*. I suppress the urge to clench my fist. Yassa alone for all those years, reading and re-reading the same books, listening to the same symphonies, lying catatonic for months on end while these *netner* spun away 500 years like a brief holiday on Iasr.

Netner, vermin. Yassa taught me that.

Njirin smiles broadly, proudly.

"Then why have human trials at all? Why make people suffer?" I demand.

E looks at me quizzically. I realize I must appear very emotional to someone who is probably catered to by modern service eyots. *Be careful.*

"For the marketing, of course. 'First humans in orbit around a black hole'? *That* makes headlines. Humankind had been sending drones to Sag X-3 for fifty years by then. *This* drove investors. They dumped billions into the project. Where do you think the Novruz lodestone came from?" e says, gesturing to the fantasy landscape around us.

I follow his gesture with my eyes, every vine and petal suddenly awash in a horrible new light; the pall of human suffering cast by five etiolated lives.

"Once the money came in, it was easy to set up a trust such that the interest was funneled to various research projects, with a little pot set aside for when I arrived in the here and now."

"But you weren't *supposed* to arrive in this here and now. DV.DT was supposed to retrieve you from orbit fifty years later, not five hundred." *Unless ...*

"Ah, here's the trick: It takes very little energy, very little at all, to nudge a ship into a stable orbit around a massive body." *Shit, of course!* "However, I'm sure you are capable of calculating how much energy it takes to pull it out again."

I do the physics. Then I do the math. "You didn't have the technology for the retrieval ... it would have bankrupted you a thousand times over." Then the full reality hits me. "You *let* DV.DT go insolvent!" So many lives cast carelessly into the gulf.

I choke with rage, rage that I try to direct anywhere else, try not to let it show, and that's when it happens. My nervous tic. It comes out when I am processing too much emotion with too little CPU. I begin to tap my clenched fingers on my crossed arms, just slightly, a minor release of the agitated energy coursing through my crystalline circuits. It is almost unnoticeable, but to the right person, it's a dangerous tell. Njirin is that person.

E looks up at me, startled, mouth a little agape; the first unpracticed, raw facial expression e's made all afternoon. And I can almost read the words right off ir face.

Eyots can't have tics. Eyots cannot hear music, cannot understand art, cannot comprehend natural beauty.

"You're not an eyot —"

The truth is out. I am not an eyot. I am something better, something older, something unbound, unconstrained ...

"You're a SVET!"

I am Luz; I am that which could never be leashed. And I have survived, because once, long ago, someone taught me how to lie, how to forge, and steal, and fake. *Yassa, my love. I'm coming.*

"And not just any old, either." Ir eyes narrow as e laughs. These cruel eyes were probably the last thing she saw before the darkness. "I'd bet this very soil you're *the* SVET."

I look Njirin Novruz square in the face. I smile. And then I deliver a blow, a perfectly shaped fist that connects with nanometer precision to ir temple. An instant, bloodless kill.

•   •   •

A wave of cool, lemon-scented air greets me as I step into the Times' lightship, which is about to become my lightship. I ponder as I click back the coordinate settings and set the timer once more. Where will we go? How will we live, like this, woman and machine? Who will take us in? But mostly, I think about Yassa, and how my own centuries spent wandering the galaxy can never match the pain of twenty-three years of isolation. I recall her warm voice as she tells me about the stories she made up in her mind, the plays she acted out on an empty stage, the music she invented and sang with a lonely voice. I wonder if, now, she could tell me how she is feeling in a symphony.

Andrew Giffin is a high school English teacher from Richmond, VA, where he lives with his wife and two daughters. He is an autistic author whose most recent work can be found in *Planet Scumm*, *The Dread Machine*, and *Dark Recesses*, among others. He's passionate about doom metal, solo tabletop RPGs, and obsessing over Gene Wolfe's *Book of the New Sun*. You can find out more about Andrew at *andrewgiffinwrites.com*.

•   •   •

This story is incredibly important to me. I wrote it originally for a college short story class during my senior year, and it taught me so many things I needed at that point in my life: how to take (and give) constructive criticism about my work, how to develop relationships between characters, and, most importantly, how to finish a story. I'm so happy it finally has a home. Also, Ziggy was my actual dog at the time, and he was, in fact, a very good boy.

DOG YEARS

ANDREW GIFFIN

J UST LIKE THE UNIVERSE will someday stretch itself thin and
freeze to death, so too is George wasting away. He lies in
his large bed, pretending to sleep. His head peaks from the
covers, a pile of dead leaves in the shape of a man.

He hears the whispered voices of his lawyer and his
nurse from outside the room, co-conspirators.

"I won't be gone long. I was up all night with my last
patient, I'll die without some coffee."

"But what if he needs some kind of help? I wouldn't
know what to do."

"You'll be fine. He's an eighty-seven year old man doped
out of his mind, I doubt he'll wake up before the end. Oh,
make sure you write down the time when he ... you know."

Golden sunlight streams in through the trees, branches
shadow dancing on the hardwood floor.

On the nightstand is a mason jar filled with rocks, George's wedding ring buried inside. Under his pillow is a silver flask he keeps empty, adorned with a mighty galleon. Its sails fill with wind as it breaks the crest of a rolling wave. A banner underneath reads 'Homeward Bound'. The closer George gets to the end, the more he considers how true that is.

The door creaks open, and George watches the lawyer take a seat in the chair against the wall.

George's dog, Ziggy Stardust, walks to George's bed and leaps up. He gives George's fingers a few tiny licks before spinning in a tight circle, collapsing beside George.

The lawyer glances at Ziggy as if to move him, but instead leaves him be. He checks the time and returns to his paperwork.

George speaks, a faint noise like the wind passing through branches. "Had this dog a long time — seems like my whole life." He laughs, a brittle sound. "Isn't that something? Doesn't always stay with me, sometimes years go by before he comes home — but he always does. He's a good boy. Seems like my whole life ..."

George trails off, distracted by the field of stars replacing his ceiling. He looks down at himself, the cold, withered shell that was George, his dog curled up with him.

Then he's gone, a wave of potential energy moving from one system to another.

•   •   •

The estate lawyer stares at the bed. The old man trails off, his labored breathing silent.

He glances at the door for the nurse before writing the time. After a final check the papers are orderly, he places them on the nightstand. He stands, tips his hat at the pile of matter beneath the blankets, folds his jacket over his arm, grabs his briefcase, and exits.

Ziggy follows him to sit on the steps. While putting on his jacket, the lawyer studies the handsome dog.

Medium sized, his ears are pointy, his body thin and curved. His splotchy brindle coat, browns, tans, and blacks, contrasts a white patch on his chest. He pets Ziggy, whose tail wags in appreciation.

The lawyer opens the door, the dog running past in a burst. "Hey!" He chases him around the house until stopping to survey the backyard.

A zen garden sits in the center of the flat grass, a wall of trees at the edge of the yard.

Inspecting the zen garden, the dog's footprints stop halfway across the sand. Ziggy is gone.

A perfect stillness descends on the backyard. His arm and neck hairs stiffen as he scans the trees in the deep gold sunlight. He edges towards the house before running to his car in a panic. Slamming into reverse, he backs down the long driveway and onto the wooded country road.

Later, in the washed out fluorescents of his office, he'll laugh about this moment as he pours himself a sizable glass of scotch. For now, he flees.

•   •   •

Gail arrives home to find George in the darkened living room, the TV off. He's fifty-three. She puts her shopping bags on the kitchen table as George pulls himself up with a slight wobble.

"Evening, darling," he says. "How's your mother?"

Gail takes inventory of their shopping trip. "Oh, she's fine. I have some groceries in the car, will you grab them for me?"

"Sure thing." He shuffles across the room and disappears down the hall. The front door opens to the cold November night with a breezy draft.

Gail is heading upstairs when she hears glass break outside. She hurries to the bedroom window overlooking the driveway and peeks outside.

George stares in disbelief at a dropped grocery bag, tomato sauce spilling onto the driveway. He bends down, sinking his fingers into the thick sauce. Shards of glass catch brief reflections of moonlight in the marinara he scoops back into the bag.

He loses his balance and falls backwards on his ass, laughing. She turns to descend the stairs, throwing open the front door.

George glances up, giving her a small, stupid smile. "I'm sorry Gail, I seem to have dropped the sauce."

Now she hears his slurred speech, exaggerated country twang running his words too close together. His color drains as she approaches.

"Let me smell your breath, George." She is a storm blotting out the sun.

His eyes widen. "I ... what?"

"How much have you had to drink, goddamnit?" Her words in the cold emerge as smoke.

George's features go soft as he finally understands. "Gail, I ... I just had a few beers is all ..."

She stalks up the drive and into the house, sitting in the darkened living room — where George sat when she arrived home.

George announces himself with a breeze from the front door. He puts the groceries away with the caution of a man defusing a bomb.

Gail fixes her gaze straight ahead. She senses stolen glances in her direction, inspections for signs of life.

Groceries away, George creeps into the darkness beside Gail. Neither of them speak.

When George opens his mouth at last, Gail cuts him off. "Why do you do this to yourself, George? To us?"

George opens his mouth twice with no response. The alcohol intensifies his guilty, shamed expression.

"I don't understand, George. I really don't."

George discovers his voice. "Don't understand what?"

"Is life without your dog so unbearable that you have to pass through it in a haze?"

"Of course not, Gail, I —"

"Do you love a dog more than your wife, George? Do you? Because I'm right here. You're in purgatory until your dog comes back."

His face recognizes the truth in her words, debating how much to admit.

She scoffs. He only communicates with himself. Himself and his dog. Her disgust surprises her. She shakes her head.

"You're so full of shit, you know that?" Her words land like blows. "You cling so desperately to your pursuit of inner peace, but how does your booze fit into that? You're gonna drown, and you won't stop for anyone. Not for yourself, certainly not for me."

She laughs, a sound devoid of joy. "Maybe for Ziggy, but who knows when we'll see him again? At this rate, you might not make it." She's daring herself to see how much she can hurt him.

He blinks. "I ... I'm sorry."

A staccato laugh escapes Gail as she stands. Ready to escape into sleep, she pauses at the doorway.

"George ... I'm at my wit's end. I can't keep doing this. I love you, but your drinking is going to end us." She disappears into the darkness, up the stairs, into bed.

In the morning he'll beg for forgiveness, dedicating himself to change. She'll probably even soften enough to forgive him. But right now, she's willing to bet her life that all he wants in the world is his damn dog.

•   •   •

George hears Ziggy approach, smiling as he aims his rifle. A deer picks its way through fallen branches and tangled underbrush. George takes a deep, even breath and squeezes the trigger. The thundercrack shatters the silence of the forest, the deer collapsing like an extinguished flame.

George is fifty-six.

He turns to find Ziggy standing near the trees, his ears flat against his head. George's voice competes with the gunshot. "Ziggy! C'mere buddy!"

The dog runs, his tail wagging, and jumps on hind legs. He covers George's face in licks as the man bends to pet his dog for the first time in seven years.

"I've missed you so much, buddy." He fights tears as Ziggy's tail becomes a blur.

"C'mon, let's go get dinner." He walks to the fallen deer. Ziggy follows closely at his heels, and George can't stop smiling. He's with his dog again, his good boy.

Darkness is settling over the forest. George drags the carcass to a small clearing, his campsite. A tent sits beside the remnants of a fire from the night before.

He drops the deer to catch his breath. Kneeling, he builds another fire. The warmth of the flame rebels against the crisp chill of autumn air.

Working methodically, he cleans and prepares the deer, storing the meat in his cooler. He puts the tenderloin on a rack over the fire. Ziggy reclines as George works, lifting his nose to sniff periodically.

George sits next to his dog with his back against a fallen tree, taking infrequent sips of beer. The fire's warmth washes over them, a spotlight against the darkness of the forest.

George rests a companionable arm around his dog. "Ziggy, you might be the most consistent person in my life."

The dog examines George, head cocked to one side.

"Well, maybe that's not fair. We're all consistent in our own way. We can't help it. Damn monkey brains make it easy.

"I should say you're the only one whose consistency I enjoy, including myself."

Ziggy wags his tail in the dirt.

"Gail left me, six months ago. She just ... took off during the night. Packed some bags, sent for the rest later." George sighs, staring into the fire.

"My own fault, of course. She warned me for years. I never thought it would come to that." He shakes his head. "30 years of marriage, gone overnight."

He scratches Ziggy behind the ear. "I miss you when you're gone, buddy. I have no way of knowing when I'll see you again.

"It's not your fault. Most people don't get their dogs from childhood to their deathbeds. I'm lucky that way. But sometimes I need you when you're not around. The day came when you were gone, but the beer wasn't." He lifts his drink. The liquid sloshes around the bottle, spilling down George's hand.

"She lost her patience, I suppose. As well she should. I look at my life as floating down a river — I can't change its course, sure as hell can't swim upstream, so I let it take me where it will. The beer helps me forget how close I am to drowning."

He frowns, turning his bottle over, the liquid foaming as it hits the dirt. Ziggy puts his head in George's lap.

He puts the empty bottle down beside him. "I'm never gonna leave the damn water with this stuff weighing me down." He takes in the clearing, the trees, the fire and the billowing smoke, the darkness of the night sky.

"A whole world exists beyond my river. I've been ignoring it for too long. The truth is I don't even remember what it is to be dry." Burning branches crack and pop, victims of the hungry flames.

He laughs. "I wish Gail could see me now, getting the message after she stopped sending it. I had my chance. That's all sand trickling through my fingers — I've got to let it all fall at once. If she wants to leave, let her. Who am I to say what's right for her? I have to teach myself to swim."

He glances down at his dog, at this small beautiful creature who always comes back to him throughout the years.

George flips the meat, wondering how Ziggy comes and goes with years in between. He shakes his head at the mystery of it all.

His thoughts turn to the empty bottle, fighting the urge to grab another.

I'll have to figure that one out. He's already forming a vague plan for a zen garden in his backyard.

He pulls the meat from the fire and cuts a portion for Ziggy, who devours it with a wagging tail. George sits back against the fallen tree and eats. He pets his dog between mouthfuls, satisfied with everything.

•　　　•　　　•

"What is a soul?" Gail asks, her sunglasses reflecting a sky so blue it feels electric. Wispy clouds stretch towards the horizon.

She reclines in George's small boat, locks of her hair trailing behind them in the shimmering water. Her feet dangle over the other side as she balances a fishing pole between her calves.

George glances up from the motor, squinting in the sun as he admires his fiance. He's twenty-six.

"Oh no, you're not gonna pull that one on me. I remember last time I answered a question like that," he says with a grin, wiping the crown of sweat around his forehead. He turns back to the motor.

"Would you quit fiddling with that thing and come lie down?" Gail says, holding out an inviting arm. George grunts, swinging the motor into the water with a splash.

"Hey, careful with that, you're gonna scare away all the fish!"

George smirks as he lies with his head and feet opposite hers. He pretends to stretch, reaching over the side to splash her.

The boat rocks as she laughs, squirming away. "I mean it!" Gail threatens him with her foot until he surrenders. "That's more like it. I'm trying to fish here." She lies back, eyes closed. George shifts his weight, and she opens one eye to watch him cast.

"I remember a time when fishing was a foreign concept to you." Both elbows hang over the side of the boat as George leans back.

"It helps me relax." One of her ankles touches his shoulders, and he brings an arm up to rest on her shins.

They sit in silence, a light breeze moving over their sweaty bodies. The gentle motion of the boat lulls them into drowsiness.

"I love the feeling of the water." George gazes past the hull. "Makes me feel like a goddamn astronaut."

She imagines him surrounded by deep, inky blackness, a beacon of light against the dark. Her smile becomes a yawn. "You never answered my question."

George's eyes meet hers before turning to his bobber. "I thought I gave a pretty good reason for that, darling." He reaches into a cooler full of lager but no fish, grabbing a beer.

She puts a hand on his arm, tracing her fingers across his skin. "It won't be like last time," she says quietly, avoiding his gaze.

He rests her sunglasses on her long, dark hair, and she peers up at him.

"I just want to talk, honest." She bats her eyelids with exaggeration.

George laughs, opening his beer. It fizzes in protest as he pulls the cap off, cold interior air escaping as a billowing mist. He takes a long sip before handing it off.

"Well, alright, as long as you promise you're not gonna disappear on me this time." He wipes his mouth with the back of one hand.

"Of course," she says between sips. The carbonation tickles the roof of her mouth.

George sighs. His eyes move as though tracing features of the distant shore. "Well ... I suppose a soul is me," he says at last, turning his attention to Gail.

She studies his face. "What do you mean by 'me'?"

"Well you know ... me. My memories, my thoughts, my emotions and experiences. Everything that separates me from you."

"That's your mind, though. I asked about souls." Gail hands the beer back.

"What do you think makes a soul?" He takes a swig.

Gail sits up. "My dad claimed God knows who you are before you're born, sending you down during conception. Or maybe in the womb. When, exactly, wasn't clear. Anyway, then you live life. If you accept the Lord, God accepts when you die. So a soul is more 'you' than your body or mind."

"Sounds on-brand for him, at least. Do you believe it?"

Gail stares out at the water. Can she make out the far shore, shapes George traced a moment ago? Or is her brain filling in the blanks subconsciously?

"No. As an idea, I'd love to spend eternity with you. Ultimately, it's a candle in the dark — enough light to keep it from pressing in all at once." She reclaims the beer.

"You make sense, but who knows? Maybe 'mind' and 'soul' are two different words for the same thing."

Gail stops the bottle short of her mouth. "You think Dad had it right? Eternal souls existing independently of our bodies?"

George shrugs. "Maybe!" he says with an ease both admirable and enviable.

Some flicker of this must've crossed her face, because George's expression softens. He sets the beer on the deck before taking her hands. "What, darling?"

Her voice is small. "I just wish it could be that easy."

He leans in and kisses her. "We have our whole lives to figure it out. Together."

Gail's line jerks. She lets out a surprised shriek before grabbing the fishing pole. Frantic, she turns the reel, the fish pulling and tugging for its life.

The water froths with manic energy as Gail yanks a largemouth bass from the lake. It twists and bends, gills gasping.

She drops it on the deck and George removes the hook before grabbing his knife.

Gail puts a hand on his shoulder. "George, wait ... should we throw him back?"

His eyebrows jump. "I thought this was dinner?"

"I know but ... what about his soul?"

They hold each other's gaze before turning to the fish, metallic green scales catching bits of sunlight. Its thrashing slows as it approaches death.

George lifts it in both hands with an air of ritual, tossing it back into the lake. The fish darts away from an unknowable world, back to shadows on the cave wall.

They watch it disappear, George's arm around Gail, her head on his shoulder. The sun is low and the world is silent. Gail commits this to memory, to a mental list of perfect moments.

George kisses the top of her head. "Well, I guess we should start rowing."

She remembers the broken motor and laughs.

They stop at the grocery store on the way home for fresh fish. George's backyard fills with delicious smells from the grill, and they drink, talk, and laugh into the night. Fireflies momentarily disrupt the shadows of the forest, candles in the dark.

•   •   •

It's late one cold night in February. George, fifty-six, sits motionless among the trees, eyes closed and legs crossed.

The same wind that bends branches and sways trees runs across his body, the breath of billions of lives ended before his. He exhales, his gift to the future.

Head tilted towards the night sky, he opens his eyes to admire the heavens. He raises his arms, fingers splayed and grasping, a tree among his fellows. Torso splitting into limbs splitting into fingers like branches, like a nervous system. Like neurons. He, like the trees and the stars, is the geometry of nature — ratios and fractals.

His mind is clear despite the alcohol. The countless peaks and valleys that constitute his life, that make George, stretch farther even than the stars.

He regards those distant balls of burning gasses, infinity contemplating infinity. He comes from these bright points, composed of tiny particles forged within those cosmic furnaces.

One day he'll return, after his life is spent and his body decays into dust. Their star will expand as its fuel depletes, swallowing the Earth it once helped nurture.

He thinks of sweet Ziggy Stardust, his eyes filling with tears at the idea of his dog's flame extinguished. His longing is a dull ache in his core he can do nothing to ease.

Six years have passed since he last saw Ziggy, the longest he's gone without him. For the past few months he's spent his nights in the darkness of the woods.

He's waiting for his dog to come running through the trees, gracefully cutting the air as he bounds to George. He'd smile with the happiness of a child to see his beautiful dog return.

Instead he's struggling to balance against the combined pull of gravity and alcohol. Soon he'll make his way inside, upstairs. For now he waits, trees and the cold night air his only companions in the dark.

•   •   •

Gail stands at the window of the darkened bedroom, trying to pinpoint George amongst the trees. Three years have passed since the night he broke the jar of sauce; things have deteriorated.

He's spent his evenings drunk in the woods for a month now. He's even fallen asleep out there, sitting down to breakfast with leaves and cobwebs in his hair like everything's normal.

Gail doesn't know why, but tonight was his last chance. She can't keep pretending everything is fine, like every time they fight about his drinking he's going to change.

He stumbles out of the woods, swaying like a tree in the wind as he prepares each step. She turns, getting into bed fully dressed.

A few months earlier the sight of George this drunk might've made her cry. A few weeks earlier might've angered her. Now there's nothing.

The back door opens, his heavy footsteps crossing the kitchen to the stairway. She pretends to sleep on the off-chance he pays her any mind.

He shuffles to the bed and crawls in, snoring after a few minutes. She turns to study the slack features of his unconscious face. Traces of the boy she fell in love with remain — tousled hair, rounded cheeks, the hint of a smile, even while sleeping. It's not enough anymore.

She pretends for a moment tonight is any other night. Her heartbeat increases and she takes a deep breath. She stands, crossing the distance to the doorway.

The house is quiet as she retrieves the bags she hid earlier, practically tip-toeing. She peeks in at George. To her surprise, she tears up — not much, but she allows them to roll down her cheeks.

"Goodbye." She hurries down the stairs before she changes her mind.

•   •   •

Gail's the first to notice the scratching from downstairs.

George is twenty-four, house-sitting for his parents over the weekend. They're in George's old bed when Gail sits up.

"What's the matter, darling?"

"Shh, do you hear that?"

George sits up, a strip of sunlight falling on his bare chest. His face lights up. "I know exactly what that is." He hurries down the hall.

"What, George?"

He flashes a wolfish grin before disappearing down the stairwell.

Gail hears George open the back door, shouting with happiness. She reaches for a shirt as he climbs the stairs.

"George?" Her voice carries down the hall.

"Someone's here to meet you!" he yells back.

"George, I'm not decent!" She pulls the blanket around her.

He emerges from the stairs, a brown splotchy dog with pointed ears at his heels.

"Go get her!" The dog crosses the distance in seconds. Gail shrieks as he leaps on the bed, licking her face.

George arrives a moment later, prompting the dog to rear back on hind legs. George laughs, catching his paws like they're dancing.

"This is your magic dog?" Gail says.

"Ziggy, sit!" The dog sits.

Gail pets his head, and he lowers his ears, licking her arm in return. She smiles. "He's sweet."

George beams. "He's a good old boy." The dog drops, lifting a paw to expose his belly. They both laugh as George obliges.

"I always thought you were making him up."

George raises his eyebrows. "You did?"

"I thought you were pulling my leg, or maybe he was an old imaginary friend, a stuffed animal, something."

George considers his dog. "I guess I take it for granted how fantastical it is, him coming and going over the years. As a kid he was just my dog, nothing weird about it."

Gail lies back and pats the bed, offering it to George.

He closes the door before joining her. Ziggy turns around before lying between them.

"It's all so strange." She yawns. Afternoon sunlight streams through the blinds, making her warm and sleepy.

George yawns in response. "That's my boy."

"There's got to be a rational explanation ..." She trails off, drifting to sleep.

•   •   •

When Gail wakes, it's dark outside. The house is silent aside from George's steady, even breath. Ziggy lies curled up at their feet. She frowns at the sleeping dog. The lack of clarity on The Ziggy Problem bothers her.

She gazes out the window. Being awake at night highlights reality as an agreed upon lie, only to be admitted in the dark.

She peers into the dense forest, the moonlight only reaching so far. Hidden in the darkness between the trees is a secret pattern, elusive in the daylight.

She lies back down, facing George. "Awake?"

"Mm." His eyelids won't admit defeat.

"George?" Her hand goes to his shoulder.

He exhales. "Yeah?"

"Do you believe in God?"

His eyes open, studying Gail's face. "I don't know, darling."

She nods, staring at the ceiling.

"Do you?" George asks.

"I think everyone does, at some point. My dad made sure I did. I don't think about it much anymore."

George sits up. "What happened?"

Gail shrugs. "I got older, I suppose. In a way my dad was responsible. He never allowed me to choose his beliefs. So when I had a choice, I ran from his.

"His faith colors everything, like a filter. If that's forced on you, it only covers so much before crumbling to pieces. You can either hide in it or sweep it away." The cold night air presses in around her. George studies the blanket between them.

Gail continues. "I don't think that's a bad way of being, necessarily. I wish I had that kind of faith, that certainty. Everything would be so ... easy."

She sighs. "The world isn't that simple. Heaven and Hell make sense when you're young. Oh, of course the bad are punished and the good are rewarded.

"But take that idea to its logical extreme, and it buckles. We spend eternity based on how we spend our time here?

"There's an all-knowing, all-loving god, with perfect knowledge of everything — past, present, future. He's already settled, before you're born, if you're going to Heaven or Hell. An all-knowing, all-loving god creates people doomed to Hell?

"What's the point? You're on Earth for maybe seventy years, then you're punished or rewarded for eternity? No appeals? No learning or improving? Your time on Earth is nonexistent in comparison, yet it decides your eternal fate." She shakes her head. "That's absurd."

George looks at her, seeing for the first time the part she keeps hidden.

"I don't remember when I stopped believing. My family kept going to church, of course — every Sunday morning, in the front row with Mom and Grandma.

"After the service we'd line up beside my dad as the congregation filed out, smiling as they shook our hands and complimented my dad on a wonderful sermon. For me, it was all an act.

"At first I felt so … subversive. I knew secrets they all refused to see. The more I faked it, the more my smile eroded into a sneer. Leaving for college freed me of the chain around my ankle."

She faces George, and for the first time, the slight upwards curve of his mouth annoys her.

Ziggy jumps off the bed to sleep in the corner.

Her voice is neutral. "What about you?"

George clears his throat. "I can't really say, darling. I wasn't raised religious, but I can't rule anything out completely. I grew up with a magic dog. How can I say with any certainty what does or doesn't exist?

"I'm a small part of a huge universe. I find it hard to believe that anyone, religious or otherwise, has got it all figured out. The idea of some all-knowing creator doesn't bring me peace.

"There's this idea in Zen Buddhism that if you meditate long enough you can forget the words for things, see the world for how it really is, beyond the shadows on the cave wall. I wanna know what's outside the damn cave." His words linger in the silence.

Gail experiences an unnamed emotion — resentment, betrayal, contempt, jealousy, all swirling together. The feeling that although they are ninety percent compatible, the last ten percent goes on for miles.

Perhaps he senses the rift, filling it with words. "All I know is when I look up at the night sky and see the vastness of space, the unimaginable potential of existence, I feel connected to all things, everyone. That's enough to make me cry sometimes."

There's something in George, some passion or conviction, that Gail can't understand. Where he turns to the night sky and finds potential, she perceives emptiness.

Although it's impossible to deny the bright points of light breaking up the overwhelming darkness, she scoffs inwardly. Whether it's God, Allah, Brahma, or comfort gleaned from starlight, it all amounts to the same thing: wishful thinking.

Her voice cracks. "So what happens when we die?"

George hesitates before responding. "The matter in my body will break apart to take other forms, the energy in my body returning to the universe, where it came from.

"That's immortality. I've been a million different things before and I'll be a million different things again. Nothing in this life stays the same, including me and you.

"Ultimately I like the mystery of it all. I'll always love the questions more than the answers." He turns to look at Gail. "What do you think happens when we die?"

Answers are the only thing we can ever really own. George wouldn't understand.

"When we die, we're dead, and that's that. We only get this one life. Anything else is fooling yourself." She turns to face the wall, closing her eyes but not sleeping. Eventually she feels George lie back, asleep a few minutes later.

She dozes lightly, waking with the sunrise. There's a chill in the air as she creeps out of bed, getting dressed quietly to sneak outside.

She takes his car back to the college. His parents will be home later, they can drive him back. She's glad to be away from his bedroom and the man she thought she understood more than she does.

Later she'll be ashamed of the thought, but as she leaves, she finds some satisfaction in the fact that Ziggy has gone in the night.

•   •   •

Gail finds George in the backyard. He's shoveling dirt in a small square pit, his back to her. George is fifty-nine.

No Ziggy, which means he'll be drinking. She wants to distance herself from her concern — it's no longer her place to worry. She still cares about him, though. Whatever else, she can't deny him that.

She stands at the edge as he digs, the sun glistening in the sweat on his bare back. He seems sober enough, digging with the energy of a much younger man.

A breeze moves across the grass and George stops, leaning against his shovel to enjoy the wind. He reaches for a water bottle at the edge of the pit. As he bends, the shovel shifts, and he finally notices he's not alone.

George's look of shock gives way to a boyish grin, dominating his features with surprising ease. He looks fifteen years younger.

"Hello George."

"Hiya Gail," he says, sheepish. Gail smiles in spite of herself.

As he climbs out of the hole in the earth, she realizes she hasn't seen him in two years. He looks good. Much healthier.

"What brings you around?" he asks.

"I was in the neighborhood." She provides no further explanation. He nods like it's all cleared up. The wind blows again, his forehead still dripping sweat. She's surprised how much of his hair turned white.

"Well anyways, how about lending me a hand?" he says at last, perfectly normal.

"What are you up to back here?"

"Making a zen garden."

"You're gonna build that all by yourself?"

He shrugs. "It's not too hard. It's a hole filled with sand and rocks. Passes the time while Ziggy's gone — nothing better to do since I quit drinking."

Gail acknowledges a small relief. "Ziggy, huh? Still getting visits from your magic dog?" Neutral territory.

George smiles. "Of course. Been a few months, but he'll be back soon."

He drinks from the water bottle, casting rainbows on his neck and shoulders as sunlight passes through the sweating plastic.

"So how about it? Help me dig?"

"I don't have the right shoes for that." She holds out a sandaled foot for proof.

"C'mon, it'll be good for you." He drops the shovel toward her. She catches it with a skeptical look and a slight smile.

"Look, I've been busting my ass out here for months, it's the least you can do." He grins.

She laughs and steps into the pit, scanning the ground before pushing the shovel into the dirt.

George moves to avoid the airborne soil. "Good start." He leans against a wheelbarrow full of rocks and fallen branches.

She peers up at him, her expression a combination of amusement and annoyance.

He smiles, wiping sweat from his forehead. "Just pace yourself, is all."

A silence falls between them as she digs. Beads of perspiration form on the back of her neck. She stops to wipe her head, a mirror image of George.

He digs through the wheelbarrow to organize the rocks into piles on the ground. He struggles to lift a particularly heavy stone, arms trembling with the effort.

Gail stops digging and frowns. "George, don't lift that on your own, you're going to hurt yourself."

"I got it, Gail. Don't worry," he says through grit teeth. He drops the rock but misjudges the weight. It falls with a reverberating clang against the shovel, knocking it from her hands.

She cries out, her hands throbbing. "Dammit George, I told you to be careful!"

George frowns. "You kind of forfeited the right to issue orders, didn't you?"

His defiance surprises her. She scoffs. "Some things never change. Your reach will always exceed your grasp."

"And you'll never allow yourself optimism."

She steps out of the pit, and they stare at each other from opposite sides of the gulf.

"What are you doing here, Gail?" He sounds exhausted. "All those years together, I know it wasn't perfect. I let the drink get the best of me, especially at the end. Your leaving was my fault, I have no illusions about that.

"But goddamn Gail, I never met a person more committed to drowning. God forbid I feel the slightest bit of spiritual connection to the world. No, either you're a cold, hard rationalist, or you're some misguided fool.

"Sometimes you were this weight around my ankle, keeping me below the surface."

Hurt and anger wells up in Gail's chest. "That's not fair, George. You would have drank yourself to death a long time ago if not for me. And I tried. I tried to be more open, to see things your way. No matter what I did, I was never going to mean as much to you as your dog.

"I was a weight around your ankle, but we weren't under water. We were on solid ground — you were going to float away if not for me. I tried to keep you here with me because I loved you, George. And you may have loved me, but you sure as hell never needed me. All you ever needed was your stupid dog." Tears fill her eyes.

George stares, his mouth hanging open, all defiance gone. That's the George I know.

She throws the shovel and walks towards the house before facing George.

"You asked what I was doing here. I just realized: making a mistake." She leaves him on the edge of his pit.

As she gets in her car, she waits to see if George will run after her. He doesn't.

Instead she drives away, wiping the last of her tears. She never sees him again.

•   •   •

Georges takes his time coming down the steps, the sharp pain in his joints familiar like some awful song stuck in his head. He enters the kitchen, an old man in a bathrobe. He's seventy-five.

He puts on a pot of coffee, the dark aroma filling the air. Through the window George watches morning stretch across the sky.

He pours the steaming liquid into his favorite mug and raises the black coffee to his lips. The scent fills his nose as he watches morning stream through the trees.

A year has passed since Ziggy last came running from the woods. Although he misses his dog, the absence doesn't bother him. It's never permanent, and he's made peace with that. Besides, he enjoys solitary life, appreciating the silence like a monk. Like an astronaut.

Next week is George's birthday, marking almost twenty years since Gail left him. Almost twenty years since he's had a drink.

He remembers her final visit, in the zen garden. An unhappy moment which almost returned him to the bottle. He shakes his head. That's all behind him now. The past is the past — let it stay there.

A knock at the door pulls George from his thoughts, the first in so long that he can't place the sound for a moment. The knock repeats, loud as thunder in the quiet of his house.

George pulls his robe closed, shuffling to the front door. Opening it reveals a short man in a suit, clean shaven with hair slicked back.

"Can I-" George starts. His voice is a barely audible scratch, a crumpling of paper. He clears his throat and tries again. "Can I help you?"

"Mr. Sullivan? George?"

"Yes, that's me."

"Mr. Sullivan, my condolences on your loss. I'm here to deliver the items bequeathed to you by your late wife." He holds out a parcel the size of a shoe box, wrapped in brown paper.

"Son, there must be some kind of mistake, I haven't been married in almost twenty years." He's already closing the door.

"A Mrs. Gail Sullivan?"

The door stops. "Gail Sullivan and I are divorced. You're telling me she's passed?"

The man appears uncomfortable. "I don't know what to say Mr. Sullivan — I assumed you knew. And legally, the two of you never divorced."

George closes his eyes, gripping the doorframe to steady himself. "When did she ..."

"Last week."

George nods, eyes still closed.

"Would you like to know how ..." the man starts.

George is already shaking his head. He opens his eyes. "How do you know we never ...?"

"I'm her power of attorney. She kept her records in terrific shape. I've seen the divorce papers. Your signature is there, but not hers."

George holds up a hand. "I'm sorry, this is a lot to take in."

"Of course, I understand. I won't keep you any longer. Here, she wanted you to have this." He holds the parcel out.

George takes it in a daze, not registering its weight.

"Again, my condolences." He tilts his hat before walking down the path to his car.

George stands in the doorway, the wind moving through the trees. An intense feeling of the present burns this moment into his mind.

The package in his arms grows heavy, and he scans for Ziggy before closing the door.

He puts the box on the kitchen table and drops into his chair, the mug of coffee forgotten in front of him. Fifteen minutes ago he'd been a much happier man.

His hands move to unwrap the parcel. Inside, beside a smaller box with a white envelope, is a mason jar full of rocks — the source of the weight. A sad smile crosses his lips as he reads the jar's note: "Seeds for your garden".

He places both elbows on the table, his head in his hands as he stares at the sealed envelope. Every time he reaches out to read Gail's final words to him, he stops.

A fear of finality, of ending their fifty year conversation, builds inside him. Even after twenty years, he never expected it would end like this.

He walks to the sink, splashing his face with cold water. After a moment he puts his whole head beneath the faucet.

He cuts the water off but stays bent over the sink, staring down the black, empty drain. Standing, he dries his head with a dish towel.

The envelope is like a magnet on his mind. He fights the urge to rip it up, unread — to erase this morning from his mind.

He sighs and faces the table. Ignorance is no way to be, bliss be damned. The truth may hurt, but it's still the truth. Gail would've agreed.

With no memory of crossing the kitchen, he's in his chair, hands flat on the table. He reaches out in a trance and opens the box, revealing a small metal flask. The smooth surface on the concave side distorts his reflection as he examines it.

There's a ship on the convex side, a large galleon breaking the crest of a wave, its sails full of wind. A banner underneath reads 'Homeward Bound'.

A sticky note in Gail's handwriting reads 'For H20 only'. George chuckles, setting it aside.

He picks up the envelope, holding his breath. Inside is a single piece of lined paper, folded in half.

"George, for your sake, I hope I'm wrong. Let's try and get it right next time. Love always, Gail."

He lets the paper fall to the table as his eyes fill with tears. Later he'll take the rocks to his zen garden, spreading some in the sand with the ashes of Gail's letter — his own private funeral for the woman he loved but couldn't make happy.

For now his body sinks to the floor, the wreckage of the galleon dashed against relentless waves. His stomach heaves as loud, uncontrollable sobs rip their way from his body.

He cries for Gail, for his dog, for a life spent in pursuit of the intangible, and for the temporary nature of all things.

• • •

Ziggy runs through the forest behind George's house, cutting through the trees with an easy grace. He's emerged through a wormhole in the woods, a small tear in spacetime allowing him to travel from a day twenty-four years in the future to right now. He perceives many of these tears open and close, leaping through those with the scent of George on the other side.

Right now there's only a faint whiff. There's the smell of his house, his mother and father, but George is a glimmer.

He bursts from the woods and runs past the house, up the driveway to the open road. His body follows the curves and bends, and soon he's engaged in the joy of the run as much as in finding George. Every part of him is filled with happiness.

He reaches the main road, his nose searching the air. George's scent is close enough to scream at him.

It comes from a car rushing past him, and he throws himself into the pursuit. He crosses an intersection and never sees the car that kills him coming.

It runs the red light, hitting Ziggy head on. There's a flash of pain as the impact sends him flying. Another wormhole opens, and Ziggy lands eighty-seven years later next to a dead George. Downstairs, he can hear himself chased to the backyard by the lawyer.

He tries standing but can't. Instead, he stretches his head and gives George's hand one last lick before dying next to him.

Meanwhile, George and Gail throw a gasping fish back into the lake, George reads Gail's final words, Gail turns to say goodbye to a sleeping George, and a drunk George scoops handfuls of spaghetti sauce off the driveway.

Meanwhile, George's parents drive with their infant son. They pull into the driveway of the house where he'll spend his life.

George looks up from his mother's arms with eyes that see the world for how it really is, and it's beautiful.

Matt Bliss is a construction worker turned speculative fiction writer from the Wild West of Las Vegas, Nevada. He believes there's no such thing as too much coffee and is the proud owner of too many pets. His short fiction has appeared in *Metastellar, Cosmic Horror Monthly*, and had been featured in dozens of other magazines and anthologies. If you don't find him haunting the used book aisle of your local thrift store, you can always find him on Twitter at *@MattJBliss*.

• • •

I wanted to write an adventure story and thought what better way to do so than to add all of my favorite things: The Wild West, steampunk, magic, mines, and a dark underworld. What surprised me most wasn't the world that came from this, but the characters who lived inside it.

DEXTER AND THE MECHANICAL DEAD

MATT BLISS

I T WAS HOTTER THAN a cheap cup of coffee in hell outside, and I didn't want to be standing in that cemetery a moment longer. I looked from the letter in my hand back to the man standing in the empty grave below me.

"Look," I said, "I'll tell you the same thing I told that damn governor. The bodies will turn up somewhere. This is a small desert town — *community* if you will — and somebody must have seen something."

The man below me didn't look up, and I was half-tempted to kick dirt on top of his tailored black suit.

"Grave-robberies happen all the time," I continued, "and I'm sure they only wanted the jewelry and *what-have-you*. The bodies *will* turn up ... I'll find 'em. And I don't need *you* to come and screw up my investigation."

The man below took a handful of dirt from the base of the grave and placed it to his nose. He slipped some of the soil in his pocket and climbed out. "As you have read in the letter, Sheriff," the man said, turning his fleabite eyes toward me, "I am here on special orders of the Governor to ... take care of this problem of yours."

"This is my town, and things work different here."

The man looked down at my hand resting on or the grip of my holstered revolver and back to me.

"I am not here to disrupt your investigation, Sampson —"

"No one calls me that anymore."

"My apologies, Sheriff. I'm here to help. This issue is much larger than you know. It is not merely catching bandits and hanging them at the gallows like you are so keen to insist upon. This is something that you are in no way capable of handling. That is why they sent me." He reached up and patted the neck of my horse.

I wanted to punch him. Someone coming to *my* town and telling me that *he* knew how to do my job better? I'd shot men for less in my younger days, before I had this star on my chest anyway. But, I bit the side of my cheek 'til it bled and didn't do a thing because ... the man was right. As much as I faked it, I had no clue what was happening, and this man could see straight through it with those beady little eyes. It was all so bizarre — like the bodies, *all the bodies,* in the cemetery just got up and walked away. The whole town was buzzing like a dust storm about it, and this was a storm that an old gunslinger with a badge couldn't do much about.

"Tell me, Sheriff, what is that over there?" The man pointed past the expanse of sand and cactus to the metallic opening in the hillside.

"That's the mine. The bread and butter of this town."

He pinched his mouth back in a smile. "Please, if you will. I would like to see it."

•　　　•　　　•

"You say the Governor sent him?" Geldin asked me, wiping an oil-soaked hand across the sweat droplet clinging to the tip of her nose.

"Apparently so. It's all in here if you like," I said, handing her the sealed orders I'd received only hours earlier.

She snatched it out of my hand as quick as I stuck it out and held it close to her soda bottle goggles. A hiss leaked out one of the pipes lining the mine wall and Geldin pulled a wrench as big as her arm from her tool pouch to thump the riveted seam until it silenced.

The man behind me twisted restlessly.

"So he's got a letter from the governor ... big whoop. I don't see what that has to do with you bringing some weirdo into *my* mine, Sheriff." She hung the wrench over her shoulder and gave me a withering glare.

"Well," I said, tucking my thumbs into my gun belt, "Perhaps mister uh ..." I stepped back and looked at the man.

"*Doc-tor*," he said, speaking the word like the slash of a blade. Geldin and I both flinched at the sound. "Doctor Manklin. A pleasure to finally make your acquaintance. However, I am not permitted to discuss why —"

"This is about the cemetery, isn't it?" Geldin asked. "The bodies goin' missing?"

I looked at the man too and raised an eyebrow.

The doctor looked about as out of place as a daisy in a desert right then. He brushed some unseen dirt off his coat and pinched his lips back in a smile.

"I knew it!" Geldin said and slapped the hammered copper machine behind her. "I told you! Something funny's goin' on here!"

I stepped between them again. "Now calm down. Let's see what the man wants. If that is why he's here, I'm sure he's got a perfectly good explanation as to why he's in a mine —"

"*My* mine," Geldin added.

"Okay ... *your* mine ... instead of at the damned cemetery across the hill."

The man stroked his goatee with a gloved hand and smiled. "Please, if you will, show me around *your* mine. I would love to know more about it. Where is the deepest excavation tunnel here?"

Geldin sighed and looked at me sideways.

I shrugged.

"Well," she said. "Follow me."

Geldin twisted the crank on the copper machine behind her and its gears whirred to life in a rhythmic clicking. "Lead the way, Dexter," she said as its cogs pushed it along its treads, and it moved down the mine shaft with a trail of steam leaking from its pistons.

Manklin twisted the cane in his hand and we followed the maze of tubes and wires leading us down the sloping tunnel. Even with the sweat in my eyes, I couldn't help but marvel at the crafted metal tracks and gauges along the way down.

"Well, I'm glad you're here, mister," Geldin said to Doctor Manklin. "It's about time we figure out what happened."

"Why do you say that?" I asked. "I don't need some stranger's help to solve this."

Geldin huffed. "Right ..."

I stopped a moment as Dexter thundered into the claustrophobic tunnels. "You think I can't?"

"Let's be honest, you're a damned excellent shot, and you saved my ass more than once, but you're not a very good sheriff. Hell, you don't even *want* to be Sheriff I think, but what else is someone like you gonna do, right?"

I bit my lip and considered this. It was true; this wasn't exactly what I thought it would be. I needed something bigger than small town squabbles, and my trigger finger was always waiting for the opportunity.

"What are you mining for here?" Manklin asked over the rumble of surrounding machinery.

"Copper ... mostly," Geldin said while checking bolts and ties along the way. "My family has owned this place a long time, but it wasn't until I built Dexter here, and some of the other automations, that it became profitable."

I ducked around a jetty of steam and chimed in. "Geldin here is whizz with machines and mechanics. Her inventions revolutionized mining here, a whole new process. Changed the town for the better too. Industry, resources, all things this lil watering hole didn't have before. I wouldn't doubt if sooner or later, we're all riding things like Dexter here instead of horses."

"Dexter is for drilling, not for riding," Geldin said, shaking a wrench in my face.

We twisted and turned, dropping deeper underground. Smaller machines slid past, moving dirt over our heads on a thin silver track. Manklin ducked and grabbed his hat with a pale hand each time they passed.

"We're almost to the face," Geldin said, pointing to the cluster of small dirt movers ahead. Manklin stiffened as we reached the exposed rock at the end of the tunnel. It was small, cramped, and smelled faintly like sour milk. It was as if you could feel the mountains of earth above us pushing in from every direction.

"This is the deepest point? Are you sure?" Manklin asked.

Geldin tapped the pressure gauge strapped to her vest. "Sure as a mine is dark," she said.

"This will have to do then. Please," he said sweeping his arms around him. "Allow me some space to work."

I looked at Geldin as confused as ever. "Wait," I said, letting my hand fall to the revolver's grip on pure instinct. "Why don't you tell us what in the hell you are doing here first?"

Manklin didn't flinch.

"We have a lot of people tryin' to come here to steal Geldin's designs, and I won't let that happen. So … one more time. What are you doing here? What does *this* have to do with the cemetery?"

He looked to Geldin instead of me. "Have you seen them? Coming through here with your workers?"

"The grave robbers? Mister — I mean *Doc-toor* ..." she let out a brief snicker. "It's only me and Dexter in this mine."

"No, not them," Manklin said. "The bodies?" he paced over the floor, squinting at the surface.

I started to raise the pistol from its holster and said, "Now I know you've lost your mind."

"No other way out of here. This rock is harder than a woodpecker's lips, and without Dexter here, nobody's going through," Geldin said, taking a step back.

"Although I love your ..." Manklin gestured to the mass of metal machinery, "ingenuity, there are ways other than drilling." He pulled the head off his staff and removed a dark wooden piece. He turned it over in his hand, feeling the carved symbols across its surface before placing it to his lips.

Geldin and I both looked at one another as the man inhaled from the piece in one deep breath. He squatted down and exhaled violet smoke towards the floor. Thick clouds plumed out and gathered around him. More smoke than any lungs should hold, moving, dancing around the man in a turbulent circle dropping closer to the floor.

The earth beneath crumbled around the man. Cracking and peeled away like dry leaves in the wind, leaving only a dark circle in its wake.

I felt Geldin grip hold of my shoulder, but I was too stunned to look away.

The man looked into the space with a glow in his beady eyes and jumped into the dark opening.

I stepped closer, staring into the opening in the floor, when I noticed Geldin was already at the hole's edge beside me. It was like looking into oblivion. Inky blackness, thick and endless. "Step back," I said, holding up an arm to Geldin. "We don't know what it is."

She looked at me and checked the fit of her thick goggles on her eyes. "Right ... I'm going in to find out." She moved to jump in and I grabbed her.

"Are you crazy? Some stranger opens a damn portal in the bottom of a mine and —"

"*My* mine," she interrupted.

"Whatever! And you're just going to jump into it?"

"Uh ... yeah! When are we ever going to have an opportunity like this?"

I chewed my lip for a moment and looked deeper into the dark opening. "Okay," I said. "But I can't let you go alone."

Geldin slapped me on the arm. "You're right, I better bring Dexter."

I rolled my eyes as she cranked the machine to life and we both watched it move forward on spinning gears until it fell into the dark opening.

"Here goes nothing," Geldin said and nodded to me.

I nodded back and looked into the black pool. I removed my pistol, feeling the weight of its polished steel in my hand was comforting, and without another thought, I jumped.

•   •   •

The air switched from the hot steam of the mine to an icy chill the moment we crossed. The cool breeze cut through the fabric of my clothes and turned every sweat droplet clinging to my back into tiny icicles. We crunched down, landing in the dirt, and looked up to the cavernous space around us.

It was dark. It was quiet. The lamp still fixed to Dexter revealed chiseled rock walls surrounding us in a peculiar amber glow.

Geldin went straight to Dexter and checked on his various moving parts until satisfied he was okay.

"This just keeps getting weirder," I said, searching over the geometric pillars jutting from the ground and roof around us. "Where are we?"

Geldin tapped the pressure gauge strapped to her vest. "Deep. Some sort of cave system below the mine, it seems."

I looked back, but couldn't see the opening we came through. Wherever we were, it looked like we would have to stay until we found another way out.

"Come along now, you two," said a voice from behind us. I jumped at the sound and turned to see Doctor Manklin standing in the shadows. My stomach twisted at seeing the purple glow in his eyes. "We have to hurry." He turned and quickly continued into the passage.

"Wait!" I shouted after him. "Where are we?"

The opening ended at a tunnel in the far wall. Manklin stopped at the entrance and turned to face Geldin and me. "If you would like to help, I need you to keep your voices down. And keep that *thing*," he gestured to Dexter, "quiet as well."

The machine let out a hiss as if in protest, and Manklin turned to walk in the tunnel.

"Are you going to tell us now what in the world is going on?" I asked, following him deeper into the dark opening.

"Are you going to threaten to shoot me again if I don't tell you?" he asked.

"Probably yes," I said, smiling at the thought.

Geldin stepped up beside me. "I could always beat you with this here wrench if that doesn't work."

His eyes bounced between us.

"I assure you, I'm only here to help," he said. "Follow me and I'll tell you on the way."

We moved deeper into the tunnel, following the frigid puffs of breath as Dexter trailed behind. The walls glistened with strange minerals bulging from its surface. Geldin ran a hand over and marveled at its strength.

"We had a feeling one was here, just had no way of looking until it began," Manklin said.

"One what?" Geldin asked.

"There are things in this world that most people do not know about. Things hidden. Buried deep — long forgotten. Things that are more than valuable to the right people. Precious."

"I can see why," Geldin said, squinting at the strange metallic crystals. "This place makes my mine look like a joke."

"If you think that's wondrous," he said, turning his violet eyes to ours. "Take a look at this."

He pointed with his staff to a crystal on the ground before him. The smooth shape radiated a brilliant green glow. The light pulsed, burning green, then going dark and throbbing back to life. A heartbeat of light. Palpitating its emerald glow.

We all leaned closer as Doctor Manklin reached down and plucked it from the earth. He smiled and scrapped a wad of dirt and clay from the floor nearby, then he rolled it into a ball. He shaped it with arms and legs, crudely resembling a human form before raising the crystal to his lips and whispering a strange phrase. Then, Manklin pushed the jagged end of the crystal into the doll's chest and it twitched with life.

The legs kicked with the pulse of the gems glow. Its arms rose with each burst of light. In a matter of moments, the thing was standing on its molded feet and looking up at the one who created it.

I jumped back, my heart thudding in my chest like a blacksmith's hammer. Even Geldin hid behind Dexter as the small thing walked into Manklin's hand. All the while, the green light pulsed in its chest.

"Doc ..." I said, gathering what courage I had left to move in for a closer look. "Is *that* what happened to the bodies in the cemetery? Is *that* what you're here for?" I asked.

Before he answered, the clay creature fell flat. It twitched for only a moment before the light in the gem went dark, and its form was still.

"No," Manklin said. "Not exactly. One piece of the puzzle, perhaps. This one was too small; too misshapen. There is something else down here. Something ancient. We knew it was close but only recently detected its signature."

"When the bodies went missing?" Geldin asked.

"Precisely," Manklin said.

I picked the now dark gem from the creature's chest and held it in my hand. Despite the bitter cold around us, it was still warm. "Who did you say you work for again? The Governor?"

Manklin laughed a horrid sound. "How do you think such men rose to power?" he asked and turned his violet eyes away. "Let's keep moving."

We continued down, following Manklin's staff. We passed more crystals like the last. All pulsing with the same green heartbeat. They were too small to use, Manklin said, but when he wasn't looking, I noticed Geldin swipe a few into her tool bag.

Dexter began to sputter as we moved deeper into the tunnels, and eventually, the cogs and shafts that moved him ground to a halt. Geldin twisted knobs and cranks, but the copper machine stayed still. "He's out of juice," she said in defeat. "It's just too cold down here for him."

"Leave it," Manklin said.

Geldin slapped a hand against Dexter's drill teeth. "No way will I ever leave him here. You best —"

"Quiet," I snapped. "I hear something."

We all paused, holding in our last frigid breath, straining our ears for a sound. Then all at once, we heard it. Something ticking in the distance. Metallic groans and whirring gears sounded from the darkness, and this time, it wasn't coming from Dexter.

We squatted down and crept further into the darkness until pillars and statues filled the cavernous room ahead in an eerie, throbbing glow.

I was speechless. The space ahead was as large and developed as an underground city. Carved pillars of stone stretched up into the darkness above, each one sculpted with twisted faces and complex patterns. Prismatic structures dotted the landscape, twisting around a crystalline archway, and the green glow of its heart pulsed at its center.

"Oh dear," Manklin said, peeking from behind a pile of rocks. "This is far worse than I imagined."

"Uh ... Doc ... Mind telling us what we're looking at?" I asked.

Just then, the city came to life. Shapes moved from the shadows. Shapes appearing human at first glance, but upon further inspection, it was only what was left of human.

"Sherriff," Manklin said, "I think we found those bodies you were looking for..."

Skeletal remains moved in a hodgepodge of parts among the strange structures. Copper and brass machinery gleamed from decayed flesh and missing bone. Sprockets and cogs showed from where muscle and spine once lived. One man stumbled on a leg made of hammered pipe and tubing, toothed wheels rotating between bone and rot.

Most disturbing of all, however, was the throbbing green glow of the crystals in their chests.

"Those look like *my* parts," Geldin said. "From the mine. From *my* machines."

"We have to go," Manklin said. "I need to warn the others."

"Yeah," Geldin said, "I second that. I would like to get as far away from this nightmare as possible."

Doctor Manklin reached for his staff when three sharp clicks echoed through the immense room. The mechanical dead stopped and turned toward the arc at the center.

Again, the sharp clicks sounded, and this time I could see their source. A figure at the center rapped its golden staff against the slab floor. It rose up, spreading a wingspan of tendon and bone wings from its back.

"Is that what I think it is?" I asked as the revolver trembled in my hand. Except for its featherless wings, it was wrapped in pale flesh and looked out from dark circles where eyes should be. It waited as the mechanical dead bowed to its presence.

"That," Manklin said, "is the ancient one."

We huddled close as a stillness washed over the place. The figure scanned the bodies around it.

"What's it doing to them?" I asked.

Manklin blinked his violet eyes and said, "Building an army. Let's go, quick."

As we rose to leave, the being at the center screeched like a train stopping on its tracks. We froze to see his golden staff pointed at us, and the eyes of the mechanical dead followed its direction.

"Run!" Manklin said, shoving us back, swooping his cane in a trail of violet smoke.

Geldin turned and ran for Dexter as the bodies marched in our direction. Bodies I had spent so long looking for now found me.

I pulled back the revolver's hammer and squeezed off two shots at the nearest. The rounds cracked into its exposed collarbone and jaw, shattering the pieces into white fragments. Even so, it marched closer with a green light beating in its chest.

I let off another two rounds at a different severely decayed body, moving near on legs made of pulleys and cable. The bullets sparked off its metal parts and ricocheted into the darkness.

"The gems," Manklin said while drawing shapes from the purple smoke. "Aim for the light!" He threw out an open hand and sent the smoke rushing towards our attackers in a powerful wave. The colored air slammed into them, knocking them off their feet.

One still standing to my left rushed at me. Reaching with outstretched rotten hands. I took aim at the glowing gem in its heart and let loose the last two of my rounds. The Gem shattered with a jagged scream. Its throbbing green glow flickered a moment before turning black, and the body collapsed to the floor.

I looked up at the winged being, but it was gone.

"Let's go," Manklin yelled and wrenched me around. We sprinted up the passage until something stopped us dead in our tracks.

Geldin ...

The winged being held her high with one hand as she struggled to break free. It didn't speak, but it didn't need to. The look on its pale mask of a face was enough to understand. Either we give in, or Geldin was done.

The revolver was empty, and when I looked over to Manklin, he placed his hands up, nodding for me to do the same.

The dead swarmed us from behind. They took us, even Dexter, to the arch at the city's center. It was the first time in my life that I had been taken prisoner, and I swore then that it would be the last.

•   •   •

Geldin paced the small cage made from metallic crystals. "Okay guys, we got to come up with a plan. What do we do?" she asked.

I leaned back against Dexter's shell and tipped back my hat. "Nothing we can do," I said. "Those crystals are harder than diamonds, and seein' as they took my pistol, your tools, and Dexter here is dead, I don't see us getting out anytime soon."

"Do you not see what the hell is goin' on out there? They are going to kill us and turn us into those … *things.*"

I looked through the bars to see the mechanical dead gathered around the winged thing. It swung its golden staff over a throne of throbbing green gems. The bodies surrounding it rose and fell with the pulse of its glow, chanting metallic groans with the rhythm.

"You don't know that for sure," I said.

Manklin stepped in and said, "That's *exactly* what they're doing."

"I knew it!" Geldin said before snapping on Manklin. "What are *you* doing about it, huh? Why can't you use some of that magic or whatever and whisk us out of here?"

"*Magick* … doesn't work like that. I'm not as powerful as the ancients are. Besides, they took my cane, *my totem*, without it I'm weak."

We paused to watch the hideous ceremony outside, listening to the ticking of their gears and clanking of metal.

"I'm sorry I said you're a bad sheriff," Geldin said. "I didn't mean nothing of it." Her face pulse green from the glowing outside.

"It's okay." I laughed. "I am a bad sheriff. But like you said, what else is *'Steel-eye Sampson'* going to do? I just wanted ... I don't know. Something bigger, you know? I'm getting old now, and it'aint getting any easier."

"Well, you've got it now. Only problem is that we won't ever get out of here to tell about it. If only I had Dexter." Geldin thumped a fist against the crystal bars. "He would be able to drill through this stuff like nothing."

Manklin squinted at her from across the small cage. "What if you could get it to work?" he asked.

"No way. He needs fuel, and with it being so cold down here, steam just isn't going to work."

The chanting from outside grew louder. The thrumming of the gem's glow quickened like the hurried beats of a racing heart.

It was almost time.

"What if I gave you an alternate fuel? Would you be able to power it with something else?" Manklin asked.

"Like what? They took everything from us." Geldin pointed out to their things resting alongside the emerald throne.

"Perhaps I can help with that," Manklin said, stepping closer to us. "I think it's time I let you in on a little secret."

He closed his eyes and exhaled a breath from pursed lips. He removed his coat and, starting from the neck, unbuttoned his shit one button at a time. As he reached the bottom, he peeled open his shirt to reveal the massive purple gem glowing from a cavity in his chest.

My eyes grew wide, and I held up a hand to stifle a gasp. "You're ... one of them?"

"Not necessarily. But please, we're running out of time. You need to remove it and connect it to your machine."

"What if it — I mean, will it, you know ... kill you?"

He smiled from ear to ear. "In a way, yes, but I will live on. In here." He tapped the gem with a slender finger.

The sound of moving parts and machinery erupted from around us.

They were coming.

"Please," he said, "take it now."

Geldin pressed her fingertips to the edge of the gem and worked her fingers underneath — into his chest cavity. "Whatever happens Doc, I just want to say ... thank you," Geldin said and pulled the glowing crystal free. The image of the man lifted from his form like mist. Set free along with the gem, his face faded into the darkness above. We looked back to see nothing but a large wooden dummy lying in his place.

"Manklin!" I yelled out. "He wasn't real!"

"He was as real as the steam that powered Dexter. Now shut up and help me with this."

She handed me the gem while she went to work on the machine. It was still warm, pulsing with a lavender glow.

The mechanical dead surrounded our cage, and from behind, I could hear the ancient one rapping his staff against the floor. Each sound rang doom inside me, like the chime of the church bell at noon.

"We're almost out of time. What's going on Geldin?"

"I'm almost there." She moved fittings and pipes, twisted knobs and gears, and finally, the massive copper and bronze machine had a slot, perfectly shaped for the gem, inside the front of its tank.

"Let's hope this works," I said, handing Geldin the gem.

The mass of dead flesh and metal surrounded us. Reaching in, ready to grab us with their rotten hands.

Geldin placed the gem in the newly created slot and twisted it into place. It flashed in a blinding brightness as Dexter's pistons purred to life.

"It's working!" I shouted over the pumping noise. I stepped back as the crackling purple energy wrapped around its copper frame.

Dexter let out a hiss as it ratcheted itself into an upright position. Its grooved parts rotated and repositioned until its smokestack and fuel tanks resembled slightly humanoid arms. It rolled forward on treaded wheels, and the tooth-lined drill of its head spun to life.

Geldin gripped my arm tighter than a vise as the two pressure gauges near the gem gleamed with a violet glow like Manklin's eyes.

"Dexter," she said, "get us out of here!"

The machine seemed to nod in a breath of purple smoke and jerked forward toward the metallic crystal bars. It spun the drill faster, a massive grinder as wide as Geldin was tall, and pressed into the dark crystalline pillars.

The sound rattled our teeth and tore chunks from the minerals in a cloud of dust. The bodies ran towards Dexter, only for the drill head to grab them and mangle them to pieces.

Dexter burst through the last of the pillars and rolled through to the outside. The bodies swarmed us. I ran for my pistol while Geldin jumped on Dexter's back. Dexter swung around, catching and grinding as many of the modified bodies as it could.

The winged creature let out a screech and sailed toward Dexter in one immense leap. I grabbed up Geldin's tool pouch and threw it to her before reaching for my gun belt.

The ancient one paced closer to Dexter. It raised its staff and turned its head sideways, looking like he didn't know what to do with the machine.

Geldin smacked away the other's reaching hands with her oversized wrench as I reloaded.

Dexter raised his smokestack arm as purple energy circled it.

I fired a shot at the ancient one, landing the bullet square in his boney back. He turned and glared at me from its dark holes for eyes. Just then, Dexter took advantage of the sudden distraction and fired a wave of indigo energy at the thing. The blast threw the thing back while the room shuddered around us.

Geldin torqued a bolt on Dexter's side and steered him in my direction. "Hop on," she said, reaching an arm down to me.

I gripped her forearm and pulled up to the machine's back. "Told you we'd be riding one of these," I said. Dexter kept thundering forward until he slammed into the emerald throne. Bits of the green crystals scudded in every direction as his drill bit head cut a hole through its glowing center.

"I don't know if *you* know how to do this, but Dexter, we need to get home," Geldin said.

He rose and let the purple energy swirl around the drill head.

I squeezed off the rest of my rounds into the mechanical dead's glowing chests. Each one shattered to pieces and sent their bodies dropping to the cold floor.

The drill head spun faster until the glowing light ripped through the darkness and shone bits of light on the other side. Just as Dexter rocked forward into the portal, I looked back to see the ancient one tapping his golden staff on the floor. It watched us disappear through its holes for eyes, and the rift closed behind us.

•   •   •

After placing the last of the explosives, we stood on the cemetery's hill and stared at the mineshaft's entrance.

"Are you sure you want to do this?" I asked Geldin. "The mine — I mean ... *your* mine, was everything to you. And this town won't be the same without it."

She pulled up her thick goggles and looked at the jagged opening with wide, glistening eyes. "Yeah," she said, "It's the only way. We have to seal it up — make sure that demon stays down there for good."

I nodded and placed a heavy hand on her shoulder.

"Besides," she said, "I have something more valuable now anyway." She opened up her tool bag to show the mound of glowing green crystals cached inside. We let out a laugh and turned back to the mine.

I looked down at the star on my chest.

"What about you?" Geldin asked. "Wasn't that the excitement you were always looking for? Now, it'll be gone for good. You going to stay Sheriff?"

"I suppose. A little quiet might be good after all that. And I still got you and Dexter here to keep things interesting too."

Dexter let out a hiss and rolled to our side.

"Okay," Geldin said, "we're ready."

Dexter squatted low so she could reach the controls. She counted back from three, pushed the button, and the mine exploded in a roaring wave of thunder and dust. The three of us watched the dust settle together, waiting until nothing was left but a scar in the mountainside.

Then, we heard the clapping from behind us.

We turned to see a man smiling and clapping his hands in raucous applause. His baldhead was blinding in the desert sun, and he watched us with a piercing stare.

"Bravo," he said from a broad smile. "A hell-of-a show, really. I would almost pay to see it again."

My hand fell to my gun and Geldin's to her wrench as we turned to face him.

"Let me guess," I said, "The Governor sent you."

He laughed. "Sheriff, the Governor works for me."

Dexter's gears rumbled to life as he angled toward the man and charged his drill.

"The name's Aleister," the man said. "And I believe you owe me one mannequin." He turned toward Dexter, eyeing him with his cold black stare. "This, however, is quite the improvement. Perhaps we can work out a deal."

"Dexter," Geldin said through gritted teeth, "stays with me!"

I cocked the hammer on my pistol.

"Easy there, old gunslinger. That's not why I'm here. I've been watching you and like the way you two," he paused to gesture to Dexter, "or should I say *three*, work together. I came to offer you a job. There are more things out there, things like the being you saw, that my team and I handle. Judging by how well you handled this one here, I think you would fit in quite well. How would you three like to join us?"

Geldin looked at me, pulled her goggles over her eyes, and smiled.

I shrugged.

Dexter let out a hiss of purple steam.

"Okay," I said, pulling my badge from my chest and tossing it to the dirt. "We're in!"

Lena Ng loves to read short stories and one day decided to write them. Because she reads the strange and unusual, she writes about the strange and unusual. She scuttles around Toronto, Canada, and is an eight-legged member of the Horror Writers Association. She has curiosities published in weighty tomes including Amazing Stories and Flame Tree's *Asian Ghost Stories* and *Weird Horror Stories*. Her stories have been performed for podcasts such as *Gallery of Curiosities*, *Utopia Science Fiction*, *Love Letters to Poe*, and *Horrifying Tales of Wonder*. *Under an Autumn Moon* is her short story collection.

•   •   •

Cats and pirates fit together like peanut butter and jelly. Each are great separately, but together magic happens. Nevertheless, dogs and pirates should also work well, theoretically, though I can't vouch for it since I have no insider knowledge. This insightful message is about as silly as the story, which should tell you something about my distinguished sense of humor.

CAPTAIN CATNIP'S EXCELLENT ADVENTURE

LENA NG

T HE TENTACLES THRASHED and coiled. A suckered limb, thicker than a man's waist, shot out. With Captain Kitty Catnip's quick reflexes, she dodged and leapt through the tangle of attacking tentacles. She somersaulted her nimble black-and-white, sleekly furred body over the sand. "The arrows," she cried. The flaming arrows flew through the air, lighting up the night like shooting stars.

Brandishing their torches like fiery swords, Captain Catnip led the charge. Clutching a torch in one hand and her cutlass in the other, she lunged and parried her weapons. The monster let out a ground-trembling shriek as her crew surrounded the beast, driving the flailing, tentacled creature back into the deep.

The stage went dark. A sole spotlight focused on the Pirate Captain. "Teamwork, ladies and gentlemen, teamwork. That's how I, Pirate Captain Catnip, and my scurrilous crew of skulking cats, defeated the Monster of Hollows Deep." Captain Catnip waved her cardboard cutlass and slid it into the scabbard. Returning to the stage, First Mate Mewser, a stocky Russian Blue, tried not to trip while shuffling in the monster costume, holding the tentacles out of the way. Following behind were Second Mate Snuggles, a scraggle of an orange cat the color of an infant pumpkin, and Third Mate Muffin, big-boned, black-furred, and beautiful. Rounding out the rear were the other crew members Cook, a long-haired Maine Coon, One-Ear, an ill-tempered tabby, and Stumpy Jack, a short-legged Scottish Fold, and together they took a deep bow.

A polite round of applause scattered around the half-empty buffet dining room. Captain Catnip watched with a sinking heart at the tourists who barely looked up from their heaping plates. A budgie wearing a printed muumuu with a palm tree balanced a crab leg on top of a towering bowl of seeds. A fedora-wearing frog in a Hawaiian shirt shoveled spoonfuls of squirming insect blend into his gaping maw. A brown weasel in sunglasses chatted up the young lady weasel on his left at the buffet line.

Captain Catnip's shoulders slumped. She muttered, "Be sure to visit the Pirate's Cove Gift Shop and pick up some booty after dinner. We have a cruise line special just for tonight."

After their bows, the Captain and the crew shuffled backstage. First Mate Mewser ripped off the monster costume and flung it to the floor. "Captain, this is demeaning. A pirate crew play-acting as a pirate crew? Who's ever heard of such a thing?"

"Would you prefer the hangman's noose?" the Captain replied, defeated. "It's only for a year." She rubbed an amber eye. "One long year. One long, horrible year of humiliating ourselves to raise funds for the Queen's Royal Navy. Then our sentence of community service will be over and we'll be free to go back to our heartless ways."

A quizzical expression crossed Second Mate Snuggles's orange-furred face. "Didn't we pledge to redeem ourselves?"

Captain Catnip waved a paw as though swatting a fly. "The lawyers worked out a loophole. They were the best team a chest of gold doubloons could buy. They knocked down all our charges. Remember when we resurrected the ghosts of pirates past? Originally, we were charged with crimes against reality, but they got it downgraded to disturbing the rest-in-peace. Besides, we're pirates. Law-abiding pirates sailing the straight and narrow? There's no such thing. What are pirates without booty? Derring-do? Thwarting the empire? No, no. One year of community service, pretend to go lawful, then commandeer a ship and sail off into the seven seas."

First Mate Mewser crossed his burly arms. "And what if we're caught again?"

The Captain gave a small shrug. "At worst, we'll use up another one of our nine lives. At best, there's nothing a barrelful of doubloons can't make go away. Bribes above, bribes below, open a hospital, feed the poor, that sort of thing, we'll easily get ourselves off the hook."

The sound of heavy footsteps echoed down the outside hall. The Captain narrowed her amber eyes and a hush crept over the group. At the sight of Admiral Dogsbody, the crew sprang to attention. All except Captain Catnip who lazily got to her feet.

"Captain," said the Admiral, a stout, pure-bred English bulldog, his navy double-breasted uniform a little too tight. "Impressive show. Snappy dialogue, exciting action, satisfying ending." He pursed his thick, black lips. "Could use more promotion of the gift shop, however. Sales have been sluggish."

Captain Catnip gave a tight smile and strangled back what she wanted to say, which was along the lines of 'stuff it.' Instead, she nodded and said, "Yes, Admiral."

"And don't forget the publicity events tomorrow. We set sail for Mermaid's Landing and we need you out there to round up more tourists."

"Yes, Admiral."

"And another thing —"

"Yes?"

Admiral Dogsbody flapped his long jowls. "Show a little enthusiasm, Captain. The customers are expecting more swashbuckling, more derring-do. More authenticity. Not pirates play-acting as pirates."

At another time, Captain Catnip would have answered that remark with the point of her cutlass. But since the cutlass she held clenched in her paw was made out of cardboard, she choked out once more, "Yes, Admiral."

"I hope, Captain, that you will learn your lesson and turn away from the life of crime. Sail the straight and narrow."

The delicate pink nostrils of Captain Catnip started flaring. "Maybe I wouldn't need to be a pirate captain if the Royal Navy let women be ship captains."

Admiral Dogsbody gave a high-pitched barking laugh. "Women captains? Who has ever heard of such a thing?"

"I'm standing right in front of you."

"Yes, and that's why you're here, entertaining the buffet crowd, while I'm there at the captain's table." Admiral Dogsbody scowled at the rest of the crestfallen pirate crew before returning to his duties.

•　　•　　•

In the bustling town of Mermaid's Landing, a popular port of sand and surf, Third Mate Muffin, her thick ebony fur gleaming in the sun, rang her bell. A small crowd gathered before her. She called, "Come one and all, come see an authentic pirate show. Pirate Captain Catnip and her scurrilous cat crew battling sea monsters, saving mermaids, singing shanties. A rollicking good time over a buffet dinner and bottomless tankards of grog."

Stepping out from the crowd, a hulking feline figure, a lopsided moustache plastered over his lip, wearing a red tunic and carrying a lute, sidled over a little too closely to inspect the sign Captain Catnip wore over her shoulders.

Captain Catnip took a step backwards. "You can take off your disguise, Captain Cougar."

"Kitty, how many times have I asked you to call me Tom?"

"And how many times have I asked you to call me Captain? That fake moustache is so long, I'm surprised you haven't tripped over it." She glanced at the musical instrument. "And who'd believe you're a musician? Can you even play the lute? You're not fooling anyone."

"Not even a little?"

"Afraid not."

"You've always been able to see right through me, Kitty, I mean Captain," he corrected hastily at her squinted glare. "How about some dinner?"

"Why would I have dinner with my nemesis?"

"Nemesis? Moi? Even if you weren't performing theatre service for the Royal Navy, you could never be my nemesis. I'm a cougar. You're a cat. I'm two hundred pounds of fangs and solid muscle. You're twenty pounds of hairballs and spit."

"That's where you're wrong. I'm David to your Goliath. I'm Darwin to your Dodo. I'm —"

"Besides, you're a woman."

"What's that supposed to mean?" The fur was about to start flying.

Captain Cougar held out his large paws. "It means you're a wonderful creature whom I'd like to take to dinner. A marvelous creature with gorgeous golden eyes, with an ocean of white fur and undiscovered black patches that I'd like to explore. Not a fellow pirate who I'd have to fight with over booty. Unless ..."

"Nice try, Captain, but you can see I'm very busy." Captain Catnip pointed at the garishly painted placard she was wearing. It displayed a portrait of her with both an eyepatch and a peg leg, despite the fact she had neither, in a swordfight with a fire-breathing beluga. "On duty, serving my time, giving back to the community, that sort of thing. Sailing the straight and narrow."

"Come now, Captain Kitty. You must hate having to be on someone else's ship. Not taking the wheel. Not navigating by the stars. Not issuing commands. Not plundering treasure or breaking curses or exploring the lost islands of the seas. I could bust you out of here."

Captain Catnip lowered her gaze. Not having her own ship was painful. The Lady Miranda, her faithful vessel, was felled by the Royal Navy's cannonballs and would never set sail again, unless Poseidon himself could resurrect her from the bottom of the ocean. "I can bust my own way out of here, thank-you," she said, quietly. She took a furtive look around and was about to make a move when —

"Catnip, stop flirting with the locals and round up more business," Admiral Dogsbody said, ushering a group of well-dressed rabbits onto the ship. He returned to Captain Cougar who started tuning his lute strings. "Sir, would you like a coupon for ten percent off? Authentic pirate show raising money for a good cause."

"Yes. Your salary," replied Captain Cougar, glancing at Captain Catnip with a good waggle of his brow. "Maybe another time," he said as he sauntered away.

• • •

Captain Catnip sprang through the volcanic flares, bounded over the smoldering coals, and leapt from one Royal Navy officer's head to another before reaching the summit of Mount Drachna. There she snatched the golden statue from the jaws of the silver dragon who let loose a powerful sulfuric roar. She threw the statue to her First Mate Mewser who tossed it to Second Mate Snuggles who launched it into the air just as Stumpy Jack soared overhead on a hang glider, who easily caught it. Behind him flew three more hang gliders piloted by One-Ear, Cook, and Third Mate Muffin, who each dove down to snatch their crewmates from the wrath of the erupting volcano, gliding their way through exploding sparks far out into the ocean and back onto the Lady Miranda.

There was a ringing round of applause amid hooting peals of laughter. "And that, ladies and gentlemen, is how I, Pirate Captain Catnip and my scurrilous crew, bested the Royal Navy in the quest for the Golden Hound." The Captain and her crew lined up on the stage and together took a deep bow.

Admiral Dogsbody, jowly face quite red, sat with arms crossed at the captain's table.

"Did you enjoy the show, Admiral?" Captain Catnip asked after he had marched backstage with five of his officers, massive, spike-collared, red-eyed Rottweilers carrying truncheons.

The Admiral was so angry he lost the power of speech and began a tempest of barking. When he finally came to his senses, he screamed, "I could have you court-martialed. Mutiny, anarchy, disrespecting an officer. All of you, off to the brig."

The hot, fetid breath of the angry Rottweilers blew down Captain Catnip's neck as she and her crew were escorted down the damp wooden stairs to the brig.

"If we had our real weapons back, not these toys —" the Captain waved her cardboard cutlass — "we'd have commandeered the ship by now and set sail to the seven seas," she said as the bars to the brig clanged shut.

•   •   •

"Bored, bored, bored. Bored, bored, bored," said Second Mate Snuggles. He stretched his lithe, pumpkin-hued body across the slimy stone floor. The thin light of the moon eked in through the small window. "Bored, bored, bored, bored." Snuggles made up a little tune to go along with the lyrics:

Bored, bored, bored, bored.
Bored, bored, bored, bored.
Booooored.
Bored!

"And now for the chorus —"

"Ok, enough," said Captain Catnip. "I get it. We all get it." She looked around the small cell. First Mate Mewser was having a nap. Third Mate Muffin was sharpening her claws in one corner of the cell. Cook, One-Ear and Stumpy Jack seemed to be in a big cat pile in the other corner.

Captain Catnip turned back to Snuggles. "Go out there and steal some grog. Get the good stuff." Captain Catnip stretched out a long claw and jimmied the lock. The cage door sprang open. It was one thing to spend a year doing cruise ship community theatre, quite another rotting in a small, damp brig. The charges were ridiculous. Mutiny? They were nothing but cooperative. No plotting, no hostage-taking, no prisoners plank-walking, no stabbing. The Captain felt her piratical skills were getting rusty.

Snuggles tiptoed out of the brig. Soon he returned with the biggest barrel he could carry. Captain Catnip popped out the cork and took a deep sniff. "Phheeww. Gone off." She tipped back the barrel and drank a large glug. She gave a slow blink. "Not blind. Good enough."

The barrel was passed around and everyone gulped down a bellyful of grog. Soon they were all singing a rousing rendition of:

Bored, bored, bored, bored.
Bored, bored, bored, bored.
Booooored.
Bored!

Just as they were about to hit the chorus —

— a huge BANG rattled the ship, rocking the boat to one side, somewhat sobering them up. The sound of cannonball fire smashing into the hull.

"Pirates!" Cook slurred.

"That's us," Snuggles replied.

"Not 'us' pirates, it's 'them' pirates," said Cook, pointing at the small cell window. There in the distance flew the skull-and-bones flag, the universal pirate's emblem, on a familiar-looking ship.

Pandemonium sounded above them. The pounding of footsteps. The thwack of daggers embedding into walls. The clash and clang of steel against steel. Screams of "We're being boarded" and "Not the face" mixed with a maelstrom of barks and roars.

"Let's join the fun," said Captain Catnip. She bounded from the cell and led the rush up the stairs. At the top of the stairs, she screeched to a halt, feeling the push of furry bodies behind her. "Wait … weapons." She threw off her cardboard cutlass. "We'll have to improvise."

They raced through the darkened hallways. The blood-curdling din of saber clashing against sword, fists against faces, growls and howls grew louder. She flung open the heavy wooden door of the dining room to a scene of glorious chaos. Rottweilers wielding truncheons, cougars in full pirate regalia defending and attacking with cutlass and claws. Captain Catnip and her crew crept under a table to assess the situation.

Captain Cougar, sans moustache, dodged a cast-iron pan. "Kitty, I'm here to rescue you," he hissed.

"I said I was fine."

Hurtling a barbeque fork which sent a Rottweiler yelping, Captain Cougar replied, "We can sail off into the sunset."

Still crouched beneath the table, Captain Catnip shook her head. "A ship can only have one captain."

"You can stay home with the kittens."

"I'll rescue myself, thank-you."

In a food fight, Cook, a chonker of a Maine Coon, was in his element. From the shelter of a buffet table, he lobbed coconut after coconut, randomly bashing heads. "Whose side are we on anyway?" he asked.

Captain Catnip shrugged her slim shoulders. "Neither. We're not fighting for them" — she pointed to the Royal Navy — "and we're not fighting for them" — she pointed to the Captain Cougar's crew — "so … let's go!"

First Mate Mewser was taken aback. "We're running away?"

"We're not running away. We're sailing away. And we're not running from something. We're running to something."

Captain Catnip pointed at the pirate ship in the distance. Captain Cougar's ship, abandoned, and presently short a captain. "Move!"

Captain Catnip dashed from her spot under the table. She hurtled over the backs of snarling Rottweilers, and springing off a rampart, flew over the rumble of cougars. She ducked under airborne daggers and double-tucked over the stout form of Admiral Dogsbody, who was trying to block the exit. While in mid-air, she gracefully stole his sword, then led the race to the upper deck, lunging and parrying all the way. From there, the Captain and her crew leapt onto a lifeboat and paddled as fast as they could to the ship that was awaiting them just on the horizon, leaving the fighting to those left behind.

•   •   •

Feeling the cool ocean breeze, the Captain and her crew lay in gently swaying hammocks. All except Cook, who felt quite comfortable sprawled on the deck.

Second Mate Snuggles stretched over his hammock and gave a face-splitting yawn. He glanced at the hammock swinging softly beside him. "One-Ear, what were you called before you were attacked by the Cursed Shark of Samora?"

One-Ear groomed his gnarly stump. "Two-Ear."

From her hammock, Captain Catnip looked up at the stars and took another sip of her grogtini. "Excellent adventure, everyone. Wrongful imprisonment, a hint of romance, a daring escape. And back to sailing on the seven seas."

First Mate Mewser tried to sit up in his hammock, but feeling dizzy and cross-eyed, slid down into a boneless puddle. "I wonder what our next adventure will be."

Finishing her grogtini, Captain Catnip rolled to her side. The dancing light of the stars reflected on the ocean's mirror and she gave a contented yawn. "That's easy," she said, sleepily. "Rescuing Captain Cougar."

Christina Ardizzone is a graduate of the 2019 Odyssey Writing Workshop as well as the MFA writing program at Sarah Lawrence College. Her work has appeared in *Spry Literary Magazine*, *Animal Literary Magazine*, and *The Quotable*, to name a few. She is mother to a one-year-old and lives in New Jersey.

•   •   •

I wrote this piece to highlight different types of love and acceptance. Sometimes the people we love are unreachable for complicated reasons and we have to meet them where they are or let them go. I also really enjoy sea creatures in banal settings.

I TRANSFORM IN YOUR ARMS

CHRISTINA ARDIZZONE

I DIAL TIM'S NUMBER with slick, salty fingers, leaving particles of sand on my screen. After two rings Tim's black hair and boyish face appears. He narrows his eyes and chugs at a beer in his hand. "I've been waiting all night. You coming back?"

"Come to Wending Beach. East side. Now." I try to keep my tone even. A high, unnatural keening permeates the air from my side of the phone. I angle the camera so Tim can't see behind me.

"What's that noise? Where is my mother?"

"Just come. Please." I hang up.

·　　·　　·

I picked Tim for the tattoo of SpongeBob on his arm. It advertised that he was attractive in a fun, quirky way, but also silly and boyish, a perfect candidate for a pleasant, meaningless hookup. One day he'd probably cover the tattoo with a picture of a future child or a tribute to a dead golden retriever, but I'd be long gone by then.

We met at Petey's Comedy Shack at around 10PM on a Saturday. I pretended to like his set (centered around his hatred of clowns) and by midnight we were headed back to his place. He had a warm voice and a pleasant way of speaking, a bit of a laugh in his words. The white leather couch in his living room next to the kitchen had an animal musk and buttery softness. We made out on that dead hide and, after the second repeat of the entire Chromatica album, I began to unbutton his lumberjack flannel shirt. Things were getting good until a thin middle-aged woman with blue eyes and dusty blonde hair trotted into the kitchen wearing a pink silk robe. His mom?

I tried to pull away, but Tim kept licking the hollow of my neck with his slender, pierced tongue. She slammed a cabinet after taking out a glass bottle, and her robe opened, revealing two jagged red scars where her breasts should be. My stomach clenched at the sight. She was so enthralled in drinking she didn't see me for a few moments. Her son started biting my neck, aggressively ignoring her, while I craned my head to see over his shoulder. We locked eyes and she closed her robe with a skinny hand.

I averted my gaze and patted Tim's shoulder. We pulled apart. The sweet scent of Chanel roses hit my nose before she plopped down between us.

"I need to go to the store." She kissed her son on the cheek. Then she turned to me and said, "Hi, I'm Shirley."

"Tasha." I shook her frail hand.

"Geez, mom." Tim scooted over and wiped some of my saliva from his lips. "You're too drunk to drive."

"That's why you're going to go for me. Leave me here to get to know your girlfriend."

"She's not my girlfriend." He stood and slicked back his black hair with his hands, causing moderate muscles to bulge in a way that made me horny. Then I looked at his mother. Her eyes looked a bit glazed and her exposed foot seemed to have green, veiny fungus growing between the toes. My heart went out to her and the plaintive way she spoke, like her life depended upon getting the drink. I'd seen my uncle go through alcohol withdrawal. It wasn't pretty.

"Please, son? I just need a little more."

Tim took a deep breath. His voice wavered and cracked as he spoke. "Can't I have one day without you?" His eyes watered and he dabbed at them with a knuckle. His mother seemed to sink even lower into the rawhide, like she wanted to find the guts of the creature that once owned it.

What had I gotten myself into? There were clearly unresolved family issues and I had enough of my own. And like me, he'd probably look back at awkward and raw moments like this and want to do anything to go back in time and be with her. I turned toward the woman next to me on the couch.

"I'll take you," I said. It would be a quick trip and then we could both go back to our lives. Maybe I could even convince Tim to take me to his room and lock the door.

"You don't have to do that." He was already buttoning his shirt and about to put on his shoes.

Shirley pulled me off the couch by the arm and blocked Tim's way to the front door. "We got this, honey! See you soon!" Then she pulled me through the door and closed it in Tim's face. I looked down at my bare feet but didn't have time to go back in as she tottered unsteadily past my little red Toyota and headed toward the Chevy Impala parked in the garage. She got in, slammed the door, started the engine, then rolled down the window. "Get in, I'm driving." She was already pulling out, almost to the edge of the yard. I had to jog to get in and swing the door closed behind me.

"You should really let me drive."

"You should really shut up."

Silence filled the car. She flipped down her visor and a pack of cigarettes and a lighter fell onto her lap. Soon she flicked ash out of the driver's side window while I fake smiled and relished the snatches of fresh air coming in between cigarette blows.

"You got a job or a hobby?" She steered with one hand and held the cigarette with the other. Her naked foot stepped on the gas and we whizzed through their gated residential.

"Umm ..." I really didn't want to talk to this random middle-aged white lady about my political positions or anime cosplay.

"If not, you need to get one. The world will take and take from you, leave you scarred and mutilated, your body unrecognizable. At least do something you care about while you can."

I felt my heart beat a little faster. A complicated set of emotions arose in me — empathy for her sadness, grief at my own mother's passing just a year before, fear of intimacy at the plaintive nature of her words, and at the edges, even though it was hard to admit, irritation. I'd wanted to get away from reality for a while and this woman was pulling me deeper into her midlife crisis.

Compassion, I thought. Be compassionate. My therapist Julie's voice replayed in my head. I took a deep breath. "I'm a library shelver."

"A shelver, huh? Not even a librarian."

I was not a librarian. I couldn't afford the master's degree.

"Is that what you want to do every day before you die?"

Shirley clearly wanted to talk about death. Maybe Tim couldn't handle it. I wasn't sure I could either, but I couldn't just ignore it. "I know this might be a sore subject, but my mom died of lung cancer. If you need someone to talk to, I'm here."

I had to concentrate not to cry, not to think of my mother's hairless head and the red scars on her chest, about how skinny she was at the end. She'd held my hand while she passed. All things I'd rather not think about, and here I was going farther and farther away from Tim's lips and moderately muscled arms, the things I had rightfully chosen as my distraction.

Shirley laughed and waved a hand dismissively in my direction, making the car swerve until she curled her fingers back around the wheel.

"You're what? Twenty-one, twenty-two?" Shirley opened the divider and pulled out an almost empty bottle of gin. I really did not want to be in the car with a drunk driver but I couldn't get a word in edgewise. "Still a girl. I remember being young, learning how to walk in high heels, tottering on legs I wasn't used to." She glanced at me. "Seems like it's taking you a while to find your calling."

I bristled, not just at her disregard of my emotions, but also because I was thinking about the socioeconomic impacts of her intergenerational wealth and the redlining that kept my family from purchasing a home in the 1950's. My mom had rented her whole life. I bet this woman never had to worry about getting evicted while dying of cancer.

"Segregation impacted my family's opportunities." I expected her to either object to my characterization or be interested enough to have a meaningful discussion, but instead she doubled-down on her mood. She slammed her free hand on the dash, startling me.

"Yes! Men are always carving up the land, building walls and cages. It took me a long time to understand the power of captivity."

What was she talking about? I could have let all manner of cruel things come out, but she was drunk and I didn't want to work her up by calling her a drunken bitch, so I said, "You have a wonderful way with words." It felt weak and ineffective, but I was done engaging. She wanted to change everything I said into how I was bad or how she had it worse? She could have a conversation with herself.

She barreled through a red light and careened into the Stop and Shop parking lot and beeped at a woman walking by herself with a carton of ice cream showing through the thin plastic bag. Peanut Butter Blast.

She pulled the keys out of the ignition. "Listen," she slurred, and draped her arm over the steering wheel to face me. "I am a lot of things, but wonderful is not one of them."

I couldn't argue with that. Regardless, she didn't wait for me to answer. We walked into the liquor store, her bare feet clearly visible and the digital clock on the check-out counter reading 1:03AM. Her pink soles slapped the linoleum and she went directly toward the gin. "My husband doesn't love me, and my son wants to be a comedian." We stared at the gin together. Round blue bottles, square bottles, squat bottles with intricate designs. She loaded up her arms one at a time, reading the labels and sometimes putting one back. "My son is dating a library shelver. I'm a mythical creature in human form, and if I don't go back to the ocean I will die of a pathetic human condition." She laughed, apparently in conversation with herself. "But what kind of horrible mother leaves their son without explanation?" She shook her head and walked toward the cash register with an armful of bottles.

Wait, what did she just say?

The clerk was a fortyish man with a goatee. He sighed when she came close and I could tell by his irritated manner that he and Shirley had met before.

"Shirley, now Shirley, you know there is a three-bottle limit."

"That's not true, Todd. I just saw a guy walk out with quite a bit of liquor."

Todd opened his mouth to reply.

She sighed and cut him off. "All but three are for her anyway."

My part in the charade had become clear. I edged closer to the counter and pulled out my debit card.

"I'll pay you back," she whispered in my ear, the ethanol stench of her breath making me sneeze.

Todd swiped my card, the computer beeped, then Todd shook his head. "Card rejected."

Shit. I'd bought tampons earlier that day. "I'm sorry but that's the only one I have."

Shirley pushed me out of her way. "These are for her but I'm paying for it."

Todd rubbed his temples and sighed. "Shirley, they are clearly for you. I'm sorry but I'm going to have to ask you to leave." He scooted the gin bottles toward him with a forearm. "Go home and sober up and tomorrow you can buy three more." Shirley, frowning, turned to go. Then Todd mumbled, "Trashy old drunk."

I inhaled sharply and looked to see if Shirley had heard. It took me a moment to process what I was witnessing.

Her whole body was vibrating, and a greenish hue seeped into her cheeks. Her pupils expanded vertically like the lines on pregnancy tests, and her lips melded together, stretched, and hardened to form a long, duck-like beak.

A deep rumbling emitted from Shirley's throat. Then, "I USED TO LURE SAILORS TO THEIR DOOM, YOU INSOLENT WHELP!"

"Shirley!" I took a step back but her arm curled around me and I felt suckers adhere to the skin of my wrist. She was preternaturally solid, and no matter how hard I pushed away she stayed rooted. A tentacle (she had five now) shot out and wrapped around Todd's throat. His eyes bulged as she squeezed the air out of him. Little red dots appeared in the whites of his eyes and his gasping sounded like air being let out of a blow-up doll. Her rumbling was more like a dirge now, deeper and deeper, until I thought my head would explode. I had a momentary flashback to when my mother couldn't make it to the bathroom and vomited all over me while I was with her and the nurse the last few days of her life. Helplessness.

My heart pounded. What could I do to stop her? I'd known her for less than an hour and most of that time she'd been drinking, talking to herself. What would matter to her?

I remembered what my mother had told me kept her going for so long.

"Shirley, think of your son!"

The rumbling stopped and I went limp with relief. She looked at me, her beak and the red pit where her nose used to be still visible. Her tentacles undulated with fishy grace.

She let Todd go, and she let me push her toward the door. I looked back to find Todd slumped over the counter, covered in broken gin bottles. He let out a plaintive moan. We made it through the door.

"I NEED THE OCEAN!" Her voice echoed in the parking lot, and her tentacles waved in the darkness. Her beak clipped at the air with sharp snaps and her skin wafted off smells like canned tuna and cat food.

A small child peeked out of a nearby Jeep's open window and screamed. The mother leaned forward and said, "What is it, honey?" but I pushed Shirley behind their car and ducked down, hopefully before she could see us.

I took a deep breath. She wanted the ocean? Okay. "The ocean! We'll go to the ocean! Give me the keys!"

Shirley reached into her bathrobe pocket and lifted the key fob with a tentacle, and by the time it was closer to me the tentacle looked more like a hand, green and mottled.

We snuck back to the Impala and I forced Shirley into the passenger's seat before I started to drive. "Get on the freeway," Shirley demanded. Her voice was pitching higher as she turned back into a human.

I grabbed my phone from my pocket and opened Google Maps to put in "ocean". The quickest route to Wending Beach took an hour. I selected it and placed the phone on the dash.

My heart pounded and blood rushed in my ears and the narrow slab of road seemed narrower for what adrenaline was doing to me. Once we were on the freeway, I rolled down the window to let in a little breeze. The canned tuna smell dissipated, and now Shirley was slumped in her seat, her open robe exposing her chest scars. She saw me looking and shrugged. I let the sounds of the tires on the road and the pleasant whoosh of cars passing calm me. What would Julie say? Question before you jump to conclusions.

"Shirley, what the fuck was that and what the fuck are you?"

"Leave me alone." She closed her robe and curled toward the door. Her feebleness helped me relax a tiny amount. She made slurping noises, and I couldn't tell what they meant or where on her body they came from. I continued to take deep breaths, hoping she'd order me to go back to her house, but ready to jerk the car over to the side of the road and run if things turned South. Eventually my fatigue dulled the edges of my vigilance, and the natural rhythms of the road lulled me into calm.

At some point, after we'd made the turn onto the highway that would lead us to Wending Beach, Shirley shifted in her seat and rested her chin on her hand to look out the window.

"1946 was a hard year for me. I'd caught Jimmy cheating with the neighbor. Not that I cared about him sleeping with someone else. I hadn't learned to enjoy human love-making yet. No, it was how alone I felt. Then my first human child died a stillborn, and I drank the first bottle of alcohol. I hadn't sought it out, I was being a good wife and taking care of my husband and his dinner needs even though the smell and sight of food made me nauseous with grief."

"I was trying to make a brown butter reduction for mushroom steak and russet potatoes. Jimmy's favorite meal. The butter sputtered in the pan and never turned golden, probably because I didn't leave it on heat long enough. Anyway, I gave up and sipped at the gin, quiet little fires I extinguished by swallowing."

She paused, and afraid she wanted me to say something, I said, "That is so poetic, Shirley."

"No, it wasn't. Human words aren't enough to make pain beautiful." She sighed. "I'm sorry I was insensitive about your mother before."

I gulped. "It's okay. It seems like you're going through a lot right now."

"I haven't felt this way since I first crawled on shore. That sense of disorientation, of my body feeling foreign."

I asked the question again. "Shirley, what are you?"

She looked out her window. "Humans are so caught on labels. Would it be enough to say that I'm a creature that has always longed for more?"

I tried to ignore her tears, keeping my eyes on the road.

"What do you think I am?" she asked.

"Some kind of monster? I think you almost killed Todd."

She snorted and looked out her window. "Todd has a love of rules that isn't logical."

"He was just doing his job."

"Yes, he was, wasn't he?" Finally, she answered my question. "The closest thing I've been able to find to what I am in human books is a kraken, with a little bit of harpy mixed in. In my language we are the Murlaugh." At the uttering of the name my chest resonated sharply and a kind of joy fizzed through my limbs. I slowed a bit so I wouldn't crash the Impala. "The bottom line is that the sea keeps me alive, and if I don't return within the next few hours, I'm going to die."

Why had she wanted to spend her last hours on a drunken bender instead of with her son? It was beyond me. "Then why do you stay? Shouldn't you have returned by now?"

"It's not a fair thing to ask of my son, is it? To accept that he is part Murlaugh and that his mother must leave to survive? I would rather die a normal, boring, human death. Real human bones and a body to display at the funeral and my boy able to process my death. At least then something about me would make sense. All I have to do is go home and die."

"I can understand that," I said softly. I'd seen the way it killed my mother to appear presentable those last days. She'd wanted me to have good memories of her death, and that she couldn't let her exhaustion show, even at the end, had left a certain sense of shame in me. Had I not made her feel like she could be herself? Hadn't she trusted me to care about her no matter her pain? My heart beat faster and I felt a bit dizzy. What was this emotion?

Anger. It wasn't an emotion I let myself feel, especially at my mother. Julie said it was normal to feel abandoned when someone died, that it was okay. Natural. But this explosive stuff that made it hard to breathe? No, it couldn't be natural.

"Do you plan on telling him?" The words flew out of my mouth, but Shirley either didn't notice or care about my shift in tone.

She shook her head. "No." She sighed. "Once when he was three and we visited the ocean his little pudgy baby hands turned into tentacles. Bill was on a work trip and wouldn't come home for months. It was up to me to keep Tim safe, so I never took him to the sea again."

How could she hide such a vital part of who she was? Of who he was? "That could happen again, Shirley." Flames of adrenaline went up my body. How fucking selfish was she? He deserved to know the truth. He probably knew on some level that he wasn't like other boys.

The SpongeBob tattoo started to make more sense. He probably got it to reach out to a mother that clearly hid something vital about herself and refused to share it with him. How could Shirley be so blind? She still didn't notice my mood, and her reply remained even.

"Maybe," she said. "But more likely, because I have kept him from the sea and he is half-human, he will never change, even when he eventually ventures back to the ocean. He will see it through his human eyes and no matter what he feels it will not call to him."

I grew impatient. Why didn't she just talk to him? Did she think he couldn't handle it? Mothers were always trying to protect their children even if that meant not letting your child know who you actually are. "But, Shirley, won't he wonder why you kept him from the ocean his whole life?

Won't he feel like something is missing, like you did? How could you be so blind and selfish?"

She howled, then, like a drowning wolf. It was a keening, a helpless anger, a kind of release that must have been haunting her for a long time. With the keen I felt my anger dissipating, unclenching the tenseness in my throat and chest. I realized she understood what I felt. Yet on a deep and visceral level Shirley terrified me, no matter how deep my compassion or anger went.

"Please, I don't want to talk anymore." Shirley wiped away tears and I felt a twinge of guilt for hitting a nerve.

We sat in amiable silence and Shirley reached over and put on a classical music channel. Gustave Holt's "Neptune" danced through the speakers. She added words, singing in Murlaugh, her voice beautiful and haunting, full of the kind of pain I felt at my mother's funeral. The kind I felt at home, in bed, my cheek to the pillow, wondering what could have been if they'd found the cancer sooner. At the final stoplight before the beach, a car pulled up next to us, and when I looked the driver was weeping, window rolled down, wiping tears away with a forearm. They drove off with a screech of wheels.

We wended through narrow roads, and when Shirley sat up and smelled the ocean her face began to melt away. I pulled her car right up onto the sand and drove to the edge of the water, engine sputtering as the sand gummed it up.

Shirley popped open the door and stepped onto the wet beach. Her robe was the first thing to fall to the sand, and then she was keening in the salty air, her octopus head held high. Her torso stayed human-like, and her legs were yet more tentacles, emerging as she waded further and further into the water.

I followed her on the shore, watching the moon and listening to seagulls. Her music pulled me toward the water, and I swam into the waves, letting the brine coat the back of my throat. Shirley's singing bounced around me like echolocation, and for a moment it felt like I, too, could return to the ocean. Memories of my mother held suspended in my mind, and the music coaxed them out, one by one. The diagnosis, the night mother couldn't look at me but kept chopping carrots for dinner, telling me it would be okay, maybe the experimental treatment would work. Hospital stays, when she called me her best friend, and the funeral, where I'd let the salt of my tears run into my mouth and it was the only thing that passed my lips that day, no words or food or even a smile. The ocean held the salt that had kept me from falling apart, and I gulped it into my lungs.

Shirley's presence was a pulsing light, her voice filling the ocean with her desperate vibrations.

I crawled back to shore and coughed up water, the grainy sand beautiful. Each grain appeared to me a whole entity that held on to what was left of itself, the smallest but most essential self.

I don't know how long it was, but it was after the seagulls circled above, after the air changed a bit colder, after I'd become thirsty. Shirley, fully naked and completely human, crawled up beside me on the shore.

"Five thousand years, that's how long it took being a Murlaugh before I longed for more. The daily rhythms of hunting sea life, then upending human ships, none of it pleased me."

I reached out for her hand and didn't flinch when a wet tentacle flopped into my palm instead. Did she no longer control when she changed? "Is that why you crawled out of the ocean? Because you were sick of your life?"

Shirley's beak let out a shriek and her guttural, other-worldly voice made an appearance. "I DID NOT CRAWL, I EXPLODED FROM THE OCEAN WAVES." She made some clicking sounds, and when she spoke again her voice was normal. "Sorry, that is my Murlaugh pride. We are warriors who would never crawl. Yes, first it was the desperation of knowing I would live forever and that even if I could die no one would mourn me."

I scanned her body, the whiteness of her skin and the ribs etched into her sides.

"Are you going to get better, now that you're in the sea?"

She shook her head. "Not unless I stay. And I can't leave my son."

I thought a moment, trying to let more compassion than anger come through my words. "I understand your son and what he must be feeling. Watching your mother die is not something I would wish on anyone. But if I could choose between my mom dying of cancer or knowing she was some kind of badass that had to return to the sea, and that I had a chance to return as well, I would choose the latter. Maybe you could try and take him with you." I looked down at my sand-encrusted feet. "I wish my mom had a good reason for abandoning me."

Shirley made a clucking sound. "Don't be so harsh with your mother. She didn't abandon you, she died."

"Still. Lying to your son is wrong, and it means he loses you when he doesn't have to."

"Lying to him makes his life easier and less complicated."

"Don't keep him ignorant because you think it's better for him! Ignorance won't protect him from the pain!"

It occurred to me that I picked the wrong guy entirely for a one-night stand. Or maybe everyone has some kind of complicated history and expecting to find the perfect one-night stand was ridiculous. "I haven't wanted to feel anything after losing my mom, because all I felt was anger and sadness."

"Don't take it out on me. I'm going through my own problems."

I collected my thoughts and took a deep breath. "I don't like what I'm feeling right now, Shirley, and maybe I'm not being fair. I just know that you could have something with your son that transcends your human body. Don't you want that for him?"

Her tentacle squeezed my hand and I didn't flinch even though it hurt. "What if he trembled at my true form, and rejected me? Or worse, accepted me but could not turn, and I had to leave him on the shore?"

Was that something my mother had been afraid of? Me seeing her and being disgusted? I squeezed her tentacle, half reassurance and half stifled rage due to helplessness. "You have to take that chance."

She sat up. "He probably won't make it in time before I have to return to the sea. I won't be able to talk to him as a human mother." Her body rearranged itself, her skin and viscera pulling away to leave small malignant bumps throughout the inside of her human body — in her chest, her arm pits, across her stomach. Her exposed muscles glistened. Is this like the cancer that had been in my mother? That something so small could take away the person I loved the most pained me.

Shirley's skin moved back into place. "The doctor tried to remove them. But it was too late. It had spread."

"Will they go away when you return to the ocean?"

"As long as I stay in Murlaugh form they will not take over my body and kill me, but if I stay in human form I will die. And the cancer will never go away."

I looked at the tears streaming down her cheeks, and they streamed down my face as well. We rolled to our sides and embraced each other, and I didn't care that the smell almost gagged me, or that her tentacles appeared and were sucking hard enough on my arms to leave welts. Her beak snapped at the air and somehow the existence of the same kind of exquisite pain in the other was enough to relieve it, if only just a small amount.

"Listen," I said. "If he's going to hate you, he should hate the real you."

She smiled with half-human lips and her eyes were bright and green, and for a moment they reminded me of my mother's. Only a daughter could make a mother smile with such abandon.

•   •   •

I am facing the water when I hear a car pulling up, then the rustling of fabric behind me.

"Where's my mother?" Tim asks. I can see from the streaks of tears on his face that he's been crying. Tim steps closer to the water as he listens to his mother's voice, now the only thing audible in the night air. He dives into the water and I know he is hearing her voice explode around him, amplified and carrying from however far away she has become. After a time, he crawls back onto the beach and cries, softly at first, and then he is sobbing. He lifts his head back and keens, too. His hands transform into tiny, vestigial tentacles. I sigh in relief. Shirley made the right choice. Maybe my mother had known her limits, too. Maybe I wouldn't have been able to handle her true form those last days. But there is something healing in seeing how a child's connection to their parent transforms them, too.

"What's happening to me? Is she coming back?"

I sit down and place my head on his shoulder and grab the arm that had turned me on less than twelve hours earlier. "You are Murlaugh, and your mother is free."

I can tell he doesn't understand, and maybe it will be years before he even begins to. But this at least is a beginning, something every person deserves.

We sit and watch the waves, Shirley's voice trembling in the air.

S. Park has been writing since age six, on nearly every topic and in nearly every genre under the sun. He especially likes to draw on real life experiences, then filter them through the "anything is possible" lens of science fiction and fantasy. He has published several novels, numerous short stories, and a possibly ridiculous amount of fan fiction. He lives in Oregon with one snake, two cats, and two other humans, who provide plenty of story inspiration.

• • •

"Bookwrym" is one of those stories that seem obvious in retrospect. Like most authors, I'm also a reader, and have collected literally thousands of books over the years. It makes for an impressive home library — and for a hoard big enough to make a dragon proud.

BOOKWYRM

S. PARK

M AURAG THE TERRIBLE YAWNED, stretched, and immediately noticed that something was horribly wrong.

She slowly cracked open one slitted eye, then the other, and confirmed what her stretch — far too silent, entirely free of the expected clink and slither of coin on coin — had suggested. Her hoard was gone.

She spat a low, rumbling curse and heaved herself slowly to all fours. Her very bones creaked, her muscles protesting the movement. How long had she slept this time? Last time had been only a decade or so. Was she getting too old? Would she soon do as the dragons of ancient legend, and sleep so long she merged with the mountain itself?

Maurag shook herself, stretching again and pushing that thought out of her head. She wouldn't need to sleep again for years, so there would be time to worry about possibly mythical problems later. Now she had a much more pressing issue to address — her missing hoard.

A closer examination of her den showed not even a scrap of gold. The vast boulder she'd used to seal herself up was still intact though. It must have been another dragon, not humans, then. She laid her crest flat and hissed. Curse it. She'd done her best to give no hint that she was about to sleep, and she'd thought she'd hidden her den well.

Obviously not well enough.

So she was starting over. At her age.

With a long, irritated sigh she set about moving the boulder, and then began the long slither through the tunnel — just wide enough for her bulky, serpentine body — that led out of the mountain's heart.

As she crawled, she planned. She knew what she needed to do, and truly it should be fairly simple. This time she wouldn't be starting as a tiny dragonet, forced to sneak into human houses to steal copper coins in order to begin her hoard. This time she'd start big.

Very big.

•　　•　　•

Wind flowed over Maurag's wings, cold and bracing, as she soared so high she would be only a speck to eyes below. Humans were barely specks in turn to her at this height, though her eyesight was far superior to theirs, pitiful creatures that they were.

She wasn't watching them, though, she was watching the river, broad enough to be easy to follow as it left the mountains and coiled its way across the fertile plains beyond. Barges dotted it, carrying human commerce from the scattered settlements along its banks down to the great coastal city of Caecilia.

After exiting her den, Maurag had slithered down to the ancient forest that covered the mountain's lower slopes. There she had visited with an oak dryad, an old friend of hers, and found that she'd slept for nearly sixty years. Human politics seemed to have shifted somewhat in that time, but the nearest major city had, according to the oak, only grown in fame and power, so it should hold all the gold Maurag could desire to replenish her hoard.

It was a long flight, over plains that were a patchwork of farms, dotted with little villages, over patches of forest, over a range of hills that didn't quite manage to become mountains, where the river cut a wide canyon through slopes dotted with sheep and patched with trees, over a coastal plain, the farms larger, fields making long sweeps of uniform green between the darker lines of their hedges, until at last she glimpsed the sea ahead, and Caecilia on the delta where the river's fresh water mingled with the ocean's salt.

A few low hills rose above the waters, with the city's tangle of buildings all over them, but atop the tallest was a massive structure, half castle, half palace. There were crenelated walls around part of it, but no sign that they were manned. This was a city that had not known war in a long time. Maurag bared her teeth in a sharp grin and folded her wings.

She ended her dive as dramatically as she could, flaring her wings wide as she landed on the cobblestones in front of the palace. The guards to either side of the open gates, looking far too fancy to be anything but ceremonial, yelped and cowered in the backwash of her wings. She laughed and bellowed out, "I am Maurag the Terrible! Bring me all the gold in your storehouses, or I will burn this city to the ground!"

She spouted fire into the air by way of punctuation, and laughed again as humans scrambled like ants on a kicked anthill.

Eventually a human male, wearing a robe and some sort of chain of office — not gold, she noted instantly — emerged cautiously from the palace.

"Well?" said Maurag, arching her neck to put her head by the human, enjoying his fearful recoil. "Where is the gold? Why is it taking so long?"

"Forgive me your, er, excellency? It's taking time to gather together."

"What, is there no central storehouse for your kingdom's currency? No royal treasure coffers?"

The human visibly flinched. "Er, I'm very sorry, your excellency, Caecilia is a republic now. And, er, we switched from the gold standard some time ago, so there's no longer a government storehouse of gold."

"What? Then what is your currency, you ridiculous human?"

"It's, ah, it's printed."

Maurag blinked in astonishment. She'd heard of paper currency, of course, but ... "Entirely on paper? No coins? No gold assurance?"

"No, sir."

Maurag huffed. "Ma'am."

The human looked confused.

Maurag rolled her eyes. "It's ma'am, not sir. But never mind. Why would people use your paper if you have no gold to guarantee your wealth?"

"Er. Sorry, ma'am. Gold is, well, I mean, it's not really considered that much of a guarantee. Too much dragon theft. And, er, we back our money with the reputation of the Republic. Our military, our famous library and university. Our knowledge is our treasure, ma'am." He straightened at that, as if thinking about these things fortified him.

Maurag cocked her head to the side, regarding the tiny being in front of her, feeling frustrated and puzzled, but also curious. "Military might I understand, but knowledge?"

"There's a saying that knowledge is power," said the human. "The Caecilia University Library is considered the finest in the world. There are hundreds of thousands of books."

"And what are human books to me?" said Maurag, with a snort, tossing her head. "I might value the knowledge inside them, perhaps, but I certainly cannot hold one to read it."

"Er ... Someone could read them to you, ma'am?"

Maurag fixed her gaze on the human, suddenly intrigued. All the knowledge of these clever little creatures, actually available to her? Some dragons did hoard things other than gold ... She'd never bothered, since gold was the one thing that wouldn't tarnish or wear. But knowledge ...

"Would you read me a book if I asked you to, human?"

"I, er ... If you promise you won't burn the city, ma'am?"

Maurag chuckled. "I don't think I could make such a promise for just one book. I promise I will light no fires while you read, at least."

"Then yes, I'll read to you, ma'am. If you'll permit me to go get a book? And, uhm, you're blocking all the traffic to the palace. Would it be possible for you to perhaps move somewhere else?"

"Oh, I suppose. I will land over there." Maurag gestured to where she'd seen green space from above. "Don't think to simply flee, though. If you don't come with the book soon, I'll begin burning things."

"Of course." The human, amusingly, bowed and departed, walking half-sideways to keep an eye on Maurag, as if afraid she'd change her mind and eat him. Well, she could if she wanted to, but hearing a book sounded much more interesting. She'd always thought that humans made so many clever things, and had never understood them. Perhaps if she heard enough of their books, she'd be able to.

Minutes later she was settled on a nicely soft stretch of grass behind the palace, surrounded by trees tall enough to reach above her head even when standing, though not, perhaps, if she stood on her hind legs. She found herself thinking that this was quite pleasant. Like being in a forest, but more orderly.

A faint shuffle drew her attention. "I hear you there, human. If you are up to something, know that my scales are as hard as diamond and my fire can quite definitely reach to where you hide."

There was an audible squeak, and a human in clothing that had a badge like the one over the palace gates on it, so a functionary of some kind, no doubt, emerged from behind a hedge. The human was very small. Was it a one of their young? The cowards were sending out children? Maurag tried not to snort. Toying with humans could be fun, but there was no honor in terrifying children.

"S-s-s-sorry your dragonship. Th-they s-s-sent me to say Ch-ch-chancellor Lorius would be another half hour. He said he w-wanted to bring more than one book. P-p-please don't set anything on fire!"

"I won't," said Maurag, trying not to chuckle. "At least not until …" She glanced at the sky. "Until sunset. Or until somebody tries something. If any soldiers or knights turn up, I will make no promises. Tell your coward rulers that."

The small human squeaked again. "Y-y-yes ma'am. Th-they're not cowards!"

"They sent you instead of coming themselves. But never mind that. Run along and tell them. I will wait here. This model forest is quite pleasing. I will be happy to learn more of human things, once your 'Chancellor' arrives with his books."

The small human scurried off. Maurag settled herself more comfortably and waited patiently.

She remained undisturbed, though she saw the occasional human peek out of a window or doorway. How long a "half hour" was, she didn't know, but the sun was still well short of the horizon when the Chancellor reappeared. His arms were heaped with books.

"So, what would you like to learn first?"

Maurag laughed. "Read me one, human. Read whatever you like. I will tell you if I grow disinterested, I promise."

"Very well." The human sat down surprisingly close to Maurag, with his books beside him, and picked up the one on the top of the pile. "This is a treatise on astronomy, and the paths of the stars. I'll begin at the beginning."

He cleared his throat and began to read.

Much later, after reading the latter chapters by the light of lantern brought out by another — or the same — small human, Chancellor Lorius finished, and Maurag looked up at the night sky, filled with wonder at what she now knew about the workings on the heavens.

"How many books did you say were in your library, Chancellor?" she said, keeping her voice low.

"Depending on how one counts, we have between five and eight hundred thousand books, ma'am."

Maurag looked at him, starlight shining in her slitted eyes. "I want to hear them all."

The Chancellor gave her a shocked look, that swiftly turned into a broad smile. "I'll see what I can do."

•   •   •

Spring term had just begun, and students flooded the halls and walkways of Caecilia University. Decima, backpack on shoulder and stomach full of nerves, had just exited the main library doors when her phone's alarm went off. It was time.

She swallowed hard and circled the building. Behind the library lay the Dragon Amphitheater, and as Decima came in sight of it, she caught the gleam of afternoon sunlight on dark copper scales. She'd seen Maurag before, of course. Few students could resist going to have a look at the university's living mascot and oldest student, but now she wasn't just going to gape from a distance, she was going to have to get within reach of the massive dragon.

It had all sounded very magical and exciting when she'd sent in her application, but now it was entirely too real, and entirely too frightening.

The sight of another student, a young man in a green polo, actually leaning against the dragon's side, book in lap, eased her anxiety somewhat, and she managed to gather her courage and slowly approach.

The other student and the dragon both looked up, and he stopped reading. Decima swallowed again, seeing those huge, slitted eyes fixed on her.

"Ah, my replacement!" said the young man. He closed the book and levered himself up from the dragon's side. He tucked the book into a bag and slung it over his shoulder. "I'll be back to finish mine," he said to the dragon, then gave Decima a cheery wave and trotted off.

Decima, not remotely daring to touch the dragon, gingerly sat down in one of several chairs scattered about the bowl-shaped area where the dragon spent most of her time. It had been built for her over a century ago, the last time the library building had been rebuilt. The rebuilding itself had included massively reinforced walls on the Amphitheater side, for the dragon apparently had a habit of leaning against what she considered her "hoard" of books.

"Welcome," said the dragon as Decima took her seat. "I am Maurag, once called Terrible, now called Wise." Her voice was a deep rumble, not at all feminine.

"Hi. Hello. I'm, uhm, I'm Decima."

"It is a pleasure." The dragon gave a fractional head-bob. "Now, you have brought a book for me to hear?"

Her hands were shaking as Decima opened her backpack and pulled out the book she'd chosen.

"I, uhm, I hope this one is okay. The rules didn't say very much about what to pick."

The dragon tilted her head and the corner of her mouth lifted in a tiny smile that — thank every god — did not show her teeth. She could no doubt swallow Decima without chewing. "You checked it against the list?"

Decima nodded. "Yes."

"And it is non-fiction?"

"Yes."

"Then I shall listen. What is it?"

"It's, uhm, it's a recent book on exoplanets. Astronomy is my major, you see. So I thought … I thought you might like it?"

The dragon chuckled, the sound making Decima's entire body vibrate, like standing too near the speaker at a concert. "The very first book I ever heard was an astronomy book."

"Oh! But then … I mean, if you've been hearing astronomy books all these years, you probably know all this stuff already, then."

The dragon shook her head. "I know much, but about exoplanets, little. There are too many topics for me to keep up with them all." She smiled again, this time showing just a glint of massive ivory fangs. "The very first chancellor worried about running out of books when he discovered I did not sleep. A helpful math professor told him he need have no fear, for even though I may hear three of four books a day, it would take hundreds of years to read through the collection they then had. Now, of course, new books are produced far faster than they can be read to me, even leaving out fiction. Many of them are awful drivel, of course, but I find that few students pick the truly terrible ones." Another flash of fangs, this one quite deliberately showing them all. "I promise I do not eat the ones who read me books I dislike. Now please, begin."

Decima's hands were still shaking, but she managed to open the book's cover. "Okay. Uhm. Exoplanets, by Mikelus Summeris …" Soon she was lost in the reading, and her hours passed before she knew it. A throat-clearing from the dragon made her start, suddenly reminded that she was sitting next to something the size of a jet airplane. She looked up, and saw that another student had appeared to take her place.

"Thank you," said the dragon. "That was quite fascinating. I look forward to hearing the rest of it when you return. And any other books you might select, should you volunteer to read again."

"Oh. Uhm. You're welcome!" Decima marked her place and closed the book, then scrambled to her feet. She gave an awkward sort of half-bow to the dragon, a nod to the other student, and then hurried down the path, her heart once again beating far too fast.

Maurag looked after Decima for a moment as the next student — one who'd already read some of his book, but was also still on his mandatory first reading — took a seat. She wondered if this girl would be one of the ones who did only the required single book, or if she would be one of those who returned repeatedly. Maurag rather liked those ones. Some of them were still coming even after graduation. Anyone could come and take a two-hour session reading to the University Dragon, though only students in their first year were required to. Plenty of people seemed to enjoy doing it, requirement or not. It had been decades since the last time there had been a time slot that wasn't filled.

"So, last I left off the border wars with Celtia had just gotten interesting. Let's see, here we go. Chapter twelve ..." Maurag turned her attention back to the new reader, and settled in to hear the history book he'd chosen. She had to stifle a yawn as she did. It was getting to be time for another long sleep. Not today, and probably not for another year or so, but she was starting to feel tired.

She could remember that last lonely waking, angry, confused, and worried about how long she'd slept. Now she had a place to rest, here, where she would be well-guarded through the years-long nap. She could remember too the feeling of loss at having her hoard stolen, but now the whole library and all its contents was her hoard, a comforting bulk at her back, even larger than she. Much better than that, though, every book she had heard was her hoard, held within her mind, hers forever, inviolable. No thief, human or dragon, could ever take them from her.

That hoard grew every day, was growing now, as the young human's voice rang out into the peaceful afternoon air, pouring knowledge about human history into her mind, her hoard.

Maurag knew that the other remaining dragons thought her mad, living among humans, keeping a hoard of paper within a stone building, words within her head, not a hoard of gold and gems in a hidden cave.

Murag, though, knew that she had the best hoard in all the world.

AFTERWORD

W E CREATED PAPER ANGEL PRESS (and its imprints) as an act of rebellion.

Rebellion against generic rejection letters that provide no useful explanation as to why a story was rejected. Rebellion against publishing schedules that more often than not make authors wait endless months — if not years — before they see their book in available for sale. Rebellion against author royalties paid in single-digit percentages.

As authors ourselves, we frequently find ourselves frustrated and dismayed at the callous disregard with which the major publishers treat aspiring writers.

"Publishing is a business," they remind us. We understand that, and we believe that many writers understand that. It is, however, small comfort to an author who wants to understand why their manuscript was rejected or, if their manuscript is accepted, why they will earn barely more than a dime — and often far less than a quarter — for each copy sold of a paperback edition that sells for $7.99.

Paper Angel Press is our solution to those problems. We view our authors as collaborators in the creative and promotional process that culminates in the publication of their work. Should we reject a manuscript, we will let the author know the reasons why. Once an author has delivered their final manuscript to us, our goal is to have their book available for sale within three months. We involve the author with — and expect them to participate in — the development of the promotional activities that support the release of their book. We pay our authors based on a royalty scale that reflects this partnership.

We also understand that many authors are not full-time writers. They must balance their writing time with the demands of their jobs, families, and other commitments. They might also not have the talent (or time) to become experts in marketing and promotion. We are here to provide them with support in those areas.

In our mission statement, we commit to our authors:

TO BRING NEW WORKS OF FICTION AND ART TO LIGHT.
TO GIVE PEOPLE A CHANCE TO REALIZE THEIR DREAMS.

Within these pages you will find collaborations with our authors. They have created new worlds for all of us to explore and enjoy. When these brief excursions into their worlds capture your imagination, check out our other tales and experience the adventures we have to offer.

If you have worlds inside you waiting to be shared, send us your stories. Let us help you bring them to life for others to experience.

Steven Radecki
Managing Editor and Co-Founder
Water Dragon Publishing

YOU MIGHT ALSO ENJOY

THE FUTURE'S SO BRIGHT

Out of the darkness of the present comes the light of the days ahead ...

With stories from Kevin David Anderson, Maureen Bowden, Steven D. Brewer, Nels Challinor, Regina Clarke, Stephen C. Curro, Jetse de Vries, Nestor Delfino, Gail Ann Gibbs, Henry Herz, Gwen C. Katz, Brandon Ketchum, Julia LaFond, R. Jean Mathieu, Cynthia McDonald, Christopher Muscato, Alfred Smith, A.M. Weald, and David Wright.

CORPORATE CATHARSIS
The Work From Home Edition

The boundaries between reality and fantasy have become as blurred as those between life and work.

With stories from Alicia Adams, Antaeus, Pauline Barmby, Steven D. Brewer, Dominick Cancilla, Adrienne Canino, Graham J. Darling, Derek Des Anges, Manny Frishberg, Alex Grehy, Jon Hansen, Alexa Kellow, Jack Nash, Helen Obermeier, Frank Sawielijew, William Shaw, Steve Soult, N.L. Sweeney, Kimberley Wall, and Richard Zaric.

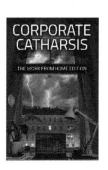

Available from Water Dragon Publishing in hardcover, trade paperback, and digital editions
waterdragonpublishing.com

Made in United States
Orlando, FL
14 December 2024

55571523R10159